P9-CBG-655

MURDER UNDER THE PALMS

MURDER UNDER THE PALMS

STEFANIE MATTESON

SOUTH HUNTINGTON
PUBLIC LIBRARY
2 MELVILLE ROAD
HUNTINGTON STATION, N.Y. 11746

BEELER LARGE PRINT
Hampton Falls, New Hampshire, 1998

LT
M Matteson

Library of Congress Cataloging-in-Publication Data

Matteson, Stefanie.
 Murder under the palms / Stefanie Matteson.
  p.   cm.
 ISBN 1-57490-137-0 (alk. paper)
 1. Large type books. 2. Graham, Charlotte (Fictitious
character)—Fiction. 3. Women detectives—Florida—
Fiction. 4. Actresses—Florida—Fiction. 5. Palm Beach
(Fla.)—Fiction I. Title.
[PS3563.A8393M85 1998]
813'.54—dc21   98-5876
                                                          CIP

Copyright © 1997 by Stepfanie Matteson
All rights reserved.
No part of this book may be reproduced in any form
without written permission from the original publisher:
The Berkley Publishing Group
200 Madison Avenue
New York, New York 10016

Published in Large Print by arrangement with
Berkley Publishing Group

BEELER LARGE PRINT
is published by
Thomas T. Beeler, *Publisher*
Post Office Box 659
Hampton Falls, New Hampshire 03844

Typeset in 16 point Monotype News Plantin type.
Printed on acid-free paper and bound by
BookCrafters in Chelsea, Michigan.

For Edie,
who's always been there

MURDER UNDER
THE PALMS

1

THE FEELING STRUCK WHEN THEY TURNED INTO AN alleyway leading off the shopping mecca of Worth Avenue, and intensified when the alleyway led them past the cloistered terraces of the old Spanish-colonial-style clubhouse of the exclusive Everglades Club. By the time they turned again, onto the narrow street lined with the columnar trunks of royal palms that overlooked the Everglades' palm-fringed golf course and caught their first glimpse of the neighborhood of Spanish-colonial homes, Charlotte Graham had begun to experience that wonderfully buoyant sensation that occurs when fantasy takes its place in the seat of reason. When they swung open the ornate black wrought-iron gate that led to the house, she was already starting to fall in love, and by the time they emerged from the walk lined with tall ficus hedges in front of which stood terra-cotta planters of lemon trees heavy with fruit, and into a courtyard that only barely managed to keep the jungle at bay, and looked up at the tower from any of whose spiraling windows Rapunzel might have let her down her golden tresses, Charlotte was fully in love.

At the foot of the tower was a quaint old wooden door studded with iron nails and set into an arched stone frame flanked by iron-grilled windows. Above the door hung a sign that read: "Château en Espagne" or "Castle in Spain." Because of the Spanish-style architecture, Charlotte assumed. But why, then, was the sign in French?

1

She had never been the kind of person who was attracted to tropical climates. A Connecticut Yankee by birth, she much preferred the vigorous climate of the temperate latitudes, and, in fact, the only other time she had ever fallen in love with a house was when she bought her cottage on a mountainside overlooking a picturesque harbor in Maine. But she was in her seventies now, and had to admit that the warm, salty breeze that wafted off the ocean just a block and a half away felt good to her old bones. Especially *this* winter, which had been the coldest and harshest in recent memory. Though she hated to admit it, she was also starting to slow down. Maybe not slow down as much as begin to entertain the notion that she might be entitled to a bit of relaxation. It was part of her nature that despite her success, she had never let herself ease up on the iron-willed ambition that had propelled her to the top of her profession. After more than fifty years in front of the cameras and on the stage, one would have thought that her reputation was secure, but in her heart, she had always been an insecure young actress combing the columns of *Variety* for the next casting call.

At last she had reached the point in her life where she might feel comfortable resting on her laurels. And laurels there were aplenty: it seemed that a month didn't go by these days that she wasn't honored by one organization or another for "lifetime achievement." Her public had come to regard her in the same way they might an historic building: as a monument to American culture. And, it struck her, as their small group stood in the courtyard soaking up the magical atmosphere, if one were to allow oneself to entertain the notion of resting on one's laurels, a house like this would be the place to do it.

"Charming," said her friend Connie Smith as she stepped up to the cool blue- and green-tiled fountain in the courtyard's center. She dipped her fingers in the water, and touched them to her forehead. "Utterly charming."

The house had the old-world air of a home that had weathered the centuries: with its ochre-colored stucco walls and red barrel-tiled roof, it might have been in old Morocco or on the Côte d' Azur or overlooking a canal in Venice. But the house wasn't in any of those places. Nor was it old. It was in Palm Beach, Florida, a block from the glittering shops of Worth Avenue, and it had been built in the 1920's, part of the Spanish revival building boom that had turned a sleepy barrier island into a winter playground of the wealthy. Charlotte's old friend, Connie, who had urged her to take refuge from the cold winter as her guest, had been imploring her for years to buy a house in Palm Beach. But she had never been attracted to the enormous old mansions, mausoleumlike Regency-style monstrosities, or glittering condos that made up most of the Palm Beach housing stock. But this was different: an elegant mansion in miniature, a little Spanish-colonial hideaway.

Connie had told her that she would love it, and she had been right. Not that it was even on the market. Which put the brakes on any acquisitive inclinations that Charlotte might have been tempted to give into. And it was doubtful there were others like it: even the other houses on the street were much bigger and showier.

The owner of the house was their dinner host, a man by the name of Paul Feder, a Worth Avenue jeweler, who had been targeted by Marianne Montgomery as her next boyfriend. Marianne was a prominent fashion designer and Connie's daughter from her first marriage. She was also Charlotte's goddaughter. It was a relationship that had demanded more of Charlotte than she ever would have expected. Marianne had never been an easy child, and as an adult she was even worse. Charlotte had spent many an hour commiserating with Connie over her daughter's escapades, most of which involved men, for Marianne was as notorious for her outrageous affairs as she was for her outrageous fashions. Connie and Charlotte may have tallied up three and four marriages respectively, but they had nothing on Marianne, who at plus or minus fifty years old, had been married half a dozen times, most recently, which was seven or eight years ago, to a twenty-year-old Italian prince.

Marianne was fond of explaining away her numerous romantic liaisons with the excuse that each was a "point of light" on her path to artistic enlightenment: the Egyptian statesmen had inspired her Egyptian collection, the rodeo star her Old West collection, the Russian dancer her Ballet Russe collection, and so on. Paul, who was known for his art deco jewelry designs (he had trained in Paris under the tutelage of Fouquet, one of France's most prominent art deco jewelry designers), was the latest source of illumination on that heavily trodden path. They had met when Marianne approached him to collaborate with her on a line of jewelry that she planned to feature as part of her new art deco fashion collection.

The group invited to dine this evening at Château

en Espagne was comprised of Charlotte, Marianne, Connie, and Connie's husband, Spalding Smith. They would be joined by Marianne's daughter, Dede, who rented the guest house on the property from their host. The occasion was a preview of the jewelry collection, which was to be officially unveiled at a society function the following evening.

For a few minutes, they lingered in silence in the courtyard, caught in the spell of romantic indolence created by the tranquil violet light of early evening, and the soothing sounds of the water trickling in the fountain and the palms rustling in the soft breeze.

Then Spalding stepped up to the ancient-looking door, and sounded the heavy wrought-iron knocker.

It was Paul himself who answered the door. Unlike many of Marianne's other lovers, who often came from backgrounds vastly disparate from her own (Charlotte in particular remembered the African nationalist, whose influence on Marianne had resulted in half the socialites in New York sporting dashikis one season), Paul seemed eminently suited to the role for which Marianne had singled him out. First, he was the right age: Charlotte guessed him to be around seventy. Rather old, but older was certainly preferable to younger in Marianne's case, since her tastes in younger men verged dangerously close to the pubescent. He was very tall—six foot three or four— and very handsome, with a strong jaw and a long, aquiline nose, a high forehead and short, curly gray-white hair. The overall impression was one of aristocratic breeding. He had a military bearing, and for a man of his age, was in excellent shape. Though he bore no title, he supposedly came from minor

Russian nobility, and was distantly related to the czars. The Russian association was emphasized by his band-collared linen shirt that buttoned, Cossack-style, down the side. He was also rich: his shops in Palm Beach, New York, and Paris were patronized by the wealthy, and were well-known for their fine jewelry designs. Moreover, he and Marianne shared an interest in the world of fashion and design. Charlotte knew that Connie, for one, found him a very suitable mate for her daughter—which was more than she could have said for any the others—and was secretly hoping that her daughter would settle down at last. Charlotte wasn't ready to place any bets on it.

After greeting Charlotte's companions warmly, Paul Feder turned his attention to her. Gazing at her with clear, pale gray, deep-set eyes, he graciously lifted her hand to his lips. "I'm very honored to have you as my guest, madam," he said, kissing the back of her hand, a gesture which, coming from this dashing gentleman, was as unaffected as a casual wave.

"The pleasure is all mine, monsieur," she replied.

"What brings you to our island paradise?" he asked. "Apart from your visit with Connie and Spalding, that is."

"A New York winter," Connie answered in her friend's behalf.

Charlotte nodded in agreement. "I got tired of maneuvering around snowbanks and chipping the ice off my front steps. Actually, I like shoveling snow. But the pleasure wears pretty thin after the twelfth snowstorm."

"We've been trying to get her down here, but it's been years since she's graced us with her presence," Connie explained. "Though we see her in Newport

6

often enough," she added, gazing fondly at Charlotte. "She arrived three days ago for an indefinite stay."

Charlotte and Connie had met years ago when they both were starting out in Hollywood. But while Charlotte stayed on, Connie had left to marry her first husband and have a family. Apart from a few old movie buffs, few would remember her now. Spalding was her third husband, the scion of a conservative old Rhode Island family. The Smiths divided their time between their oceanfront house in Newport, where Charlotte was a frequent guest, their home in Greenwich, Connecticut, and their place in Palm Beach, where they spent the "season," which ran roughly from New Year's Day to Easter.

"It took the worst winter in twenty years to finally get Charlotte down here," said Spalding as he shook Paul's hand. A big man himself, Spalding was nevertheless forced to look up to their host.

After a few more moments of conversation, Paul ushered them into the foyer, with its beamed ceiling and cool floor of black Spanish tile, and then into the living room. At one end, French doors gave onto a walled swimming pool surrounded by tropical plantings, whose brightness contrasted with the somber, meditative air of the room.

As she took a seat on the sofa, Charlotte found herself being seduced by the magical atmosphere of the house. The room seemed subterranean, surrounded as it was by the dense vegetation that pushed up against the windows. It was cool and dark, and furnished very simply and sparingly with heavy Spanish-colonial-style furniture.

Most of all, it was serene. It had the feeling of a medieval cloister. A place of refuge. It was a place

7

where she could easily imagine spending the rest of her days.

Once everyone was seated, their host poured rum cocktails from a silver pitcher into gleaming antique silver mint julep cups, which were perfectly suited to the mood of the house, and placed them on a tray that he brought around to each of his guests.

After serving the cocktails, Paul took a seat next to Marianne on a sofa facing the pale stone medieval-style fireplace. Then he removed a cigarette case from his pocket and held it out to Charlotte. "Do you smoke, Miss Graham?" he asked. "It know my other guests don't."

Spalding and Connie shook their heads in acknowledgment, and Marianne looked mildly put out at the attention Paul was playing to Charlotte.

"Yes, thank you," Charlotte said, taking a cigarette from the magnificent gold case, which was inlaid with diamonds and enameled with a multicolored art deco sunburst design. She wondered if it was part of the new collection.

Reaching over, Paul lit her cigarette with his lighter.

"I'm charmed by your house," Charlotte said, savoring the smell of the tobacco. Since she smoked only a couple of cigarettes a day, she made the most of them. "What is the significance of the name Château en Espagne? I was puzzled that it was in French, rather than Spanish."

Paul nodded as he fitted a cigarette in an ivory holder and placed it between his lips. "It's a passage from a rondeau written by Charles d' Orleans when he was imprisoned in England," he explained. "In the fifteenth century."

After lighting his cigarette, he proceeded to quote the passage in perfect French, and then in English: " 'All by myself, wrapped in my thoughts. And building castles in Spain and in France.' "

"In other words, castles in the air," Charlotte said.

Paul nodded again. "In fact, the translation in English for 'Château en Espagne' is 'Castle in the Air.' I don't know for certain why the person who built the house chose that quote, but I suspect it's a reference to Mizner."

"Mizner?" said Charlotte.

"Obviously, you haven't spent much time in Palm Beach."

"Addison Mizner," Connie explained. "Palm Beach's founding father."

"You might call him that," Paul agreed. "He was the architect who designed this house. He came here in 1918, completely broke, supposedly to die. He struck up a friendship with Paris Singer, the heir to the sewing machine fortune, who had also come here to spend his final days."

"He was exhausted by his romance with Isadora Duncan," offered Marianne, for whom the dancer's countless love affairs had been a lifelong inspiration.

"Yes," said Spalding. "He called her Isa-bore-a-Drunken." He took a sip of his drink and smiled at Marianne.

She shot him a dirty look.

Though Spalding affected a limited tolerance for Marianne's sexual escapades, Charlotte suspected that this strait-laced, old-fashioned man harbored a secret fascination for his stepdaughter's antics.

"Anyway," Paul continued, "the story goes that, as they sat in their rockers on the porch of the Royal

9

Poinciana Hotel, fanning themselves and waiting to die, they started budding castles in the air."

"In what way?" asked Charlotte.

"They were seduced by the climate. The climate here is as close to perfection as you can get. It's moderated by the Gulf Stream, which flows closer to land here than anywhere else on the East Coast. They dreamed of a playground devoted to the pleasures of affluent northerners on their winter holiday."

"Let me guess the end of the story," Charlotte said. "As a result of their dreams, their spirits revived and their health improved and they went on to realize the winter playground that they had envisioned."

"Exactly. Hence the name Château en Espagne. With Mizner's artistic talent and Singer's money, they created a building boom that didn't let up until the hurricane of 1926."

"What do you call this style, exactly?" asked Charlotte as she looked around the room. She had noticed what seemed to be Spanish, Moorish, and Mediterranean elements.

"You could just call it Mizneresque. Or you could call it—as they did then—bastard Spanish, Moorish, Romanesque, Gothic, Renaissance, bull market, damn-the-expense style." Paul smiled.

"I like that," said Charlotte.

"Mizner's aim was to create the air of antiquity," Paul went on. "He didn't really care what brand of antiquity it was, as long as it was antiquity. He liked the sense that a building had been added onto over the centuries by waves of conquerors. He even built factories in West Palm Beach where he manufactured antique reproduction furniture, roof tiles, and iron work."

"Is this Mizner furniture?" Charlotte asked, running her hand over the rich, heavy wood of the coffee table. Like the rest of the furniture, it looked as if it had been found in a crumbling European villa.

Paul nodded. "Beaten with chains to give it that antique look. All of the furniture on the first floor was designed by Mizner specifically for the house. He insisted on it." He pointed to the vaulted ceiling. "The native cypress ceiling is a Mizner trademark."

"It's called pecky cypress," Spalding added. "It's very rare now."

Charlotte leaned back to look up at the hand-painted ceiling, and smoked the last of her cigarette. She had the feeling that she too, having come here to escape, was starting to spin dreams. She wondered if other houses like this were available. If she could afford it. If she would be happy here.

Most of all, she wondered if this feeling would last. It was a lot like a love affair. The question was, would she feel the same in the morning, or was it "just one of those fabulous flings," to quote a line from one of her favorite Cole Porter songs.

She almost hoped it was just one of those flings. It would make life easier. Castles in the air took a lot of energy. They were expensive to build, and even more expensive to keep up.

But then, maybe she was ready for a castle in her life.

2

THEY WERE DISCUSSING MIZNER—PAUL WAS SAYING that his house was unusual in that it was a small Mizner house—when they were interrupted by the arrival of Marianne's daughter, Dede, who entered through the door from the kitchen in the company of a large German shepherd on a leash, which she stooped down to unhook. Marianne had sometimes been called the ugly daughter of a beautiful mother. With her black hair styled in a severe Cleopatra cut and her geisha-white skin, she was striking, but at the expense of slavish hours to her appearance at the beauty salon. By contrast, her daughter, Dede, was a natural beauty, a throwback to her lovely grandmother, who, with her pale blue eyes and delicate skin, had been considered one of the great beauties of her day.

Dede stood now in the arched doorway to the kitchen, a tall, tawny beauty with mysterious yellow-blue eyes—the color of sunlight shining through a wave—and long, curly, golden-brown hair that flowed over her bare shoulders. She had a perfect smile that was made all the more charming by the presence of a slight gap between her two front teeth. She was wearing a sarong-style dress in a black and gold batik pattern that emphasized the exotic, almost feline, quality of her loveliness.

The last time Charlotte had seen Dede she had been an awkward, long-limbed teenager, and now, within the space of only a few short years, she had been transformed into this exotic swan.

"I took her for a walk down to the beach," Dede said, looking up at Paul. When she had finished unleashing the dog, she stood up and crossed the room to kiss first her mother and then her grandmother. Then she poured herself a cocktail from the pitcher on the tray.

"Shall I get more ice?" she asked, and when Paul nodded, she disappeared through the door to the kitchen with the ice bucket, reappearing with it a moment later.

Charlotte noticed Dede's easy familiarity with the house. She also noticed Marianne noticing the same thing. Her sharp, dark eyes followed Dede's every move with the intensity of a bird dog stalking its prey. Did Dede have a thing going with Paul, or did Marianne just think she did? Charlotte wondered.

If she did, it would be a case of the apple falling not far from the tree. Charlotte remembered the way in which Marianne as a young woman had flirted with Connie's second husband, Count Brandolini, who had probably been as old as Paul at the time. In fact, it was probably on account of competition with her mother that Marianne had been prompted to marry her own Italian count.

If Dede did have a thing going with Paul, her motives were probably the same as Marianne's had been before her: to rankle her mother.

"You seem to know your way around here pretty well," Marianne said icily, as Dede set the ice bucket on the tray. Marianne was not one to disguise her feelings. She sat next to Paul, wearing a chic black and white cocktail dress with a square neckline from her recent collection.

"Mother, I live here," Dede protested.

13

"Not here, I hope," Marianne said.

"You know what I mean, Mother," Dede responded, her low voice tense. "I mean that I live out in back."

"Dede lives in the guest cottage at the rear of the house," Connie broke in, in an attempt to thaw the icy atmosphere. "Maybe you'll take Aunt Charlotte out there later on and give her a little tour."

"I'd be happy to, Nana," Dede said. She gave her mother a daggered look and then bent down to kiss her step-grandfather, who sat next to Connie on the tapestry-upholstered couch.

As she did so, Paul introduced the dog, who sat at his feet, as Lady Astor. "There was a time when I would have described her as my dog," he said as he scratched the animal's neck. "But I'm not sure that I can make that claim anymore. Dede seems to have replaced me in her affections."

"That's only because I'm around more than you are," Dede said. "If you'll pardon my saying so, someone who travels as much as you do shouldn't even have a dog," she chided.

"That's why I had the good sense to rent my guest house to you," was Paul's good-natured retort.

"What do you think of my granddaughter, Charlotte?" asked Connie proudly, as she patted Dede's hand.

Seen beside Connie, Dede's resemblance to her grandmother was striking. Their coloring was different—Connie had blue eyes, and, as a young woman, had had a peaches and cream complexion—but the features were virtually identical.

"She's exquisite, and a dead ringer for her beautiful grandmother."

14

"Let's all compliment Dede," Marianne said acidly, provoking an angry stare from her own mother.

Charlotte remembered Dede once describing her mother as "toxic," and she could now see why. She recalled how shocked she had been by Marianne's apparent indifference to Dede as a child. Now that Dede was an adult that indifference seemed to have hardened into outright animosity.

But Dede seemed oblivious to her mother's barbs.

"Hello, Aunt Charlotte," Dede said, leaning over for a kiss. Then, embarrassed by the attention, she swayed across the room in her graceful sarong to a chair by the fireplace and took a seat, crossing one long, tanned, lovely leg over the other. Every eye in the room was upon her.

With Dede's entrance, the energy in the room had undergone a subtle shift. She had that magnetic quality that would have made her a natural in front of the camera, but her interests lay in another direction.

Because of her grandparents' residence in Newport, which could boast some of the country's finest architecture, Dede had developed an interest in historic preservation, and after studying that subject in college, she had landed an enviable job—with the help of Spalding's connections—at the Historic Preservation Association of Palm Beach.

In fact, it was because of Dede that they had gathered at Paul's. Dede's boss at the preservation association, a Palm Beach socialite named Lydia Collins, was a collector of Normandiana, art deco mementoes and artworks from the French ocean liner, the *Normandie*. She displayed her collection in an art deco house that had been built in the same period as the ship itself.

15

The year before, Dede had suggested to her mother that she collaborate with Paul on an art deco jewelry collection to be previewed at a dinner dance at Lydia Collins' home, which was called Villa Normandie. The party, at which prominent guests would display the jewelry, would have a *Normandie* theme and would be a fundraiser for the preservation association.

The idea had been a big success. In a town in which social life revolved around charity functions, the quest was for a novel idea. Apparently, the combination of the *Normandie* theme and the jewelry collection debut was just the ticket to appeal to jaded Palm Beach socialites. The party was to take the form of a captain's dinner that had been held on the 100th sailing of the *Normandie,* which had taken place in the summer of 1938.

"How are the plans coming, my dear?" asked Connie of her granddaughter, who was the assistant to Lydia Collins, chairman of the benefit.

"Fine," said Dede. "A few last minute glitches, which is to be expected. But we've sold out all three hundred tickets at five hundred dollars apiece. We expect to net about a hundred thousand dollars, which is good since we need the money desperately. We've been having a serious budget shortfall."

"To put it euphemistically," said Paul. "Without this benefit, Dede wouldn't be getting her next paycheck."

"Paul is the treasurer of the association," Dede explained. "And he's on the board of the Palm Beach Civic Association, as well." She looked over at him fondly. "He's known around town as Mr. Palm Beach."

Paul smiled. "It's good for business."

16

"Speaking of business," said Marianne, "I think we should look at the collection now." She turned to Paul. "How much time do we have before dinner?"

He checked his watch. "About twenty minutes," he replied, then rose and led his guests to a heavy Spanish-style side table on which half a dozen jewelry boxes were set out. "I've taken the liberty of choosing the pieces that each of you will wear. But I can assure you that only the finest pieces will be modeled by those present."

"Oh, what fun!" said Connie, clapping her hands in anticipation. She gazed eagerly at the assortment of various-sized boxes on the table. They were made of lapis-blue calfskin with the words "Feder Jewelers, Fine Jewelry Since 1924, Paris, New York, Palm Beach" embossed in gold lettering on the lid, along with a family crest.

Paul picked up one of the boxes and held it out in front of Connie. "For Madame," he said as he opened it. Resting on the white satin lining was a magnificent bracelet of diamonds and sapphires set in a chevron design, with earrings to match.

Connie removed the earrings she was wearing and clipped on the new pair. "They're gorgeous," she said as she admired the earrings in a gilded mirror that hung over the table. Then she fastened the bracelet around her wrist, and held it up to the mirror.

The blue of the sapphires perfectly marched her eyes.

"Do you like them?" Marianne asked.

Connie leaned over and kissed her daughter. "You've done it again, my dear. I'm so proud of you."

Marianne stood by with arms folded, assessing the effect of her creations on Connie's image in the

17

mirror. "It helps to have someone in mind to design the jewelry for," she said graciously.

"You designed these for me?" Connie asked, and her daughter nodded.

"And for Monsieur. . ." Paul said. He opened a small box to reveal a diamond-and-jet pinkie ring, also in an art deco design. He slid the ring on Spalding's finger. "This collection is unusual in that there are almost as many items for the gentleman as there are for the lady," he explained.

"That's Paul's doing," Marianne commented.

"Very nice," said Spalding, holding out his hand to admire the ring. "Do we get to keep these as party favors?"

Paul smiled and shook his head. "They're due back in the shop by noon on Monday. I'm afraid that I'll have to ask you to sign a memo to that effect—a mere formality. But you're welcome to buy it. It's only"— he checked the price tag in the box—"twenty-two thousand dollars."

"I don't think so," said Spalding, who despite his affluence came from the kind of old Yankee stock that didn't believe in pretentious displays of wealth. He didn't even drive a new model automobile.

Dede stood looking on, the dog at her side.

"Next," said Paul, turning to her. Picking up another box from the table, he opened it to reveal a delicate diamond choker, which he proceeded to fasten around the smooth, tanned skin of her exquisitely long neck. No one could have shown such a necklace off to better effect.

"It's beautiful," she murmured, turning to admire it in the mirror.

Though everyone else made admiring comments,

18

Charlotte noticed that the young woman's mother refrained from saying anything. Which she supposed was better than her earlier, sarcastic remarks.

"Now I will show you what Marianne and I will carry," Paul said, turning back to the table. "First, for Marianne." Picking up the largest of the boxes, he removed a small, colorfully enameled pocketbook. The inside was divided into compartments for lipstick, mirror, and comb.

"How lovely," Charlotte said.

"And relatively inexpensive," he added.

"It's called a *minaudière*," Marianne explained. "It has compartments for everything a lady might need for an evening out."

"And for yourself?" Charlotte asked Paul.

"I have the honor of carrying the second most expensive piece in the collection," he replied. "But if I may say so, Marianne, it is the most beautiful item in an absolutely stunning collection."

Marianne nodded in acknowledgment of the compliment.

Reaching into his pocket, Paul pulled out the diamond-inlaid gold case from which he had offered Charlotte a cigarette earlier in the evening.

"How much is that worth?" Spalding asked.

"About two hundred thousand," he replied. Opening it, he offered Charlotte another cigarette, which she declined. "But well worth every penny. Not since Fabergé has there been such workmanship, if I do say so myself."

"And what's the most expensive piece?" asked Spalding, who, though much too polite to ever say so, was clearly astonished that anyone would pay so much for something as frivolous as a cigarette case.

19

"This," Paul said, picking up the remaining box. "Five hundred thousand. But it's not the most unique—that honor belongs to my cigarette case. This is actually a copy of a piece that was designed by Cartier in the 1930's. They gave us permission to reproduce it."

"Little did we know when we planned to include it that we would have the ideal model," Marianne said.

Paul smiled and turned to Charlotte.

"*Moi?*" she said, clapping a hand to her chest. Having only arrived at the last minute, she hadn't expected to be included at all.

"Yes," said Paul. Standing before her, he slowly opened the lid.

Charlotte gasped. Inside was a replica of the necklace she had worn in the film, *The Normandie Affair,* which had been shot on the ocean liner in 1939.

"The original is on display at the Musée des Arts Décoratifs in Paris, as I'm sure you know," Paul said.

Charlotte nodded. The necklace had been on loan from Cartier, which had displayed it at the 1939 New York World's Fair. They had also lent it to her when she received the Oscar for her role in the film.

"Let's hope that no one steals it tomorrow night," said Paul, referring to the movie plot, in which the necklace is stolen by an enterprising jewel thief with whom Charlotte falls in love.

"I hope not," Charlotte said.

"Don't worry," he reassured her, "there are going to be security guards there. If you don't mind, we'd very much like to photograph you wearing the necklace," he continued. "It would be wonderful publicity to have the actress who wore these jewels in

20

the movie wearing them again at our party."

"I'm afraid I look a little different now," Charlotte remarked. She had been twenty then, younger than Dede was now. Young, and still so innocent. Though she had already made two films, it was her role in *The Normandie Affair* that would make her a star.

"Not much, if I may be so bold as to comment," Paul said as he fastened the necklace around her neck.

"Thank you," she replied. Though she was not without wrinkles, her skin was well preserved, and she considered the fact that time had treated her face so well as one of the great benisons of her life.

The necklace was of a flexible openwork geometric design of diamonds in various cuts mounted in platinum and accented with cabochon rubies. From the center hung a single cabochon ruby the size of a small hen's egg. There was also a diamond and ruby bracelet to match.

"I remember this necklace very well," said Connie, who had met Charlotte earlier in 1939, just after they had both arrived in Hollywood. She looked over at Charlotte. "It brings back memories."

"It certainly does," said Charlotte as she gazed at her reflection in the gilded mirror.

Though the passage to Europe had been memorable enough for a twenty-year old—it had been her first ocean voyage—it was the passage back that was the stuff of Charlotte's memories. It had been her own private *Normandie* affair. She was married; he was married. And despite their youth—he was only a few years older than she—both marriages were already on the rocks. Her marriage to her hometown sweetheart had started to fall apart when she'd gone to

21

Hollywood the previous year, and by the summer of 1939 was as good as dead. He had been separated for a year, but was planning to go back to his wife to give the marriage one last try. His name was Eddie Norwood, and he was a piano player with the ship's orchestra: the George Thurmond Orchestra. Their affair had lasted four glorious days, days that she would remember for the rest of her life. Four days, twelve hours, and twenty-eight minutes, to be precise. It was the first time she had really been in love, and there was to be only one other real love in her life, though she had been married four times and had had more lovers than she cared to admit to. It might have lasted longer, had the war not intervened. Instead, it had ended up being "just one of those fabulous flings." "Just One of Those Things" had had been their song. She remembered now how he had played it for her on the baby grand piano in the Café-Grill as the sun rose in the east on their first morning out. They had been up all night. She had been wearing the Cartier necklace, which she would be returning to New York for display at The World's Fair. After they arrived home she never saw him again, though their paths had crossed, like ships in the night, many times. He had just been starting out then, as had she, but he had gone on to become one of the most famous bandleaders of popular music history. She'd once read that he had sold over a hundred million records. For a time it seemed as if he was everywhere: he had hosted his own radio show, and later his own television show; he had starred in several dance band movies; he had arranged the music for many of Hollywood's best-known movies, including some of Charlotte's own; and his All-American Band

22

had played every major hotel, theatre, and ballroom in the country, to say nothing of the White House and Buckingham Palace.

Their lives had been like two arcs whose trajectories occupy the same plane in space and time but never intersect. Charlotte had often felt that fate must have been conspiring to keep them apart, so unlikely was it that their paths never crossed again.

And if they had? Would she still have felt that spark? Or was she past the point of feeling sparks anymore? She turned to Paul, her fingers raised to the cool, smooth ruby. In retrospect, the necklace seemed to have a magical quality, like an amulet. It was with this necklace that all that was good in her life—romance, fame, wealth—had begun. "May we keep our jewels on?" she asked, reluctant to relinquish the necklace that had set loose such a flood of memories.

"Of course," he replied with a gracious smile. "The necklace is yours until Monday at noon." He turned to Connie and Spalding. "The same is true for you. The point of fine jewelry is to enjoy it."

"We certainly will," said Connie enthusiastically.

The swinging door to the kitchen opened, carrying with it the aroma of fine cuisine. A young man in a starched white jacket appeared, no doubt from one of the many companies that catered Palm Beach's private parties.

"Dinner is served," he announced, and proceeded to shepherd the guests in the direction of the dining room.

If Charlotte was already in love with Château en Espagne, she fell for it even harder once she saw the dining room. Like the rest of the house, it was simple almost to the point of being austere. But its severity was relieved by the rich paneling, which Paul said Mizner had imported from a Spanish monastery. The dining room table had also been designed by Mizner, in his heavy antique Spanish style, with sling-back chairs of rich Spanish leather. Wrought-iron candelabra stood in the center of the table, no doubt another product of the Mizner workshops, and the French doors opened on to a terrace lush with tropical foliage, including an orange tree whose fruits hung like gumdrops from the branches. Charlotte was surprised that she was so drawn to this style of house. It was quite masculine, and much more restrained than she was accustomed to. But she had found that the older she got, the more she wanted to strip away the excess. Elegant simplicity was her credo. She was way beyond chintz and knickknacks. It was her theory that this impulse to shed belongings that tended to overcome people in later life was a consequence of the accumulation of experience. If one went according to the premise that there was a finite amount of *stuff* with which the human mind could cope, then it became necessary to shed baggage as one accumulated more experience, and exterior baggage was easier to shed than the interior kind.

The table was set with handsome Spanish stoneware, whose rustic style matched the mood of the room. The meal, which was quickly and efficiently served by white-jacketed waiters, was simple but delicious: a perfectly cooked filet of beef, with fresh vegetables, green salad, and crusty focaccia.

Over the meal, which included an excellent cabernet, they talked about the *Normandie*. Or rather, *Normandie*. The name of the ship had inspired much

24

debate. Though it was named after the French province in which its home port was located, and therefore should have been *La Normandie,* it was a ship and therefore should have taken the masculine article (the names of ships being masculine in French), *Le Normandie.* The powers-that-be had settled on *Normandie,* with no article at all, but Charlotte had always thought of the *Normandie* as a she. Despite the ship's size and power, she was every inch a female.

Charlotte was the only one among them who had actually sailed on the renowned luxury liner.

"What was she like?" Marianne asked.

"In my humble opinion, she was simply the most magnificent thing ever built by man," Charlotte replied. Then she went on: "At the time, she was the biggest ocean liner ever built. If you can imagine the Chrysler Building turned on its side—that was how big she was. And the fastest. But she was much more than the biggest and the fastest. She was also the most beautiful, the most elegant, the most gracious. She was—"

"The world's most perfect ship?" Spalding broke in. "That's how a friend once described her to me."

"Yes," Charlotte agreed. "Perfection. A floating work of art. The greatest French artists were commissioned to design the artworks and the furnishings: Lalique, Dupas, Dunand. Each of the cabins was different and they were all exquisite." She thought back to her own two-bedroom, two-and-a-half-bath luxury suite—all highly polished woods, smooth upholstery, gleaming surfaces, and curved lines. There hadn't been a rough edge in all five rooms. That was life aboard the *Normandie:* no rough edges.

"The French considered her the pride of France," Spalding said. "So much money was spent on the ship that they called her 'the floating debt.' "

"I didn't know that, but I can understand why," Charlotte said. "And the service! She had the largest crew of any passenger ship that ever sailed. The crew-to-passenger ratio was something like one-and-a-half to one."

"When did you sail on her?" Paul asked.

"I was a passenger twice. The first time was the eastbound crossing in early August of 1939. That's when we filmed *The Normandie Affair*. The shipboard part of it, that is; the rest was shot in Paris. I was a passenger again on the return crossing, which left Le Havre on August twenty-third, 1939."

"I'm surprised you remember the exact date," Marianne commented.

"It's an easy date to remember. Unforgettable, in fact: the day after Germany and Russia stunned the world with the announcement of their nonaggression pact. France was mobilizing, Britain was preparing to blockade Germany, and the rumors were that Germany would invade Poland by that evening."

"Which they actually did on September first," Spalding put in.

"Yes. The ship was filled with people who were getting out while the getting was still good—German and Czech refugees, draft dodgers, Americans desperate to get home before war broke out. Everyone was very apprehensive. Then, the first morning out, the *Bremen* was spotted on our port side. The crew was certain that she was bird-dogging for a German sub."

"The *Lusitania* all over again," said Spalding.

Charlotte nodded. "We were all afraid that we'd be torpedoed. As the trip progressed, the mood turned from one of apprehension to one of near hysteria. The rumor on board was that war had broken out. Passengers were spotting illusory U-boats every five minutes, and every sighting resulted in a mad stampede for the life jackets."

Charlotte paused while a young waiter refilled their wineglasses, and then continued with her tale:

"To avoid subs, the reserve boilers were brought on line, and the ship set a new zigzag course, which was supposedly the recommended strategy for avoiding a torpedo hit. We also followed a course that took us a hundred miles farther north than the ship had ever sailed before, which of course set everyone to worrying about hitting an iceberg."

"What a trip!" said Marianne.

"It was exciting," Charlotte agreed. "Radio communication was cut off for the entire trip for fear that a German sub would use the radio signal as a beacon; and when night fell, passengers were ordered to turn off the overhead lights in their cabins and draw their curtains," she added, remembering the eerie mood of the long, hushed, dim corridors.

"Did you manage to lose the *Bremen?*" Spalding asked.

Charlotte nodded. "We left her behind during the night. But that didn't stop the sub worries. For some reason, the officers were convinced there was a spy on board who was signaling our position to a sub, and they passed their theories on to the passengers."

"That must have made for great passenger camaraderie," said Spalding facetiously.

"Everybody was convinced the person next to them

27

was a spy. I've never seen such paranoia." In retrospect, Charlotte imagined that it was this charged atmosphere that had allowed two otherwise respectable married people to let down their guard. Neither of them thought they would live to see the next day.

"That was the *Normandie's* last crossing," Charlotte said. "But it wasn't the last time I saw her," she added, as she laid her knife and fork across her empty plate. The meal had been delicious.

"You saw her in New York, you mean?" Connie asked.

"Oh yes, I used to see her in New York," Charlotte said. Unlike many other film stars, Charlotte had always made her home in New York, where the *Normandie* had been docked for safety during the early part of the war. "But the last time I saw her was on February ninth, 1942. Saw her alive, that is."

"The day she burned," Spalding commented.

Charlotte nodded. "After Pearl Harbor, the *Normandie* was seized along with the other French ships in U.S. ports. The Navy was converting her into a troopship when a fire broke out. The fire was extinguished, but so much water was pumped into her holds that she capsized in her slip. As I'm sure you all know."

"But it's fascinating to hear about it from someone who was there," said Marianne, who sat at the opposite end of the table from Paul.

They had finished their dinners, and the waiters entered to clear the table for the dessert course. Once their places had been cleared, Paul offered Charlotte another cigarette from his exquisite case. *There goes tomorrow's ration,* she thought as she helped herself to

28

her fourth of the day.

"I remember that day as if it were yesterday," she said as Paul lit her cigarette. "We all knew the *Normandie* was burning, of course. There was this acrid brown haze hanging over midtown. I had an appointment with a producer in Rockefeller Center that afternoon, and I could see the decks burning from his office window. Later on I went down to Pier eighty-eight to watch. The Navy had painted her hull in a camouflage design, and they had painted over her name. She had been renamed the U.S.S. *Lafayette*. But as the fire burned, the new paint blistered, revealing that wonderful red and black of the funnels and the gold lettering that spelled out her name."

Charlotte paused, took a puff of her cigarette, and looked out at the darkening foliage, remembering that icy February afternoon. Then she turned back to her audience. "It was as if her soul were shining through that drab paint. She was like an elegant lady who's still elegant, despite her age, despite the indignities that have been heaped upon her, despite the arrogance and stupidity that were determined to kill her." It struck Charlotte that she might have been speaking about herself; no wonder she had felt such an affinity with the lovely ship. The only difference was that she was still forging on ahead, despite the indignities she had suffered over the course of her fifty years in Hollywood.

"Later that evening, I went out to dinner and a show. I was with Will," she explained, naming the man who would become her second husband and who would die prematurely of a heart attack. She remembered how hard it had been to concentrate on the meal when the *Normandie* was burning just a few

29

blocks away. "The show was Cole Porter's *Let's Face It*. At the Imperial."

"With Danny Kaye and Nanette Fabray," said Spalding. " 'Ace In the Hole.' " Pleasantly lubricated by the rum cocktails and the wine, he began to sing the popular tune from the show.

"Enough, darling," said Connie, tapping him on the arm. "Charlotte's telling us a story. Please go on, Charlotte."

Spalding harrumphed and turned back to his wineglass.

Seated next to Charlotte, Dede was surreptitiously feeding bits of leftover filet to Lady Astor, who sat quietly under the table, thumping her tail.

"It was a bitterly cold night. Afterward, we walked down to Twelfth Avenue to watch. I'll never forget the sight. The charred and broken-up hull, still steaming in places, the cascades of ice, all illuminated by the eerie glare of the floodlights. And the crowd! If I remember right, it was estimated at fifteen thousand. The fire had been under control since six-thirty, but the tugs and fireboats were still pouring water into her. Even an idiot could see that if they didn't stop, she would keel over from the weight of the water."

Charlotte's audience sat spellbound by her tale of the death of the magnificent ship. The candles had burned down and flickered in the breeze that wafted in through the open French doors.

"Just after midnight, the admiral in charge ordered all hands to leave the ship. By that time she was listing seriously to port. The wonderful French-Line gangplanks had fallen into the water, and the hawsers that held her to the wharf had snapped and hung

30

down from her sides like spaghetti. Will and I stood there and watched as she slowly tilted farther and farther over. With each lurch, there were these terrible groans and crashes as she began to break up. They were like the death rattles of a living thing. Then she slowly edged over, her great funnels coming to rest just inches above the water."

Charlotte was surprised that tears had actually come to her eyes. She must be getting sentimental in her old age. Or maybe she'd just had too much to drink. "It was one of the most tragic events I've ever witnessed," she continued. "she was like a magnificent beached whale that no one could help. I remember that as she came to rest in her slip, a wisp of smoke drifted over midtown, like the last breath of an expiring creature. She lay there on her side in the mud for eighteen months before they finally righted her and towed her to Brooklyn, where she was auctioned off for scrap."

"I remember seeing her from the West Side Highway when I was on leave in the city," said Spalding. "The police had erected a fence at the pierhead to prevent rubbernecking, but you could still see her. What impressed me was that vast expanse of her flank." Addressing Charlotte, he asked, "What would you say her length was? Over a thousand feet?"

Charlotte nodded.

"And how pathetically useless those gigantic propellers looked sticking up above the surface of the water," Spalding added.

"I always felt as if a part of my past had died with the *Normandie*," Charlotte said. "A part of everyone's past. It was the end of an era. Literally, because the advent of regular transatlantic flight put an end to the era of the grand ocean liners, and figuratively as well. I always saw the death of the *Normandie* as the end of American innocence."

"I would think that most people would consider Pearl Harbor the end of American innocence," Spalding submitted.

"Of course," Charlotte concurred. "But I always linked the two events in my mind. Everyone thought it was sabotage, you see. Pearl Harbor in Hawaii, and, two months and two days later, the *Normandie* in New York. The press had been warning that she was a target. One reporter even slipped aboard without being challenged, to plant imaginary bombs and set imaginary fires."

"The Germans took credit for it, didn't they?" said Spalding.

"Yes," Charlotte acknowledged. "But the conclusion of the investigation conducted by the New York District Attorney's Office was that it was an accident. If I remember right, their wording was 'Carelessness has served the enemy with equal effectiveness.' "

There was silence for a few moments while everyone at the table pondered the sad fate of the *Normandie.* Then Dede stood up to leave, the diamond choker around her swanlike neck gleaming in the candlelight.

"I'm sorry I have to run," she said. "But I have a few last-minute details to iron out with the bandleader. Thank you, Aunt Charlotte, for telling us about the *Normandie.* And thank you, Paul, for the wonderful dinner."

"Who's the band going to be?" asked Connie as the waiters served the dessert: a sinful-looking chocolate

32

mousse cake. "Not Grant Martin again, I hope. People are tired of the same old boring dance band all the time."

"No. At your suggestion, Nana, we've gotten someone different. We're really lucky, in fact. We're going to have a famous big-band leader who's down here because he's being inducted into the Big Band Hall of Fame at their annual ball, which is in two weeks."

Connie turned to Charlotte "The Big Band Hall of Fame is one of Palm Beach's charities," she explained. "They hold a ball to raise money for a Big Band Hall of Fame museum; it's going to be in a beautiful old Mediterranean-style building at Palm Beach Community College in West Palm Beach."

"Who is this bandleader?" Charlotte asked, wondering if the two separate trajectories might finally be about to intersect.

"Eddie Norwood," Dede replied.

3

CHARLOTTE WAS STAYING AT THE BRAZILIAN Court, an old Mediterranean-style hotel built around a charming fountained courtyard, and located in a residential section of Palm Beach four blocks from the ocean. She had chosen to stay at a hotel rather than with Connie and Spalding in order to spare them the burden of her constant presence. Though Connie and Spalding's house was large—in fact, it might have been called a mansion—she knew that if she had stayed there, they would have felt obligated to entertain her. A measure of privacy might have been provided by their guest house, Grace and Favour, but at the moment, it was occupied by Marianne, who like Charlotte, spent most of her time in New York. When Charlotte had asked Connie where she should stay, Connie had recommended the Brazilian Court, and Charlotte had been very pleased with the accommodations. The hotel had been a Palm Beach landmark since the twenties and had the charming, unpretentious feel of old Florida. She wasn't the first movie star who had stayed there: the hotel had a reputation for discreetly pampering the rich and famous. She occupied a one-bedroom suite on the first floor whose stucco walls were painted lemon-yellow, and which was charmingly furnished with French provincial furniture painted a cheerful green and white. A bay window in her sitting room looked out over the courtyard through a thicket of jungly vegetation that left no doubt that she was a visitor to the tropics.

She had spent the day on nearby Worth Avenue, which rivaled Rodeo Drive's reputation as the most expensive shopping street in the country. She had been trying to forget the subject that was uppermost in her mind: her anticipated meeting with Eddie that evening. Now she sat in one of the rattan chairs in her bedroom, looking at the gown that was spread out on her bed. It was the Fortuny gown that she had worn in the Grand Salon scene of *The Normandie Affair* and again on the return trip, the night she had met Eddie. Both times she had worn it with the Cartier necklace. For fifty-three years, the dress had hung in its garment bag in the closet in the spare room of her Manhattan town house, a memento of those four short

34

days just before the outbreak of the war. And now she would be wearing it again, to a dinner dance at a house filled with artworks from the *Normandie* at which Eddie Norwood would be leading the orchestra. Little had she known that she would be meeting Eddie again when she had unearthed the gown from her closet. Her instructions from Connie when she had called to invite Charlotte for a visit had been to pack an evening gown that one might have worn to a gala dance on board the *Normandie*. Though she knew the plans for Eddie to play must have been made long in advance of Connie's call, she nevertheless felt as if it was her decision to wear the Fortuny gown that had set in motion the series of events that would result in her reunion with the first man she had ever fallen in love with.

She had retrieved the necklace from the hotel safe on her way back from Worth Avenue and now laid it out on the bed above the neckline of the dress and draped the ensemble with the silver fox stole that she had also worn on that voyage. The effect was stunning: the deep red of the ruby pendant was a perfect complement to the faded rose of the delicately pleated dress. The gown was one of Fortuny's Delphos designs, a long sheath of silk so fine that it had to be weighted down with tiny beads sewn into the hem. Fortuny had always been one of Charlotte's favorite designers, and she had several other Fortuny gowns that she still wore from time to time. They were worth a fortune now, collector's items. One advantage of a Fortuny gown was that the pleats were forgiving of extra pounds—not that Charlotte was overweight, but she wasn't twenty years old anymore either.

Her thoughts were interrupted by a rap on the door. It was room service with the Manhattan she had ordered a few minutes before. Drink in hand, she sat down, put her feet up, and indulged herself in the memories that the vision of the dress evoked. It had happened in the Grand Salon, the first night out. Eddie had been noodling on the piano in between sets. A mutual acquaintance had introduced them. Charlotte and the acquaintance had been standing beside the piano, waiting for Eddie to finish. Then he had gotten up and turned around to meet her. The acquaintance later said it was the only time in his life that he'd ever seen two people fall in love right before his eyes. If he'd filmed the event, he joked, he could have sold the footage to colleges for use in their behavioral science classes. Later, she and Eddie had danced. Oh, how they had danced! On that wonderful parquet dance floor, the pattern of which was an exact replica of the one on the floor in the Fontainebleau throne room. Eddie was a wonderful dancer. Afterward they had walked on the covered promenade, talking. When the orchestra had stopped playing in the Grand Salon, they had gone to the circular Café-Grill at the stern of the ship and danced to the music of a French tango orchestra. That was the night they'd had the unforgettable thrill of watching the sun rise over the sea through the curving wall of bay windows surrounding the room. Eddie had played "Just One of Those Things" on the baby grand piano.

After that there had been three more wonderful days—and nights. And that had been it: four days in a lifetime. An isolated piece of time, an isolated piece of space. The elegant surroundings, the gourmet food, the threat of war. She had often wondered if it would have been different had they met somewhere else.

Her reverie was interrupted by a telephone call. It was the front desk calling to tell her that a courier would be dropping something off at her room.

When she peered through her peephole a moment later, she could hardly believe her eyes. It was a pageboy from the *Normandie*—or rather, a catering company employee posing as a pageboy from the *Normandie*—dressed in the same scarlet livery with the same polished brass buttons and the same jaunty little scarlet pillbox cap with the chin strap.

It was as if she'd pressed a button on a time machine. They had been everywhere on board the *Normandie,* these quick-footed servants, always on hand to meet the passengers' every need and request.

For a moment she just stood there in surprise. Then she opened the door. With a white-gloved hand, the page handed her that evening's dinner menu, along with a card showing the table seating and a copy of the ship's daily newspaper, *L'Atlantique.* Just so had the pageboys on board the *Normandie* delivered the same information to the passengers fifty-three years ago.

"Courtesy of Mrs. Harley T. Collins of Villa Normandie," he said as he saluted sharply. Then he spun on his heel to leave, but not before Charlotte had tipped him generously.

She looked at the seating card first. She would be sitting at the captain's table. Then she opened the card to see who the other guests at her table would be. They were Mrs. Harley T. Collins; Admiral John W. McLean III (USN, retired), whom she supposed to be the "captain"; Mr. and Mrs. Spalding L. Smith; Mr. Paul Feder; Ms. Marianne Montgomery; Ms. Diana Montgomery; a couple she didn't know; and, at the bottom of the list, just below her own name, Mr. Edward Norwood. No Mrs. Norwood was listed.

Taking a deep breath, Charlotte went back to her chair and picked up her drink and the copy of *L'Atlantique*. The headline was "100th Crossing of *Normandie*." The front page featured a story on the crossing, along with photographs of the ship. The middle two pages were taken up by a photo layout of celebrities who had sailed on the ship in the one hundred crossings since its maiden voyage in 1935. They were displayed according to category: stage, screen, society, sports, diplomatic service, and so on. The back page listed all the records that had been broken by the *Normandie*, including 572,519 bottles of wine and champagne consumed in one hundred voyages.

Setting down the paper, she then picked up the menu. The cover was the same as the menu aboard the *Normandie:* a colorful drawing of fish, poultry, game, fruit, and wine. Seeing it brought back memories of that marvelous dining room, which had been the length of a football field—supposedly the largest single room ever built aboard a ship.

Inside, the menu was headed:

SS Normandie
Diner de Gala
Samedi 16 Juillet 1938

The menu was typical of the first-class dining room, with eight courses, ranging from *hors d'oeuvres* and *potages* to *fromages* and *pâtisserie*.

"Yes," she thought, "it's going to be quite an evening."

Spalding and Connie picked her up in front of the Brazilian Court at five-thirty. Marianne would be going with Paul, and Dede would be going on her own. Charlotte was waiting for them as they pulled up in Spalding's ten-year-old Cadillac. Though he came from wealth, Spalding was a throwback to an earlier, more conservative era of society in a Palm Beach that was rapidly being taken over by junk bond financiers, German industrialists, and fifteen-minute celebrities. It was typical of Spalding's old-money social stratum that they drove cars until they fell apart. Charlotte was enormously fond of him. He sat now behind the wheel, portly, rubicund, and comfortingly dependable, attired in the same English-tailored tuxedo that he'd been wearing to social events for as long as Charlotte had known him. Finding a thirties-style tuxedo wouldn't have been a problem for Spalding, since his own was probably of that vintage. Though Connie had been married three times, her marriage to Spalding had lasted now for more than twenty years and seemed as solid as the Rock of Gibraltar. In fact, Charlotte suspected that her own subconscious envy of their marriage had been one reason she had married her fourth husband. As with Spalding, Jack Lundstrom's appeal had been his dependability. But Charlotte should have known that what worked for Connie wouldn't work for her. Though she and Jack had worked very hard at making a go of it, they'd eventually come to recognize that Charlotte wasn't cut out to be the wife of a Midwestern businessman—she especially hadn't been cut out to live in Minneapolis!—and Jack was unsuited to play the part of Mr. Charlotte Graham. After several years of vacillating, they'd parted amicably a couple of years ago.

After four husbands, Charlotte figured it was time to put the whole "men" issue to rest. It had taken her some time to come to terms with this decision, which is why she was finding the anticipated meeting with Eddie Norwood so disturbing.

"You look beautiful this evening, Charlotte," said Spalding politely as the doorman helped her into the back seat. "As always," he added.

"Thank you," she replied. "This is the gown that I wore in *The Normandie Affair*. I haven't had it on in fifty-three years."

"I'm amazed you could still fit into it," said Connie, referring to her own plump figure, which was clothed in a diaphanous blue gown that matched the sapphires in her gem-encrusted bracelet.

Though Connie was still a pretty women, the years hadn't been as kind to her as they had to Charlotte. She had the kind of delicate skin that doesn't stand up well to time, and she had put on a lot of weight in her later years.

"Actually, so am I," Charlotte said as the doorman closed the car door behind her. "But the pleats help."

After crossing the width of the island, Spalding headed south on South Ocean Boulevard, which ran along the oceanfront, with the rolling turquoise sea on their left and, on the right, the gated mansions that were screened from the road by the tall hedges that were the foremost manifestation of Palm Beach's fierce desire for privacy. The mansions, whose turrets and upper stories were visible above the hedges, were a stylistic mishmash: Old Spanish next to Venetian

40

Gothic next to Palladian Revival next to French Regency; money next to money next to money next to money—an unremitting display of wealth. And growing everywhere were the mop-headed coconut palms, their lithe, slender trunks leaning this way and that like dancers frozen in exotic poses. Charlotte had read that Palm Beach had its origins in the misfortune of a Spanish ship that had been swept ashore during a storm in the late nineteenth century with a cargo of coconuts. Two enterprising homesteaders claimed the coconuts, and started selling them to other settlers for a few cents apiece. The settlers planted them along the beach and the lakefront. When Henry Morrison Flagler, the Standard Oil tycoon, visited some years later, he was so entranced by the palm-fringed coral island that he decided to transform it into a resort mecca for the wealthy. Though in recent years many of the island's palms had died as the result of a blight, the community had recently launched a campaign to replant the roadsides with the trees that had come to symbolize the exotic, languorous mood of their town.

As they headed downtown, Connie and Spalding filled Charlotte in on their hostess, Lydia Collins, who lived around the corner from them: hers was oceanfront property—in fact, it stretched from ocean to lake—while theirs was on a side street. Lydia belonged to a distinctive Palm Beach type that Spalding and Connie disdained, though they would never have come right out and said so. Palm Beach had often been called the back door to society, and Lydia was one of those people who, having been snubbed at the front entrance, had gone around to the rear. Spalding especially, with his snobbish, old-guard sensibilities, could not abide the kind of affectation

41

that led people like Lydia to pretend to social connections they didn't have. She was the widow of a businessman from Flint, Michigan, who had made his fortune in the manufacture of automobile bumpers. "The bumper king," Spalding called him, with a hint of contempt. For Spalding, anybody who made their money from anything other than clipping bond coupons was *déclassé*. But along with the Smiths' disdain came the recognition that it was social aspirants like Lydia Collins who kept Palm Beach oiled and running and devoted their time to the charity functions around which the town's social life revolved.

As for Charlotte, she had long ago removed herself from the social game Or rather, she'd been removed at an early age by virtue of her mother's divorce. Her lawyer father had been wealthy, but her mother hadn't had two pennies to rub together after he deserted them. Moreover, Charlotte had spent most of her adult life in Hollywood, where an actress friend of hers had once quipped that anyone with a high school diploma was considered society.

After a pause in the conversation, Connie turned to face her friend, who had the spacious back seat all to herself. "I did a little investigative work today," she announced.

"On what?" Charlotte asked, turning away from the view of the sea, which had turned a deep violet blue in the late afternoon light.

"I called up Sally Wardell. She's the chairman of the committee in charge of the Big Band Hall of Fame Ball this year."

"And?" Charlotte asked.

"I found out that Eddie Norwood is a widower. His

wife died of cancer last spring. Nor does he have any"—Connie paused to fish for a word—"love interests."

Connie, bless her heart, was a strong proponent of the institution of marriage and had been very upset when Charlotte's last marriage had broken up. She had wanted Charlotte to be with someone.

Charlotte said nothing. She only raised a dark, flaring eyebrow in an expression that was one of her screen trademarks, along with her broad Yankee accent and her forthright, long-legged stride.

Connie reached over the back of the seat to clasp Charlotte's hand. "Nervous?" she asked.

"Yes," Charlotte admitted. "I am."

The house was down around Delancey Street. At least, that's how Charlotte thought of it. It hadn't taken long for a New Yorker such as herself to realize that Palm Beach was, at fourteen miles, roughly the same length as Manhattan (though it was much narrower) and bore striking similarities in its layout. Instead of the Hudson River to the west there was Lake Worth, and instead of the East River to the east, there was the Atlantic Ocean. The north end was not unlike Manhattan's Upper West Side, a residential neighborhood of middle-class professionals—middle class for Palm Beach, that is, where an average home cost several million dollars. The oceanfront neighborhood at the northern end of the island, which was lined with spectacular mansions, was Palm Beach's equivalent of Sutton Place—a tropical Upper East Side—and the faintly urban shopping district was in a location that corresponded roughly to Herald Square. Even the location of the local theatre, the

Royal Poinciana Playhouse, corresponded to the location of Lincoln Center, and as Royal Palm Way (the main east-west thoroughfare) was to Palm Beach, so was Forty-second Street to Manhattan.

They were now headed downtown on South Ocean Boulevard, which was the Palm Beach equivalent of FDR Drive, with minor differences, such as that the road was lined with mansions and beach cabanas. There was no Alphabet City here, folks. Charlotte hadn't confided this idiosyncratic view of the island's geography to Connie and Spalding. With their frame of reference limited to the heavily traveled path between Newport and Palm Beach and the Connecticut suburbs, she was sure they would have no understanding of the geographical centrism of the typical New Yorker.

After fifteen minutes, they reached their destination: a large house which, were Charlotte to extend her Manhattan analogy, would have been located at the foot of the Williamsburg Bridge. The house was set back from the road at the rear of a manicured lawn planted with coconut palms on a lot that stretched to Lake Worth. This was the island at its narrowest, probably no more than five or six hundred feet. The house, which was set sideways on the lot to take advantage of the water views to the east and west, was built in the art deco style of the 1930's, but with a marine twist. Nautical balconies ringed each of the three oval-shaped stories, and a gangway led to the door on the second deck, as it were. Where Paul's house strove to create an impression of antiquity, this house strove for an impression of modernity: a 1930's modernity that now seemed quaintly out of date.

They pulled up to the entrance, where they were greeted by a valet wearing a French sailor cap with the words SS *Normandie* imprinted in navy blue on the brim. Lydia had really gone all out, Charlotte thought. The French tricolor flew from a flagpole on the deck of the second story.

"Looks like a ship, doesn't it?" commented Spalding, as they emerged from the car and walked up the gangway to the house, which was aglow with lights that shone through the porthole-shaped windows.

"Yes," Charlotte agreed. With its sleek, curving lines and three increasingly narrow stories, it looked like an ocean liner that was sailing down the island. "I can see why it's called Villa Normandie."

As she spoke it struck her that the *Normandie* and Palm Beach had a lot in common: they both represented a way of life with no rough edges.

They were greeted at the front door by an elegant-looking older gentleman wearing a navy blue uniform trimmed with gold braid and brass buttons. "*Bon soir,* Miss Graham," he said with a gracious smile and a little bow. How had he known who she was? Charlotte wondered. Though she was often recognized, it usually took people who were familiar with her only from her movies a minute or two to make the connection. Then it was her turn to recognize the face under the visor of the officer's cap. It belonged to René Dubord, who had been the *sous-commissaire,* or assistant purser, aboard the *Normandie.* Though his temples were now gray and his face was fleshier, he still had the same dashing waxed mustache and the same expressive brown eyes that had sent the women

45

passengers into a swoon. Since the *commissaire principal,* or chief purser, had been occupied behind the scenes, keeping the accounts and meeting the payroll, the job of keeping the passengers happy and entertained had fallen to his assistant. Though he was quite young at the time, René had acquitted himself with distinction in this position and had developed a well-deserved reputation for thinking of everything—including names. He had known the name of every passenger aboard the ship—at least every first-class passenger—and, it was clear, still remembered them fifty-three years later.

"René!" Charlotte exclaimed, stepping forward to kiss him fondly on each cheek. "It's been a long time." In fact, René had been as much a friend as a member of the crew. A witty conversationalist and an excellent dancer, he had mingled easily with the passengers and had become the doting overseer of the romance that had blossomed so quickly over the course of that short voyage.

"My dear Miss Graham," he said, clasping her hands in his and gazing at her with his warm brown eyes. "It has been a long time," he agreed in his slightly accented English. "But, if I may be so bold: tonight you will *still* be the most beautiful woman aboard *Normandie.*"

"Thank you, René. It's wonderful to see you again. You're looking very well yourself. And you're just as flattering as always." Charlotte turned to Spalding and Connie, who were standing just behind her. "I'd like you to meet my good friends, Mr. and Mrs. Spalding Smith."

Stepping forward, René grasped first Connie's hand and then Spalding's. "Ah," he said. "But I am already

46

acquainted with Mr. and Mrs. Smith. What I didn't know was that they were acquainted with you!"

René must have been the friend who Spalding said had described the *Normandie* as the world's most perfect ship, Charlotte thought. "How do you know one another?" she asked.

"The Smiths are members at Château Albert," said René.

Spalding explained: "René is the owner of Château Albert, which is a private dining club here in Palm Beach. Connie and I are charter members. How long has it been now, René? Fifteen years?"

René nodded.

"You'll have to come with us one night, Charlotte," Spalding continued. "The food is the best on the island." He smiled at René and corrected himself: "Make that the best food in the South."

"You could bring Miss Graham with you to our Normandy dinner on Thursday evening," René suggested. He turned to Charlotte. "It's going to feature the food and wines of my native province in France."

"Excellent idea," said Spalding as he removed Connie's and Charlotte's wraps and passed them to a young man dressed in the white-jacketed uniform of a *Normandie* steward.

Behind the steward stood a stocky man in an ill-fitting tuxedo whom Charlotte took to be one of the plainclothes security guards hired to protect the guests from jewel thieves.

"How did you ever end up in Palm Beach?" asked Charlotte, turning her attention back to the former assistant purser.

"It's a long story," René replied.

"I'd like to hear it."

He glanced up at the next group of arrivals and greeted them warmly. *"Bon soir,"* he said with his little bow. "Welcome to *Normandie.* The most perfect ocean liner ever to sail the seas."

Clearly he had lost none of his flair, Charlotte noted.

Turning to the young steward, René asked him to take over. "I'm ready for a break," he announced. Removing his cap, he gestured to a sitting room off the foyer. "Would you like to sit down?" he said to Charlotte and the Smiths.

When they replied that they would, he caught the eye of a passing waiter and asked him to bring them some champagne.

A moment later, they were comfortably seated in the art deco-style chairs of a small sitting room, flutes of bubbly French champagne in hand. They talked for a few minutes about the upcoming Normandy evening at Château Albert, and then, at Spalding's urging, René began his story:

"I stayed with the ship until 1941. I was part of the skeleton crew. There were only a hundred and fifteen of us, compared to an original crew of one thousand three hundred and fifty, but we did as good a job as a crew ten times our size. She was our pride and joy. In truth, we had nothing else to do except worry about what was going on back home. We used to say that the ship was interned but we were marooned." He smiled. "We wore out every deck of cards on the ship. Then, after Pearl Harbor, all the French ships in American ports were seized, as I'm sure you know."

"Were you upset about that?" Connie asked.

He shrugged. "We would rather have given

48

Normandie to the Americans than let the Germans have her. We volunteered to stay on. We were the ones who knew how to run the ship. The Americans knew nothing," he added with contempt. "But they didn't want us. They gave us two hours to pack up our belongings. For me this was the accumulation of nearly six years on board. I had come aboard just before the maiden voyage in June, 1935, when I was nineteen years old, and I had never left. *Normandie* was my home. Then they loaded us into a Coast Guard cutter, our sea bags on our shoulders, and put us ashore on Ellis Island. They treated us like stowaways." His voice was bitter. "They could have learned from us, but they thought they knew everything."

He paused for a moment to sip his champagne and then went on: "I still remember that day perfectly. December twelfth: it was cold, a gray sky, light snow. As we pulled away from *Normandie,* we stood up on the afterdeck, removed our hats, and sang 'La Marseillaise.' There wasn't a dry eye among us."

"Why didn't they want to take advantage of your knowledge?" Charlotte asked as René refilled their glasses.

"They were afraid we were Vichy sympathizers, that we would sabotage the ship. Vichy!" He turned his head aside as if to spit. "To assuage their fears, DeGaulle even offered to crew the ship with Free French troops, but they weren't having any of it. They were afraid that *we* would sabotage the ship, and they killed her with neglect within two months."

"Did you go back to France then?" Charlotte asked.

"Not right away. I had no place to go back to. My native village was occupied. Besides, I couldn't leave

49

Normandie. She was my love, my life. I stayed at the Twenty-third Street YMCA. I would go down to Pier eighty-eight every day to visit her. Then she burned. It was the saddest day of my life." He stared pensively into his glass of champagne for a few seconds, then drained it before going on. "There was nothing to stay for anymore, so I booked passage on a ship to Marseilles and joined the Maquis."

"The Maquis!" Charlotte exclaimed. Centered in southern France, the Maquis had been the fiercest of France's many resistance groups. They had specialized in blowing up railroads.

René nodded. "I fought the Boches for two years." Lifting a finger, he pointed to the the red and black rosette pinned to his lapel. "The *Médaille de la Résistance,*" he said. "So much for my being a saboteur, eh? Then I was captured. I sat out the rest of the war in a Nazi prison." He gave a world-weary Gallic shrug.

Charlotte thought back to the René of before the war: gay, charming, devoted to a life of pleasure. On the surface he still seemed the same, but the superficial gaiety cloaked a war-wounded soul.

He held up the empty bottle of champagne. "We have finished the bottle, but I have not yet finished my story. I warned you that it was a long one." He glanced over at the staircase that led to the room on the third floor where the party was in progress. Newly arrived guests were still streaming upstairs. "I'm afraid I must excuse myself," he said as he stood up. "I'll have to finish my story another time. Perhaps when you visit Château Albert."

"I hope so, René," said Spalding, giving the former assistant purser a hearty thump on the back. "You can't

50

leave us hanging. I understand that you're catering the party. That means the food is bound to be excellent."

"Thank you," René replied. "We are serving a duplicate of the chef's menu suggestions for the one hundredth voyage in 1938."

"We're looking forward to it," said Charlotte.

As she rose from her chair, René leaned over to look at her necklace "I see that you are wearing the same necklace that you wore on the return crossing in 1939. It's very beautiful."

"I'm surprised you remember!" she said, raising her fingers to the ruby pendant.

"Every detail of that voyage is permanently engraved in my memory," he said. "I think you will agree that it was a most memorable crossing."

"Yes. Actually I wore it on the voyage over too, but as you point out, that trip wasn't nearly as memorable. It's not the same necklace, actually. It's a copy of the Cartier original. It's from the new *Normandie* collection that's being previewed tonight."

Connie held up her arm to display her bracelet. "Many of the guests will be wearing pieces from the collection, which was designed by my daughter, Marianne Montgomery, in collaboration with Paul Feder of Feder Jewelers," she said. "We're going to model them after dinner."

Connie was an indefatigable promoter of her daughter's creations.

"Ah, yes!" said René. He had leaned over again to look at Charlotte's necklace. "I remember noticing the necklace as you descended the grand staircase on our first night out." He paused before adding, "If I remember correctly, that was the night that you met M. Norwood."

51

The *Normandie* passengers had entered the dining room by way of a dramatic staircase, which allowed them to make a grand entrance. Charlotte remembered well the nightly challenge of descending those stairs into the cavernous room. "René, you have a memory like an elephant."

He smiled. "The crew always takes delight in a shipboard romance, and yours was one of the most romantic. Such a handsome couple!"

And all the crew knew exactly what was going on, Charlotte might have added.

"Have you seen M. Norwood in the intervening years?" René asked.

"Not since August twenty-eighth, 1939. If you don't count seeing him on television, that is." She looked over at Connie, who wore the motherly smile of a matchmaker anticipating the imminent culmination of her efforts.

"Aha!" said René. "Did you know that he is here this evening?" he asked with a mischievous little smile that set the debonair mustache under his long nose to twitching.

Charlotte nodded and glanced up at the stairs.

"Well, you know what they say: 'True love never dies.'" Stepping up to Charlotte's side, René offered her his arm. "Shall we?" he asked.

4

THE STAIRCASE WAS NARROW AND WINDING, WITH A low ceiling, like that on a ship. As they ascended it, Charlotte was beset by the same sensations that she used to have on the opening night of a Broadway play, which was to say that her legs felt like rubber and the back of her throat seemed to be locked in a vise. People who weren't in the theater had the mistaken idea that stage fright was an affliction of the inexperienced. Not true. It was like allergies or myopia: if you were unfortunate enough to suffer from stage fright at all, you would probably suffer from it your entire life. It had nothing to do with one's level of experience or one's ability. The best actors fell victim to it, as well as the worst. In truth, she was inclined to think that the best actors suffered from it more, because they put more of themselves on the line. But she was fortunate in that she had a cure, the secret of which had been imparted to her years ago by her friend the actor Larry Olivier. It was to think of your feet. She had once seen an article in which Larry was quoted to that effect, in response to a question about the secret to consistently fine acting. The reporter had treated the quote as if it were a flip remark, but in fact Larry had been quite serious. There was something about shifting the attention to your feet that served to anchor you to the earth. The negative energy was conducted downward, just as a lightning rod draws lightning downward into the ground.

The staircase her feet were ascending was magnificent—a gracefully curving spiral with a polished brass handrail—and Charlotte could feel her nervousness diminish with each step. But the staircase was nothing by comparison with the room at the top. As in many oceanfront houses, the public rooms were located on the top floor to take advantage of the views.

"*Magnifique, n'est-ce pas?*" commented René, as

they paused at the top of the stairs to pose for the photographers who were covering the event for the local society pages.

"*Oui,*" Charlotte answered reflexively in French, too taken aback by the splendor of her surroundings to realize how dumb she must have sounded.

The room was a replica of the Grand Salon of the *Normandie,* but smaller. There were the same chairs covered in red-and-gray floral needlepoint tapestry; the same twelve-foot-high ruffled glass Lalique light fountains, each with a circular settee at its base; and the same art deco glass murals, or one of them anyway. The Grand Salon had featured four of these striking murals; this room had one, at the south end. At the north end was a stage, at one side of which a piano player was seated at a baby grand. Seeing him, Charlotte's heart skipped a beat before she realized that he was too young to be Eddie.

Once she had regained her composure, she scanned the room full of ladies with bare shoulders and gentlemen with starched shirt fronts, but she saw no Eddie Norwood there, either.

Turning back to René, she asked, "Is this an original Dupas mural?" She was referring to the French artist who had designed the famous glass panels for *Normandie's* Grand Salon.

"The very same," he replied.

"But how did they . . . ?"

As she spoke, a woman detached herself from the party of guests that had immediately preceded them, and headed toward Charlotte's party.

"I'll let our hostess explain," said René, as the woman joined them. "This is Miss Charlotte Graham," he said to her. "She was a passenger on

54

Normandie's last crossing. And this is our
Mrs. Harley Collins, chairman of the pres
association and noted collector of Normandiana

"Please call me Lydia," said the woman
shook Charlotte's hand. In her other arm she cradled a
tiny silky terrier. "And this is Song Song," she added,
introducing the dog, whose silver topknot was tied
with a yellow ribbon that matched her mistress's
gown, "I'm very pleased that you could join us
tonight, Miss Graham."

Charlotte returned the compliment. Lydia was one
of those women whose most notable physical feature
was her bouffant platinum blond hairdo, which was
worn in a style that had once been described by
Charlotte's acerbic hairdresser as "fried, dyed, and
shoved to the side."

Apart from her hair and the dog, there was little to
remark about Lydia: she was fashionably thin;
expensively, if a bit ridiculously, dressed in a yellow
off-the-shoulder gown with pouf sleeves and a
billowing skirt in which she looked like an extra for
Gone With the Wind; and attractive enough if one
discounted the facial skin that was taut from too many
face-lifts.

Charlotte could see why she wasn't Spalding and
Connie's type.

After their hostess had greeted Connie and Spalding
with kisses to the air on either side of their cheeks,
Charlotte said, "I was just commenting to Mr.
Dubord about the Dupas panels. I didn't realize they
had been saved."

"Most of the artwork from the *Normandie* was
removed at the time of the conversion in 1941," Lydia
said. "But it still wasn't easy locating the individual

els that make up this mural. A lot of the *Normandie* artwork has disappeared." She looked up at the mural, which must have measured twenty feet high by at least as wide. "This is half of one of the four murals that originally decorated the walls of the Grand Salon."

The glass panels showed silver gods and goddesses riding on the back of an enormous sea serpent which was swimming in a scalloped sea set against a background of puffy clouds and the billowing sails of golden ships. The back of the glass was painted with gold and silver leaf, which caught the light from the light Lalique fountains.

"The murals depict the story of navigation in mythological terms," Lydia explained as she scratched the dog's neck with a hand whose most conspicuous feature was a huge emerald-cut diamond. "This is half of 'The Chariot of Poseidon.' The other half is in the Metropolitan Museum of Art."

"That's right!" Charlotte exclaimed. "I'd forgotten. It's in the dining room, over the bar." She had often admired it there.

Lydia nodded her bouffant head.

"My half consists of fifty individual panels. Harley and I bought the first twenty-six from an antique dealer in 1977, and seven years later, we bought another twelve at auction. But for eight years, I'd been missing the twelve panels from the center of the two bottom rows."

"That must have been frustrating," Connie sympathized as she gazed up at the shimmering mural. "To have all but that one section. The mural wouldn't have made sense."

"Yes, it was frustrating," Lydia agreed. "There was

a great big hole in the center, just where the sea serpent is." She removed her hand from the dog's neck to point out where the gap had been. "The missing panels finally surfaced at Christie's, and I was able to complete the mural."

"You were lucky you weren't outbid," said Connie. "Wouldn't it have been awful if someone else had gotten them?"

"I made sure I wasn't outbid," Lydia replied. "They were expensive, but I just *had* to have them."

"And the Lalique light towers?" Charlotte asked.

"The light towers aren't original. I had them copied from photographs of the originals."

"You would never know," Charlotte said. "The mood is exactly the same." Like a crystal box, she had thought then. The room even had the same tall windows as the Grand Salon, from which one could easily imagine an uninterrupted ocean view.

"Thank you," said Lydia. "I've tried to make it as authentic as possible."

Her escort had joined her, and she proceeded to introduce him. He was the Jack McLean of the table-seating card, and he was a retired rear admiral and another acquaintance of the Smiths'. Despite its veneer of sophistication, Palm Beach was at heart the kind of small town where everybody knew everybody else.

He was a formidable-looking man, with a square jaw and deep-set gray eyes shielded by craggy gray eyebrows. He was tall and still very handsome, though he must have been close to seventy.

"I presume it's the U.S. Navy that you're retired from, and not the French Line," Charlotte said, nodding at his flawlessly cut dress uniform, with medals and gold buttons and a black tie and a stiff, snow-white shirt.

"Oh, yes," he assured her with a smile, his voice carrying a hint of a Southern accent. "It was Lydia who persuaded me to wear the uniform. I'm to play the role of the captain tonight. For the sake of verisimilitude."

"It's hard to have a captain's gala without a captain," Lydia trilled. "Lacking the real thing, we substituted a home-grown version."

"Well, Lydia's certainly done a wonderful job planning the party," Charlotte said. "I especially liked it when the *Normandie* pageboy came to my hotel room with the menu." She turned to her hostess. "That was a very nice touch."

"Thank you," Lydia responded. "Your necklace is lovely, by the way," she added, obviously having been briefed on who would be modeling the pieces from Marianne's *Normandie* collection. "We'll be having the jewelry show right after dinner, just before the dancing."

"Your brooch is lovely too," said Charlotte. Their hostess was wearing another piece that was obviously from the collection, on the bodice of her flouncy gown: a diamond pavé brooch in the shape of the *Normandie*.

"Thank you," Lydia said. "Paul has generously given it to me to keep." Then, mindful of her social obligations, she glanced away to briefly scan the room, then excused herself and moved off to mingle with the other guests, the dog still cradled on the crook of her arm.

Following Connie and Spalding, Charlotte moved over to a table of *hors d'oeuvres,* the centerpiece of

58

which was an enormous ice sculpture in the shape of the *Normandie*, filled with Beluga caviar. After heaping a cracker with the caviar, she stood back to survey the crowd.

She spotted Paul Feder right away. He stood out by virtue of his height. He was talking with Dede, who looked like a princess in a long, simple white satin sheath with a crisscross back that fit her like a glove and which was a perfect complement to the simple elegance of the diamond choker.

Then she spotted Marianne, who was wearing a pleated lavender gown of her own design. The fact that it was very similar to Charlotte's was no surprise: Marianne was known for her revival of the Fortuny look.

Marianne stood at the bar, watching Paul and Dede. The black eyebrows beneath the straight bangs of her Cleopatra cut were drawn together in a frown, and her narrow red lips were pressed together. Her fingers tapped a nervous tattoo on the surface of the her, as if to say, What are we going to do about *this?*

Knowing Marianne as she did, Charlotte would be willing to bet that the fur would be flying before the night was out.

She was watching Paul take a cigarette out of his elegant cigarette case when she spotted Eddie standing near the piano.

His hair was no longer black, it was now silver-white, but worn in the same close-cropped style. He was a bit heavier than he had been then, but otherwise he still looked much the same. But then, Charlotte had known how he would look from television. He was wearing a white tail-coat and white tie, the same attire she'd first seen him in fifty-three years ago.

She was trying to decide what her next move should be, when he looked up and met her gaze. Their eyes locked across the crowded room, just as in one of her sappier movies. All that was lacking was a camera lens to shift the rest of the room into soft focus.

He smiled and then turned to mount the step to the stage. Still moving with the same athletic grace, he leaned over to speak in the ear of the piano player, who rose to relinquish his place. The murmur of conversation died down as the guests turned their attention to the well-known pianist and bandleader.

Charlotte wasn't sure that he would remember; it had been so many years. And then the opening refrain came, delivered in Eddie's mellow, intimate baritone, a little weaker than it had been, but still as smooth and easy: "As Dorothy Parker once said to her boyfriend, 'Fare thee well.' "

The song was "Just One of Those Things."

He played the piano as he always had: so smoothly, so effortlessly, his long fingers seeming to ripple over the keys, and radiating the charm and showmanship that had endeared him to audiences for half a century. Except that in this case, he was playing to an audience of one.

Charlotte suddenly was conscious of her feet again. They were no longer on the ground. In fact, they were ten feet in the air. *Oh-oh,* she said to herself. *I thought I was done with men.*

After playing a couple of other old favorites, he stood up and bowed to the audience, which applauded enthusiastically. Then he stepped down off the stage and wove his way through the admiring crowd to Charlotte, removing two flutes of champagne from the tray of a passing waiter along the way.

Reaching her, he handed her a glass.

Seeing him standing there before her, Charlotte felt as if fifty-three years had magically evaporated.

Then he wordlessly took her by the elbow and steered her out to the deck. If the house could be thought of as a ship that was sailing down island, they would have been on the aft sun-deck, looking out over the port side toward the Atlantic. The sight before them was lovely: a generous deep green lawn of Bermuda grass dotted with slender coconut palms whose swaying crowns were silhouetted against the orange-violet sky, in which a perfect crescent moon was suspended like a Christmas ornament.

For a moment, they stood silently at the railing, looking out, their champagne glasses in hand.

Charlotte found herself acutely aware of his physical presence. His smell; his size—much smaller than her former husband, who had been a bear of a man; how his skin had aged. She was surprised at how comfortable she felt with him. Nervous, and comfortable at the same time. She remembered how sick she had been on that long-ago voyage—unable to eat, unable to sleep. She had had all the symptoms of seasickness, except that it had been lovesickness. Now that she was back in his presence, she had the feeling that that sickness was about to flare up again, after lying dormant for over half a century.

He looked up and then turned to her. "All that's missing are the lifeboats dangling overhead."

"It's true," she said, as she leaned over the pipe railing, which was strung with canvas, just as on a ship. There were even the cane-seated deck chairs from the *Normandie,* covered with rust-colored cushions stamped in beige with the CGT logo of the

French Line, Compagnie Generale Transatlantique. "And the blackout," she added.

The bright light that spilled out onto the deck from the party inside was a far cry from the intimate atmosphere created by the dimness of the enforced blackout on the *Normandie's* last voyage.

He nodded. "But you look just the same." His long fingers reached up and gently touched the ruby pendant. "You're wearing the same necklace, too. I remember how beautiful it was. How beautiful you were. Still are," he added.

Charlotte explained about its being a reproduction, then said, "I'm even wearing the same dress."

He looked down at the dress, and said, in mock exasperation, "Well, you can't expect me to remember everything."

Charlotte smiled. "It's been hanging in my closet for fifty-three years."

He looked at her and then turned to the view. "I wanted to call you, Charlotte. Or to write. I almost did, a number of times. All I thought about was you. But I thought I owed it to Celia to give our marriage one last chance, and I knew that if I saw you . . ." He looked back at her and his voice trailed off.

"You don't have to explain," she told him. "I didn't expect to hear from you." He had made it clear that he felt an obligation to try to work things out with his wife. She smiled at him and then quoted a line from their song: " 'As Columbus announced when he knew he was bounced, It was swell, Isabelle, swell!' "

"Touché," he said.

Below them, the guests had started to drift out onto the patio at the foot of the gangway to smoke. A few could be seen crossing South Ocean Boulevard to the beachfront cabana that went with the house, no doubt to admire the view of the crescent moon over the sea.

Occasionally a car or a chauffeured limousine would pull into the driveway that ran alongside the tall hedge that screened the property from its neighbor, the headlights illuminating the figures gathered on the patio.

Standing there, Charlotte remembered how dreamlike that voyage had seemed, the sense of timelessness. Every day the clocks had been stopped for sixty minutes, with the result that one never knew what time it was. Some passengers were on Paris time, some on New York time, some in between.

And because of that timeless quality, what a shock it had been when they'd sighted the Nantucket lightship in the fog early that last morning. It was an anchored ship that had been painted red as a kind of lighthouse, and the first sign that they had made it home, that the dream was over.

" 'It *was* swell, Isabelle,' " said Eddie, still looking at her.

She nodded and looked into his eyes. She felt that same way now, as if she were on a cruise. The only trouble was that she had no idea what their destination was.

Thinking back to that last morning, she remembered how relieved the other passengers had been. For them the lightship had meant the end of a dangerous crossing, not the end of a love affair. Six hours later they'd passed the Ambrose light at the entrance to the port of New York, and they were home.

"We came so close to meeting so many times," she said. "I always thought that fate must have been conspiring to keep us apart. Remember that awards dinner in Chicago? You left only two minutes before I arrived."

He nodded. "I didn't find out that you'd been there until later," he said. He deposited their empty champagne glasses on the tray of a passing waiter, then placed his hands on the railing, his fingers tapping out a rhythm.

She remembered how his fingers had always been tapping, tapping. Even then he'd had music in his soul.

For a few minutes they watched the guests coming and going below as they exchanged anecdotes about all the times they had just missed one another.

Among the guests below were Paul and Dede, who, after lingering for a moment on the patio' headed down the driveway toward the beach. Charlotte watched for a moment until they disappeared down the path that led through a thicket of sea grapes to the cabana on the other side of the road.

Eddie placed his hand over hers on the railing. "Like ships passing in the night," he said of their missed encounters.

Charlotte noticed that there were scars on the back of his right hand and wrist. With the forefinger of her free hand, she gently touched the scar on either side of his sleek gold wristwatch. "A burn?" she asked.

He pulled up the sleeve of his dress shirt. The scars ran up his forearm almost to his elbow. "They're from the *Normandie*. I was very lucky my fingers didn't get burned. If they had, I might not ever have been able to play again."

It took Charlotte a moment to grasp what he was saying. "You were on the *Normandie* when it burned?" she asked, astonished.

He nodded. "I enlisted right after Pearl Harbor. I was assigned to the *Normandie,* or the U.S.S. *Lafayette* as she was then called. I was in the Grand Salon when the fire broke out. I tried to help put it out. That's how I got burned." His expression had turned pensive.

"Were you badly hurt?" she asked.

"I almost died," he replied. "One of the rescue workers stumbled over me in a corridor in tourist-class and hauled me out. I have no idea how I got there. All I remember is feeling my way along those long, dark, smoky corridors, trying to find my way out. I still have nightmares about it. By that time, the ship was listing ten, fifteen degrees So the corridors were tilted, like in a funhouse. You lost all your bearings."

"I remember," she said.

He looked at her oddly.

"I was there," she explained. "In the crowd on Twelfth Avenue." She remembered the long lines of ambulances, moving like a line of cabs at a taxi stand through the smoke-filled side streets to the pierhead, and the stretcher bearers running up to them from the smoke-choked pier shed with their cargos of injured men. "I probably saw you being loaded into an ambulance."

"Like ships passing in the night," he commented ironically. "I was in Bellevue for three months," he continued, shifting his glance away from her. "A fractured skull and second- and third-degree burns. By the time I was well enough to write to you, you were married to Will. Then by the time he died, I was married to my second wife." He looked back at her.

65

"We could just never seem to connect, could we?"

"Until now," she said.

"Yes," he agreed. "Until now." He paused, and then went on: "Maybe it wouldn't have worked out. I was too hard-driving, a perfectionist. I saw everything in black and white then; there were no grays. I've mellowed," he added.

"So have I," said Charlotte.

The sound of conversation drifted up from the patio below. Marianne had descended the gangway and appeared to be questioning a couple who were standing off by themselves at the edge of the driveway.

Charlotte saw the woman raise an arm and point in the direction of the beach. *Uh-oh,* she thought, then watched as Marianne marched down the driveway, crossed South Ocean Boulevard, and headed down the path to the cabana. A hurricane was brewing, and it wasn't even the season.

She returned her attention to Eddie. "Did you go back into active service after that?" she asked.

He nodded. "Playing in a Navy band."

"It's odd that so many people from the *Normandie* have ended up in Palm Beach," she remarked. "I nearly fell over when René Dubord greeted me at the door. He's been telling me his life story. He was quite bitter about the fire. Now he owns an exclusive private dining club in Palm Beach."

"So he told me," Eddie said. "He looks great, doesn't he?"

Charlotte nodded in agreement. She was looking down at the crowd on the patio two stories below. The heads of the men were either bald or white. On second thought, she supposed it wasn't so odd that so many

Normandie alumni had ended up in Palm Beach: the population here was certainly of prewar vintage.

"There's another guest here who was on the *Normandie,* too," Eddie said. "Our hostess's escort, Admiral McLean. He was my commanding officer. I'm looking forward to seeing him again."

"I met him," Charlotte said. "An imposing-looking man."

"A good officer, too," Eddie added. "We used to call him Big Jack McLean."

"There he is," she said, looking down at the tall man in the elegant uniform who was headed out toward the beach.

"He still looks the same," Eddie said, looking down at the admiral. "He was one of the officers who ended up taking the blame for the fire. But I always thought he was a scapegoat. Yes, the Navy was careless. But it's hard to dot every i and cross every t when you're under orders to convert a luxury liner to a troop carrier in five weeks."

"René Dubord wouldn't agree with you. He had nothing good to say about the U.S. Navy."

"No. I suppose he wouldn't." Eddie turned to her. "And what about you?" he asked. "Are you still married?"

Of course, Charlotte thought. How would he have known? She had the benefit of Connie's espionage, but he had no spies working for him. Nor was she such big news anymore that her divorces were splashed all over the newspapers. Or maybe it was that she'd had so many husbands, nobody cared anymore.

"I was divorced three years ago," she said. "From my fourth husband. The first and second you knew about. The third was a very brief-lived mistake. And the fourth . . . The fourth was a mistake too, I guess I'd have to say. But not quite such an ill-considered mistake as the third."

"I heard about number three," he said. "I never heard about number four."

"Well, no use in boring you now. It was boring enough for me." She looked over at Eddie. "I guess I kept trying to find what I had with you."

"Did you ever?" he asked.

"Yes, once. But not with any of my husbands." The other love of her life had been Linc Crawford, the cowboy actor. Funny how different the two men were. Linc: tall, quiet, serious. Eddie: short, garrulous, charming. "He died in 1957," she said. "And you?"

He shrugged. "Celia and I. Well, you know about that. I guess I could say that I loved Mary, my second wife. She died just last spring—in Pasadena, where we lived, where I still live. We were very comfortable with one another. But I didn't love her the way I loved you."

"How long will you be here?" Charlotte asked.

"Until after the Big Band Hall of Fame Ball. It's at the Breakers, where I'm staying. I came down here early for rehearsals. I'll be going out on tour for two and a half months right after the ball, which is on February twenty-second, two weeks from yesterday. Would you like to be my date?"

"Very much," she said.

"I'm playing," he added. "So it will mean a lot of sitting around."

"I don't mind." She smiled at him. "I'm sure the music will be good."

"Not just good—great," he said. "But I'd like to see

you before that. I have to go away on a little trip, but I'll be back on Thursday. Would you like to go out to dinner on Thursday night?"

Charlotte nodded. "René is having a special Normandy night at his private dining club that night," she said. "Featuring the cuisine of Normandy. My friend Spalding Smith says the club has the best food in Palm Beach. He and his wife Connie are members."

"Could he arrange for us to eat there?" Eddie asked.

"I think so," said Charlotte. As she smiled at him, she noticed that her heart was pounding.

Their conversation was interrupted by one of the white-jacketed stewards, who announced that dinner was about to be served. Passing through the sliding glass doors into the Grand Salon, they joined the throng that was drifting into the dining room through the doors on either side of the mural. Like the Grand Salon, the dining room was a large, high-ceilinged room in which a couple of dozen round tables seating ten or twelve people each had been set up. Though it was a beautiful room, with sliding glass doors that stood open to the deck, it was not decorated in the style of the *Normandie*. Charlotte could just imagine what the Dupas mural must have cost if its other half was hanging in the dining room at the Metropolitan Museum of Art; apparently even the resources of the bumper king were not extensive enough to decorate two large rooms with original *Normandie* artworks.

They were greeted at the door by René. "Aha," he said, his face radiant. "I see that the two lovebirds have met up again after all these years." He spoke with the appreciation for romance that only a

Frenchman could have. "Please come with me."

Winding his way among the tables with the authoritative air of a man who is in charge, he led them to the far end of the room, where Connie and Spalding were already seated. "The captain's table," he announced, as he pulled out a chair for Charlotte.

After Charlotte had introduced Eddie to Connie and Spalding, they sat down. The place settings were identical to those on the *Normandie,* with elegant Lalique stemware and Haviland porcelain, each item bearing the CGT logo of the French line. A silver-plated coupe in the center of each place held an elegant tropical fruit cocktail.

They were joined a minute later by Lydia, *sans* Song Song, and the admiral, and by a couple whom their hostess introduced as the president of the preservation association and his wife. Dede arrived a moment later. She looked as if she had been crying, and Charlotte wondered if there had been a scene at the beach.

Introductions were made all around.

"Nice to see you again, sir," said Eddie when Lydia introduced him to the admiral. He went on to reintroduce himself: "Edward A. Norwood, Lieutenant J. G., U.S.S. *Lafayette,* Third Naval District. Assistant to Commander Jack McLean."

The admiral broke into a smile and extended his hand. "I remember you, Norwood. But I never realized that my junior officer and the famous bandleader were one and the same. Well, here we are on the *Normandie* again."

"Yes," said Eddie as they started eating their fruit cocktails. "After fifty years. Did you realize that today is the fiftieth anniversary of the fire?"

70

"No," said the admiral. "I didn't. But you're absolutely right, Norwood."

"Really?" said Lydia. "I hadn't realized that either. If I'd known, I would have changed the date. We're supposed to be celebrating the life of the *Normandie,* not her death."

"February ninth, 1942," said Eddie.

But Lydia's attention was occupied by the two empty seats at the table, whose place cards indicated that they were intended for Marianne and Paul. "I wonder where Ms. Montgomery and Mr. Feder are?" she said, clearly perturbed by their tardiness.

"The last I saw them, they were out at the beach," offered Dede, with more than a hint of petulance in her voice.

"We'll be having the speeches soon. They'd better get back here," Lydia said. She thought for a moment, and then summoned one of the stewards and asked him to go out to the beach to fetch Marianne and Paul.

Then she gave a discreet signal to René, who was still stationed at the door, and the phalanx of waiters sprang into action. Within minutes, their empty fruit cocktail coupes had been cleared and they were served the next course, a classic *soupe á l'oignon.*

"Are the place settings all original?" asked Charlotte as she picked up her heavy Christofle soup spoon.

Her hostess nodded. "I bought most of them at an auction in Monte Carlo in 1979, and I've added to them over the years. Unfortunately this is the only table that's set with originals. I only have a complete service for fifteen."

"That strikes me as a substantial number," Charlotte commented. She had once been tempted to buy a Lalique goblet from the *Normandie* as a memento until she saw the price: $400. "How did you come by your interest in collecting *Normandie* art?" she asked. "Were you a passenger?"

"Regretfully I was never a passenger," Lydia replied with a saccharine little smile. "I wasn't even born when the *Normandie* burned."

Charlotte doubted that, but she wasn't about to challenge her.

"It started with an egg cup, actually. A silver-plated Christofle egg cup. Harley and I bought it at an antique shop for three dollars. Now it's probably worth three hundred. I fell in love with that egg cup. We had been collectors of art deco furniture and *objets d'art* for some time, because of the house."

"This is quite a place," Eddie commented.

"Thank you. It was built in 1935, the same year that the *Normandie* made her maiden voyage. It was designed in the streamline moderne style and is meant to resemble a ship. We found that we needed to narrow the focus of our collecting, and it seemed fitting to collect art from the *Normandie* because of the nautical theme of the house. From the egg cup, we went on to other silver, and then to glasses, porcelain, furniture, and finally to the art itself."

"It's an obsession," explained the admiral. "Lydia doesn't know when to stop. She lives and breathes her *Normandie* collection."

As they continued to chat about Lydia's collection, Charlotte noticed that the steward whom Lydia had sent to find Paul and Marianne had appeared at the door and was talking agitatedly with René. Then she saw René leave his post and wind his way through the tables in their direction.

Arriving at their table a moment later, he leaned over to speak in Lydia's ear. "May I speak with you for a moment in private, madam?"

Excusing herself, Lydia left the table to talk privately with René in the nearby corner. When she returned to the tab]e a moment later, her skin was the same platinum color as her hair. "Mr. Feder has been murdered," she announced in a hushed tone.

Paul Feder murdered! Charlotte couldn't believe it.

"He's lying out on the beach right now—dead," Lydia continued. "He was stabbed in the chest." Her blue eyes widened as if she were looking at the gruesome sight. Then she started to cry.

Charlotte wasn't sure if she was crying out of grief for Paul or because his death meant that her party would be ruined.

Lydia turned to the admiral. "Oh Jack, what are we going to do?"

Across the table, Dede looked crushed. Her yellow-blue eyes welled with tears, which flowed silently down her lovely cheeks.

"Nothing, at the moment," Jack replied. "Get a grip on yourself, Lydia," he told her sternly. "We don't want a panic situation here." He looked at everyone around the table, commanding them with his glance to keep calm. "We want to keep this a secret among ourselves for the moment."

Lydia sniffled a couple of times and regained her mask of social composure, while Dede blew her nose in a handkerchief provided by the gallant admiral, who seemed quite taken with the beautiful young woman seated at his side.

"Has Mr. Dubord called the police?" the admiral asked.

Lydia nodded. "He told them not to use their sirens, and he's going to try to keep them downstairs for the time being. But he said he thought that at least some of the guests would have to be interviewed. He said he would try to get the police to wait until Mr. Norwood is playing."

Thank God for René, Charlotte thought. A lifetime of experience in damage control. She remembered an incident on board the *Normandie* in which an elderly woman at an adjoining table had fallen over face-first into her dinner plate, the apparent victim of a heart attack.

With a nod from René, two members of the dining room staff had quietly come over, picked the woman up, chair and all, and discreetly whisked her out of the dining room. René hadn't missed a beat: the incident had simply been erased.

But a murder wasn't as easy to erase.

A group of waiters had fanned out over the dining room to remove the soup bowls. They were immediately followed by a second group, who served the fish course: Loire pike with clarified butter. It was a pity that Charlotte had suddenly lost her appetite.

"Did you know him?" Eddie asked.

Charlotte shook her head. "Not really. I just met him at a dinner party last night. He collaborated with my god-daughter, Marianne Montgomery, on the *Normandie* jewelry collection. Marianne is the daughter of my friend Connie,"—she nodded at Connie—"who used to be Connie Montgomery."

"The actress?" Eddie asked, looking over at Connie, who was talking with the president of the preservation association.

"Yes," Charlotte replied. She shifted her glance to

74

Dede. "Dede is Marianne's daughter and Connie's granddaughter."

"I can see the resemblance," Eddie said, looking from the lovely granddaughter to her lovely grandmother.

Dede looked up briefly and then back down at her plate. She was picking at her fish and biting her lip to keep from crying.

"Do you have any idea why he might have been killed?" Eddie asked.

Charlotte shook her head, though her glance shifted involuntarily to the empty place at the table marked with a card on which the name Ms. Marianne Montgomery was written in hand-lettered calligraphy.

5

THE FACT THAT A MURDER HAD OCCURRED JUST A few hundred feet away did not stop the party, though a damper had been put on the festivities at the captain's table by the absence of their hostess, who had been summoned by the police. The waiters cleared away the fish course and served the entreé, *le caneton a l'orange.* Led by the president of the historic association, the guests at their table, who had been instructed by Lydia to behave as if nothing had happened, carried on a stiff and uncomfortable conversation about the quality of the food aboard the *Normandie* and how this evening's meal compared. As the only guests present who had been passengers aboard the ship, Charlotte and Eddie answered questions about the wines, the cheeses, and the pastries. *As if they had been paying close attention to the food,* Charlotte thought. Though Eddie was obliging enough with his answers, Charlotte's mind was elsewhere. She was eager to question Dede, who sat silently across the table in her white satin sheath and diamond choker, picking at her food and occasionally sniffling into the admiral's handkerchief. What had happened at the beach that caused her to return with such red and swollen eyes? Had Marianne confronted Paul and her daughter with her suspicions?

Fifteen minutes later, Lydia returned on René's arm. She looked quite composed for a hostess at whose party a murder had just taken place, but Charlotte had already pegged her for a cool customer. After resuming her seat, she flashed a wooden smile and then asked how they were enjoying the food.

René had moved around the table and now leaned over to whisper in Charlotte's ear. "The police would like to see you next, Miss Graham." Then he graciously pulled out Charlotte's chair and offered her his arm.

Charlotte was not surprised at the ease with which René was handling the situation. "Remember the storm on the westbound crossing in August, 1939?" she asked as they threaded their way among the tables. She was thinking of how he had raced around making sure everything was secure.

"Very well. I remember everything about that crossing. Including making my first acquaintance with a beautiful young American movie star. Are you implying that a murder at a dinner party is nothing by comparison?"

"I guess that's what I *was* thinking," she admitted.

"I think you're right. At least I don't have to cater

to seasick passengers," he said.

"The man who can handle anything," Charlotte said as they began their descent of the stairs.

René smiled.

"I wonder why the police want to talk with me before the other guests?" she asked as he led her past the room where they had talked earlier in the evening.

"I think you'll find that your reputation has preceded you," René replied.

René delivered her to the door of the library and then returned upstairs to resume the job of damage control. Opening the door, Charlotte found herself in a book-lined room in which a young woman with thick, dark blond hair done up in a French braid sat behind a desk crafted of blond wood in the same moderne style as much of the other furniture in the house. She was broad in the shoulder and big in the bust: not overweight, but definitely stocky. She was also very pretty, with a wide face, large hazel eyes, and a glowing complexion. She wore a short-sleeved blue denim blouse and gold hoop earrings. Beside her, an older policeman wearing the brown shirt and khaki Bermuda shorts that comprised the uniform of the Palm Beach police sat on a loveseat holding a notebook. The young woman didn't look like the typical detective, but then, the Palm Beach police department wasn't typical. With a year-round population of only 10,000 (a figure that doubled during the season), Palm Beach was in reality a small town in which the police knew almost everybody. Charlotte remembered Connie once telling her about a friend who had drunk too much at a party. He had been escorted home by the police and tenderly tucked into bed. Nor was there much crime on the island. Though the occasional sensational crime made the headlines, basically it was a place in which stealing bicycles and going shirtless within one hundred feet of the beach (a violation of a local ordinance) were the most common infractions.

At Charlotte's entrance, the young woman stood up and extended her hand across the desk. She was taller than Charlotte's own five foot eight: about five foot ten, she guessed. All in all, a sturdy-looking young woman. "I'm Detective Maureen White," she said as she shook Charlotte's hand.

Though she may have looked as if she belonged here, Detective White's accent told a different story. She was from New Yawk, probably the Bronx. There was no r in Maureen. Charlotte guessed that her father was a cop. Also her brother, her uncle, her brother-in-law. That's the way it was with women cops in New Yawk.

She nodded at the chair facing the art deco desk. "Please have a seat, Miss Graham," she said, then seated herself. "I think we have a friend in common," she began.

"Oh?" said Charlotte. "Who's that?"

"Jerry D'Angelo," the detective replied with a wide smile.

"You know Jerry!" Charlotte exclaimed with pleasure.

Jerry D'Angelo was a former cop whom Charlotte had met when he was working as a trainer at a spa in upstate New York. Charlotte had been invited there by her friend, the beauty queen Paulina Langenberg, to look into an attempt to sabotage her spa business. The investigation had turned into a murder case. In

78

the course of solving the murder, she and Jerry had become friends.

"We worked together in New York," Maureen explained. "He was the head of my team in Manhattan South Narcotics. I was the undercover," she said, rolling her eyes. "Your basic buy-and-bust. Which is why I'm down here now. It gets to you after a while: acting like a junkie, looking like a junkie. And you have to, because otherwise you're dead meat."

Charlotte couldn't imagine Maureen ever looking like a junkie, though she, more than most, was aware of how different people could be made to look.

"He told me all about you. I also read *Murder at the Morosco*."

Murder at the Morosco was the best-selling book about the murder of Charlotte's co-star on stage at the Morosco Theatre. It was Charlotte who had shot him: a real bullet had been put in a stage prop. In an effort to clear her name, Charlotte had not only solved the murder, but established a reputation as an amateur sleuth that later led Paulina to call on her in the spa case.

"That's why I wanted to talk with you first," Maureen went on. "I thought you might have some insights into what's going on here." She lifted her chin to the ceiling, where the party was going on overhead. "I understand that you're an old friend of the Spalding Smiths, who are the parents of Marianne Montgomery. I also understand that Marianne and the victim were lovers."

It appeared that Lydia had already filled Detective White in. "Yes," Charlotte said. "I'm here visiting the Smiths. Marianne and Mr. Feder were business partners in the jewelry line." She proceeded to tell the detective about Marianne's fashion business and about the new jewelry collection. "But as for their being lovers, I couldn't say. Though I suspect they probably were."

"What makes you suspect that?"

"Marianne's history," Charlotte replied. "She's notorious for her many love affairs. If she wanted Paul—and it appeared to me that she did—she wouldn't exactly have played hard to get. Also, she behaved in a"—she thought a moment for the proper word—"proprietary manner toward him when we were together at a dinner party at his house yesterday evening."

Maureen was leaning back in the desk chair She picked up an ivory Japanese netsuke in the shape of a monkey and started turning it over in her hands. "Miss Graham," she said, looking up.

"Yes?" Charlotte said.

"In my experience, if a woman acts in a proprietary manner toward a man, it's usually because she thinks there's someone out to steal the goods. Was there anyone at the dinner party who Miss Montgomery might have perceived as a threat to her relationship with the victim?"

This woman is sharp, Charlotte thought. "I don't know," she answered. It looked as if Lydia had already done a good job of setting up Marianne, however unwittingly. Charlotte didn't want to contribute to a scenario that featured Marianne as the jilted woman.

"Let me put it differently. Who else was at Mr. Feder's dinner party?" Maureen asked and nodded at the policeman on the loveseat, who pulled out his pencil.

"Mr. and Mrs. Smith; their daughter, Marianne Montgomery; Marianne's daughter, Dede—her real name is Diana—and myself," Charlotte replied. "In addition to Mr. Feder, of course."

"Tell me about the daughter," Maureen directed.

"She's in her mid-twenties, has her master's degree in historic preservation, and she's worked as the assistant to Lydia Collins at the preservation association for the last couple of years."

"I understand that the victim was treasurer of the association."

Charlotte nodded.

"Does Dede have a boyfriend?"

"I have no idea," Charlotte replied.

"Pretty?" asked the detective.

"Extremely," Charlotte said. She failed to volunteer the information that Dede lived in the cottage behind Paul's house, though she was sure Maureen would find that out soon enough.

The detective looked at Charlotte appraisingly. "Could you have been the woman who the victim was interested in?" she asked

Oh brother! Charlotte thought—though it was true that she was more Paul's age than Marianne was. She shook her head.

"Okay," Maureen said, abandoning that line of questioning, much to Charlotte's relief, "let's get back to tonight. Do you have any idea what time it was that the victim went out to the beach?"

"It was six minutes past seven."

Maureen looked surprised. "How do you know?"

"I saw him go out there," Charlotte said, and went on to explain about standing at the rail with Eddie and noticing his burns. "I was looking at the burns on Mr.

Norwood's wrist. And I noticed the time on his wristwatch."

"Was anyone with Mr. Feder?"

Charlotte nodded. "Dede Montgomery."

Maureen gave her a disapproving look. "Why didn't you tell me that right away?" she scolded. "Remember, we're not jumping to conclusions here. We're just gathering the facts."

Charlotte nodded contritely.

"And where was Dede's mother at this time?"

"She was inside. She came down the gangway to the patio a few minutes later. I saw her talking with some guests, a couple. Apparently she asked them where Paul and Dede had gone, because they pointed in the direction of the beach. Then she followed them."

"She followed them out to the beach?"

Charlotte nodded.

"Did any of the other guests go out to the beach? You must have had a bird's-eye view of everybody's comings and goings."

"We had a pretty good view, but there's a lot of vegetation along the driveway, so somebody could easily have gone out there without our seeing them. Also, I wasn't paying attention every minute—*boy, was that ever true*—but I did see a number of guests going out to the beach, yes."

Maureen was still toying with the netsuke. "The cabana is quite unique," she said. "It's also in the art deco style. There was a write-up on it in an article on cabanas in the Living section of the paper recently. I imagine some of the guests might have gone out there to have a look at it."

"I wondered why they were all headed that way. I thought it might be to smoke, but they could have smoked on the patio."

"Do you remember who you saw?"

Charlotte nodded. "Most of them I don't know by name, of course. But I did see Admiral McLean wander out there, and the man who's head of the preservation association and his wife. There were a number of others. I wasn't able to see if they just went to the cabana, or if they continued on down to the beach."

"I understand that Marianne didn't return."

Charlotte nodded again. "I didn't see her."

"And Dede?"

"She came back about twenty minutes later. Just before the soup course." Charlotte thought for a minute and then volunteered: "She looked upset." She saw no point in holding out anymore. Maureen would find out anyway, and there was no point in alienating her.

"Crying, you mean?"

Charlotte nodded.

"Do you think there had been a scene at the beach?"

"I would guess that's what happened, yes," Charlotte replied, thinking that it certainly wasn't looking good for Marianne.

"What was Marianne wearing?"

"She was wearing a dress of her own design. It was long, pleated, a soft purple color. With a ruffle at the hem and a big mauve flower at the waist. Very pretty." What was Maureen getting at? Charlotte wondered.

"Any accessories—a handbag, anything like that?"

"Yes, she was carrying a *minaudiére*."

Maureen gave her a look. "A mini-what? I'm just a

83

girl from da Bronx. Can you please tell me what the hell that is?"

Charlotte smiled. "I didn't know what it was either. She was carrying it at the dinner party last night. It's from her new collection. It's a box with compartments for everything a woman might need for an evening out: lipstick, powder puff, comb, and so on."

"It's worn on a chain, like a pocketbook?"

Charlotte nodded. "Marianne's was gold, enameled with an art deco design and inset with diamond's."

Maureen looked her in the eye. "Miss Graham, are you squeamish? What I mean is, do you have any objection to looking at a dead body?"

"Not particularly."

"Then I suggest we take a little walk."

With Maureen in the lead, they followed the winding driveway out to South Ocean Boulevard. By now it was dark, though the undersides of the low-lying clouds that had moved in over the last hour were still tinged a dusty rose. The clouds had obscured the moon, and a stiff ocean breeze had come up, rustling the fronds of the coconut palms that dotted the lawn. From the direction of the ocean came the dull roar of the surf pounding against the shore. It was one of those unsettling South Florida nights. A line of cars, including several police cruisers, was parked on the beach side of South Ocean Boulevard. After speaking briefly with a cop sitting behind the wheel of one of the police cars, Maureen led Charlotte through a wooden gate and down a stone-paved path that passed through a miniature grove of feathery Australian pines, swaying palms, and stubby palmettos. Another path led off to the right, to the art deco cabana, which

84

was surrounded by a thicket of sea grapes. At the foot of the path they were following, a steep set of wooden stairs led down to the wide, white stretch of beach twenty feet below.

At the bottom of the stairs, Charlotte paused to remove her high heels. The sand, still warm from the sun, felt wonderful between her bare toes. (She was one of those women who hated pantyhose and avoided wearing them whenever possible.) Then they turned north along a path in the sand that was demarcated by the yellow plastic tape used by police to rope off crime scenes. The path led to a spot about 100 feet up the beach where a cluster of policemen was gathered at the foot of a steep bank covered with sea grapes and the wheatlike stalks of sea oats. Other policemen were stationed up and down the beach to keep away the curious, and floodlights had been set up to illuminate the scene, which was encircled with the yellow plastic tape At the center of the scene, a body lay on the sand at the foot of the embankment.

As Charlotte and Maureen approached, one of the policemen withdrew from the group and came down the path to greet them.

"Anything new?" Maureen asked, and he shook his head.

They paused at the edge of the crime scene, about ten feet from the body, which lay in a pile of seaweed and palm fronds and other debris that had been deposited at the foot of the embankment by the tides. Charlotte noticed that the location would have been hidden from the view of anyone at the cabana, which was set about fifteen feet back from the summit of the embankment.

The body lay on its back with with its knees bent to

one side and its arms outstretched. It always struck Charlotte as odd how one tended to notice small things about a corpse, as if the death itself was too much for the mind to comprehend. This evening, it was Paul's satin-lapeled tuxedo with its white pocket-square and his shoes, elegant patent leather tuxedo pumps with small grosgrain ribbons. The shoes had already been half-buried by blowing sand from the stiff offshore breeze.

"We're waiting for the medic unit to take the body away," said Maureen. "They should be here any minute. The medical examiner has already been here."

The mouth and the clear gray eyes were open and the skin was already beginning to turn gray, but otherwise Paul looked in death as he had looked in life, the exception being the small red-ringed wound in the center of his starched white shirt front, just above the third gray pearl stud, and what looked like fingernail scratches on his right cheek.

"Very neat," Charlotte observed.

"Yes, it is," Maureen agreed as they gazed down at the body. "It looks like a direct in-and-out thrust. No defense wounds. The perpetrator must have caught him by surprise. Though there *are* signs of a struggle." She nodded at the sand, whose surface had been disturbed by a chaotic jumble of footprints.

"Looks like somebody held a dance here," Charlotte commented.

"Yeah," Maureen said. "Some are the footprints of the crime-scene investigators, but most of them were here already. The photographer was here before the sand was disturbed." She nodded at the policemen who were combing the vegetation on the bank with flashlights. "We're looking for the weapon, but we haven't found it yet. We're planning to come back tomorrow."

"What are you looking for?"

"The ME says it's probably a dagger with a six-inch blade, though he won't know for sure until he measures the depth of penetration." Borrowing a flashlight from one of the crime-scene investigators who were sifting the sand around the body, Maureen aimed the beam at a point a few feet to the right of the corpse. "This is what I wanted you to see."

Lying on the beach, partially covered by sand, was Marianne's *minaudiére*. The rich colors of its distinctive geometric cloisonné design gleamed in the light of the flashlight's beam.

"Is this Marianne's minny?" Maureen asked.

Charlotte nodded.

"Can we bag that now?" one of the crime-scene investigators asked.

Maureen nodded, and he proceeded to pick up the *minaudiére* in a rubber-gloved hand and put it in a plastic evidence bag, along with a cigarette butt that was also lying in the sand.

Maureen then guided the flashlight beam along the ground to a spot where a photographer was aiming his lens directly downward at the sand. Then she moved the flashlight beam along the sand. The beam illuminated a line of footprints that went from the body to the stairs leading up to the next cabana, about fifty feet to the north.

They were the prints of small bare feet, feet that might have belonged to a petite woman, a woman of about Marianne's size. The woman must have been carrying her shoes, just as Charlotte now was.

"As you can see, these footprints lead to the stairs up to the next of the cabanas lining this stretch of oceanfront. We'll be coming back tomorrow to make plaster of Paris castings of the impressions. Also to do another search; it's hard to conduct a thorough search in the dark."

Charlotte could see the flashlight beams dancing in the vegetation crowning the embankment at the head of the stairs. Presumably, policemen were searching the area around the neighboring cabana. It was a cabana that she was very familiar with: she had spent all day there just two days before.

It belonged to Spalding and Connie.

It was a long evening—or so it seemed. Using three of the second-floor rooms, Maureen and her assistants took written statements from all the guests who had gone out to the beach themselves and all the guests who had seen others go out to the beach. The remaining people—guests, security guards, and catering staff—were asked to give their names and addresses to the police stationed at the front door on their way out. But the party had gone on. After dinner came the jewelry show, for which Charlotte was drafted as mistress of ceremonies in the conspicuous absence of either Paul or Marianne. Since she didn't have a script, she improvised, relying on a combination of descriptions from the catalog of the collection that had been prepared by Feder Jewelers, and whispered prompts from Connie on the names and backgrounds of the socialites who modeled the jewelry on runways that had been set up between tables. The guests at the captain's table had succeeded in keeping the news of the murder under wraps for the duration of dinner, but once the police started interviewing the other guests, the secret was out. Watching the news spread across the room had been like watching a wind rise across a wooded plain: at first, just a few eddies of movement, and then all the leaves rustling. The fact that guests were being interviewed by the police downstairs added a titillating air to the party that, rather than putting a damper on it, made it all the more lively. Three of the guests, however, were clearly not amused by the prospect of a murder in their midst, and they were Connie and Spalding and their granddaughter, Dede.

After the jewelry show, Spalding suggested that they leave, and since Charlotte and Dede had already been questioned, they did. Charlotte went up to the stage and briefly said goodbye to Eddie. Then they thanked Lydia and went back downstairs, where Connie and Spalding provided the policeman posted at the door with their names and address, following which a valet in a SS *Normandie* sailor cap promptly fetched their Cadillac. Within minutes they were heading uptown on South Ocean Boulevard.

As they headed back to midtown, Charlotte's mind was swirling with questions, foremost among them being: Had Marianne killed Paul in a jealous rage? And then: Were those scratches on Paul's face from Marianne's fingernails? How could she have stabbed him if she was carrying her shoes? Charlotte found it difficult to imagine a scenario in which Marianne had set down her shoes, pulled out a dagger, and stabbed Paul, all without his taking notice. How would she have concealed the weapon? The *minaudiére* wasn't big enough to hide a dagger with a six-inch blade.

Why didn't she come back to the party? Had any of the guests who wandered out to the beach witnessed the murder? Or had any of them seen anyone suspicious in the vicinity? And where was Marianne now? Though the police had been busy all evening, they had yet to interview the most important witness: Marianne Montgomery.

"Okay, Miss Diana, let's have it," said Spalding sternly the minute they were underway, using the name he had called Dede as a child. "What happened out there?" he asked, looking up at her through the rearview mirror. "I want every detail, minute by minute."

Dede started to sob, and Spalding pulled out a handkerchief and passed it to her.

After a minute, she began to speak: "I was with Paul out on the patio. We were talking about the preservation association. Our financial problems. I had seen Mother standing on the deck, and I knew she was watching us. That's when I asked Paul if he wanted to walk out to the beach."

She sat for a minute, the delicate diamond choker gleaming in the light from the headlamps of the oncoming traffic. "I knew it would piss her off. That's why I did it: to provoke her." She sobbed again. "She had been so obnoxious the night before at Paul's."

Connie looked at her sympathetically in acknowledgment of Marianne's bad behavior and reached over the seat to grasp her hand.

"I wanted to get back at her, to make her think that there really *was* something between Paul and me, which there wasn't. The idea is ridiculous: he's old enough to be my grandfather!"

"Not quite *that* old," Spalding observed.

Dede forced a smile. "Anyway, we stood on the terrace by the cabana for a few minutes, and then we went down the steps to the beach. We were walking along the beach—again, we were talking about the preservation association—when I heard someone coming up behind us." She looked out at the ocean for a moment and then back at her grandparents. "When I turned around, I saw that it was Mother. I knew there would be trouble; I had been asking for trouble. She grabbed Paul by the arm and spun him around."

Connie shook her head in disapproval.

"Was she carrying anything in either of her hands?" Charlotte asked. "Like her shoes, for instance?"

"Yes," Dede replied. "She *was* carrying her shoes. In her left hand." She looked at Connie. "Nana, do you think she could be taking anything?"

"Like drugs, you mean?" Connie asked.

Dede nodded.

"What makes you think that?"

"It's just that she's been acting so crazy lately. I know she's been under a lot of stress with this jewelry debut, but she's been under a lot of stress before and she's only acted mildly crazy."

"It could be," Connie acknowledged. "I gave up long ago trying to account for my daughter's behavior."

Spalding turned his head toward Dede. "I've been saying that for a long time, but your grandmother refuses to acknowledge that her darling daughter could be a druggie," he said. "I know she takes pills by the handful."

"Nana, she was like a . . . a pit bull," Dede said. "She stood there with her fist clenched, staring him in the eye, snarling at him about . . ." Tears started

91

rolling down Dede's cheeks, and she wiped them away with Spalding's handkerchief. "I don't even want to tell you what she was saying—it was so sick."

"What then?" asked Connie.

"She ordered me to go back. She was screaming at me."

"And did you?" asked Charlotte.

Dede nodded. "That was the last I saw of them."

"Do you think we should contact our lawyer, dear?" asked Connie, who by now was an old hand at getting Marianne out of trouble.

"Let's wait," said Spalding.

"I can't believe Mother would have stabbed him," Dede said. "Poor Paul," she added, and started bawling again. "If only I hadn't set out to provoke her, none of this would have happened."

Charlotte didn't think Marianne had killed him either, but the truth was, with Marianne, you never knew.

"Let's not jump to conclusions, Dede," said Spalding. "Just because they had an argument doesn't mean that your mother is a murderer. For one thing, she doesn't carry a dagger around with her."

Dede looked at him hopefully. "You mean, it might have been someone else? But then, why didn't she come back to the party?"

"She was upset, that's all. Think about it. If she really was the murderer, don't you think she would have come back to the party in order not to attract attention to herself?"

He had a point, Charlotte thought.

"I'm sure she just walked home," Spalding went on. "We'll talk to her when we get back and find out what happened. Maybe it was a robbery. Remember

92

that couple who were held up on the beach last year, Connie?"

"What happened?" Charlotte asked.

"They were held up at gunpoint. They'd been walking home from a party. The wife's diamond ring was taken, and some other jewelry. I don't think the police ever solved that case, did they?"

Connie shook her head.

Remembering the *minaudiére* lying in the sand, Charlotte hoped for Marianne's sake that that was what had happened.

It was eleven-thirty when Spalding and Connie pulled into the circular driveway in front of Charlotte's hotel. The doorman opened the door for her, and she walked into the old-fashioned lobby with its beamed ceiling, crisp black-and-white tiled floor, and yellow walls, where she was greeted by a young, tanned, handsome bellboy. She paused in the lobby for a moment, and then, lured by the music of a jazz combo, headed toward the hotel's Rio Bar at the far end of the lobby. She wasn't sleepy, and felt as if she needed to sit quietly for a few minutes before she went to bed, to sort out the evening's events in her mind. A maître d' greeted her at the door and escorted her to a banquette at a small table at the back, where a waiter promptly appeared to take her order. When she explained that she only wanted to listen to the music, he graciously brought her a glass of ice water. Putting the murder out of her mind for the moment, she sat quietly, sipping her glass of ice water and studying the handsome, well-dressed, older couples who were swirling around the tiny dance floor. Watching them, Charlotte decided that the element that most characterized this island paradise was the quality of grace—grace, in the sense of acceptance. Though there was still quite a bit of inherited money, there was less than in the past, and most of the inhabitants of Palm Beach were people who had worked hard all their lives to fulfill their dreams, achievers who had reached the pinnacle of their field. At peace with themselves and with all the comfortable accouterments that went along with wealth, they were at last free to quietly enjoy what time was left to them. It seemed as if the marvelous climate, the elegant buildings, and the tanned, handsome young men who were always standing at the ready—to open a door or fetch a glass of ice water—were there to pay homage to this quality of grace that seemed to hover in the gentle tropical air like a magic spell.

It was a spell that was quietly working its magic on Charlotte, like "that old black magic" of the song the jazz combo was playing. She had sensed that the island was casting its spell on Eddie too. They had both worked hard all their lives and they had both reached the top, in part because they had outlasted everyone else. Were they ready now to sit back and quietly enjoy their place in the sun? Eddie had admitted to being a different person now. They wouldn't have gotten along back then, he had implied. They had both been too driven. She thought back to those four short days on the *Normandie:* their lives had been all ahead of them then. For Eddie, a career as one of the most famous bandleaders of his day. For Charlotte, dozens of movies, four Oscars. And now it was all behind them. Or mostly behind them. Charlotte wasn't ready to throw in the towel quite yet. Had

Eddie also been implying that they *would* get along now? she wondered. She was unsettled at how easy it was for her to imagine that it was she and Eddie swirling around that dance floor.

She had left the party without really speaking to him again; he'd been too busy with his band. The band had played on, despite the corpse on the beach. Charlotte thought of those shoes: the elegant patent leather tuxedo pumps buried in the sand. Handmade by the looks of it, and Paul's long, thin fingers. His noble profile, with its high-bridged nose, still so handsome even at his age. His elegant house, and his gracious manners. Most of all, his talent. A creative life that it had taken decades to nurture, obliterated in a second.

It made her sick.

6

SHE HAD DREAMED THAT NIGHT OF THE *NORMANDIE*. The ship was speeding through the misty gray waters of the North Atlantic, the threatening silhouette of the *Bremen* lurking off her port side. The *Bremen's* immense red flag rippled in the breeze, a black swastika circled in white at its center. René had been in the dream. One by one, he'd summoned the passengers into a small stateroom, but instead of being interviewed by the police, they'd been individually fitted for life vests. Clamping a row of pins between his lips, he had fussed and fretted over every detail of the fit, like an overbearing French couturier. Then they had all assembled on the deck to model their vests. One by one they'd pranced down the promenade, twisting and turning like fashion models on a Paris runway. Dede was there, and Lydia, and the couple from the preservation association. Charlotte had been asked to be the mistress of ceremonies, but she found herself in the unfamiliar position of being at a loss for words. Despite the customized fittings, all the life vests looked the same to her. Except for Marianne's. Her life vest was enormous: it pushed up under her pointed chin and reached down almost to her knees. It was so thick at the sides that her arms stood almost straight out. With her straight black bangs and blunt-cut hairstyle, she looked like a five-year-old in an overstuffed Halloween pumpkin costume.

Usually Charlotte didn't remember her dreams, but she'd awakened that morning with this one fresh in her memory. She was sitting at the small table in the bay window of her sitting room, pondering its significance and dining on a breakfast of a boiled egg and toast with marmalade when she was interrupted by the ring of the telephone.

It was Connie Smith.

"I need to see you," she announced without even bothering to say hello. Her voice had an hysterical edge.

"Where are you?" Charlotte asked.

"At the front desk."

A few minutes later her distraught friend was sitting on the other side of the table, telling her story. It seemed that the police had come by the Smiths' house a short while before and asked that Marianne accompany them to the police station for questioning.

Which hardly meant that Marianne was about to be

charged with murder, but Connie didn't know that. Charlotte poured her a cup of coffee from the pot on her breakfast tray.

"They also talked to her late last night, but this time they seemed more serious," Connie said. "Charlotte, you have connections with the police," she went on, referring to past episodes in which Charlotte had helped in murder investigations. "Can't you do something?" she pleaded.

"What's Marianne's account of what happened?"

"She admits to arguing with Paul. She even admits to scratching his face, which is when she thinks she dropped the *minaudiére*, but she denies murdering him. It was just as Spalding said: she climbed back up the steps to our cabana and headed home. She said he was smoking a cigarette when she left him."

"Why didn't she go back to Villa Normandie?" Despite Spalding's explanation, this struck Charlotte as the most puzzling aspect of Marianne's behavior. It seemed to her that the designer of the jewelry collection would have wanted to be present at its debut.

"She said she was plotting," Connie replied as she added cream and sugar to her coffee.

"Plotting?"

"Knowing that her relationship with Paul was over, she was trying to figure out how to divvy up the business to her advantage."

For Marianne not to return because she was upset over a quarrel was a scenario that Charlotte found hard to accept, but for her not to return because she was trying to make sure she got the best of a business deal—now *that* made sense. "Have you called your lawyer?" she asked.

"Marianne insisted on her own lawyer. But he's in New York. He won't be able to get down here until tomorrow. I was hoping you could smooth things over. I'm worried," Connie said. "Especially after . . . you know."

"You know" was the murder in Newport, four years earlier, of Shawn Hendrickson, one of Marianne's boyfriends. Marianne had also been a suspect in that case. Charlotte had been called to the rescue then as well and had succeeded in identifying the real culprit.

Tears had welled up in Connie's cornflower-blue eyes.

"Okay, I'll go down there and see what's going on," Charlotte agreed. She swallowed the last of her coffee and set down her cup. "But if I get the sense that Marianne's in real trouble, I want you to call your lawyer. Pronto."

Connie nodded.

Charlotte looked over at the clock on the desk. It was 9:15. "What time did they come by for her?"

"It was only about half an hour ago. I'm sure she's still there." Connie had stood up to leave. "Please call me the minute you find out anything. I'm not going out. I'll be waiting for your call."

Charlotte nodded as she escorted Connie to the door. So that's what the dream had been all about, she thought as she closed the door behind Connie. The oversized life vest no longer seemed as silly as it had.

Marianne was going to need it.

As Charlotte drove to the police station a short while later in her rental car, it was in a state of—not amusement exactly; more like anticipation. Since

98

she'd been a teenager, Marianne had been causing scenes, shocking the bourgeoisie, and getting into tight squeezes. Scandals, love affairs, arrests—you name it. For all his apparent disapproval, her stuffy stepfather harbored a morbid fascination with Marianne's antics, and Charlotte had to admit that she did as well. For those who played by the rules, there was a thrill attendant to being an observer of Marianne: it was like watching an adventurous cat that's fallen off a tree limb. You know that the cat is ultimately going to land on its feet, but it's the contortions it has to go through to achieve that end that provide the entertainment. Marianne would land on her feet. She always had; she always would. She had succeeded in skirting scandal her entire life. The question was, what was she going to do next? "With Marianne, you never know," was a constant refrain of the Smiths.

The police station was located a short distance from Charlotte's hotel in an elegant, relatively new Spanish-style building across from the town hall. The building overlooked a park that occupied the center of the road behind the town hall, and which featured a long reflecting pool and a spectacular fountain into which four galloping steeds, forefeet upraised, spouted water.

It would have fit in beautifully at the palace of Versailles.

Though the elegant architecture of the police station matched that of the rest of the town, the quality of service was a letdown. There weren't any tanned, handsome young men to park Charlotte's car. What was the place coming to? she wondered as she drove around in search of an elusive parking space.

She had found a spot at last, and was collecting her things when the blue leather box in her tote bag caught her eye. She stared at the box for a few seconds before it dawned on her. As was usually the case at this hour of the morning, her conscious brain had yet to kick into full gear.

It was Marianne's life vest. Of course, it didn't *look* like a life vest. It looked like a rectangular, gold-tooled, blue leather box: the box that held the necklace that she was supposed to return to Feder Jewelers by noon. But its contents provided Charlotte with the answer to the question of how to get Marianne out of her latest predicament.

The lobby of the police station was cool and serene. Stepping up to the dispatcher's window, Charlotte asked for Detective White. The dispatcher telephoned upstairs, and a moment later, an elevator door opened and Maureen emerged. As before, her thick, honey-colored hair was done up in a braid that hung down almost to her waist. Except for the fact that she was a little overweight—chunky would be a better word—her wholesome good looks would easily have qualified her as a model for a shampoo or skin-cream ad.

They exchanged greetings. Then Charlotte said, "I understand you're holding Marianne Montgomery for questioning. Her mother told me that you picked her up at the Smiths' house earlier this morning." She tried to sound collegial rather than threatening.

Maureen nodded warily, waiting for Charlotte to go on.

"I can understand why you would want to question her more thoroughly, given the circumstantial evidence," Charlotte continued, alluding to the scratch marks on Paul's face and the *minaudiére*.

Maureen nodded again.

"But I thought of another avenue of inquiry that might be worthwhile looking into."

Maureen perked up at attention.

"May I see her?" Charlotte asked.

"She's upstairs," Maureen said, turning back to the elevator.

A moment later, they had arrived at an interrogation room, where Marianne was sitting in a tan plastic chair with her chin down and her arms folded. She had that stubborn that's-my-story-and-I'm-sticking-to-it look about her. A uniformed policeman sat at one side of the room, keeping guard.

"Miss Graham is here to see you," Maureen announced, taking a seat behind the desk. "She says she has some information that might help you."

Marianne looked up at Charlotte with an expression that was as close to gratitude as her hardened face would ever allow.

Since there were no other chairs in the small room, Charlotte stood near the door. "Tell Detective White about the *Normandie* collection," she said.

Marianne looked up again, puzzled.

"How it came about, and so on," Charlotte added.

Marianne explained the genesis of the idea and the *Normandie* theme of the collection. She also mentioned that it was her first venture into jewelry design. Then she stopped, unsure of what else Charlotte wanted.

"And the purpose of the party last night was to introduce the jewelry?" Charlotte prompted.

Marianne nodded. "Some of the guests were asked to model pieces from the collection. After dinner, there was a show. Which I was unable to attend," she

101

added, looking defiantly at the detective.

"And what was the most valuable piece in the collection?"

Marianne's sulking face broke into a grin as the aim of Charlotte's line of questioning dawned on her. As Charlotte had suspected, she had been too rattled to think of this angle for herself.

"It was a diamond and ruby necklace based on a Cartier design from the 1930's that was modeled by Miss Graham," Marianne replied. "It's valued at half a million dollars."

"And the second most valuable piece?"

Marianne proceeded to don her safety vest. "It was a gold cigarette case inset with diamonds valued at two hundred thousand dollars."

"And who was to display the cigarette case?"

"Paul Feder," she replied with a look of triumph.

"Do you know if he was carrying the cigarette case when he went out to the beach?" Charlotte asked.

Marianne nodded. "When I was climbing the stairs back up to our cabana, I turned around to look at him. He was standing there, smoking a cigarette."

"We found a cigarette butt," Maureen offered. "It was his brand."

Charlotte turned to the detective. "Did you take an inventory of the items that were found on the victim's person?"

"We always do that right away," she replied. "The last thing we want is for a relative to claim that the police stole something."

"And did it include a gold-enameled cigarette case?"

Maureen shook her head and then turned to Marianne. "You're sure he had it on him when you

102

left him?"

Marianne nodded again.

"For what it's worth, I saw him take a cigarette out of the case earlier in the evening as well," offered Charlotte. "When I first arrived, about an hour before he was murdered."

Maureen thought for a minute. "Okay, let's say for the sake of argument that the murder was committed by a jewel thief. How would he have known the case was that valuable? A diamond ring, I can see. But a cigarette case isn't something that you usually think of as being worth that much."

"Maybe he read the newspaper," Marianne suggested. "There was an article on the *Normandie* collection on the Style page of the *Palm Beach Daily News* last week. It included a photo layout of the most important items from the collection, including the cigarette case."

"Did it give prices?" Maureen asked.

"Yes," Marianne said. "It also mentioned that the jewelry would be shown at a benefit dinner at Villa Normandie."

Maureen rolled her eyes. "Talk about asking for trouble."

It was an easy scenario to imagine, Charlotte thought. The jewel thief hiding in the undergrowth, waiting for a bejeweled party guest to wander out for a breath of fresh air. He sees Paul light up, remembers the cigarette case from the article, and boom—that's it.

"Did any of the other guests see anyone or anything?" Charlotte asked Maureen.

"Zilch," The detective replied. "Which isn't surprising, considering the fact that you can't see the crime scene from the cabana. None of the other guests actually went down to the beach."

"Any other recent jewel thefts?"

"We had an incident last year in which a couple was robbed when they were walking home after a party, but no one was hurt." She looked pointedly at Marianne. "Nor had they advertised what jewels they would be wearing."

"We realized there was a risk of theft. We arranged to have security guards at the party," Marianne said defensively. "But we didn't realize that the guests would be wandering out to the beach," she added with a sigh.

"Did you solve that case?" Charlotte asked.

Maureen shook her head.

Maureen dismissed Marianne, but she asked Charlotte to remain behind.

She wasn't convinced, she confided after Marianne had flounced out in triumph. It wasn't that she thought Marianne had done it, but that she didn't think a jewel thief had. First, it was unlikely that the typical jewel thief would read the *Palm Beach Daily News*, which was aimed at the social community. Second, even if he were the sophisticated kind of thief who studied the social pages, it was unlikely that he would have been able to identify the cigarette case at night, especially if he was hiding in the undergrowth some distance away. He would have had to be standing right on top of the victim to identify the case, and even then it would have been difficult. It was far more likely, Maureen thought, that the murder had been committed for some other reason, and that the perpetrator had stolen the cigarette case in order to make it look as if the murder had occurred during the course of a jewel theft. Or, if the murder *had* really occurred during the course of a jewel theft, that the murderer had known Paul would be carrying one of the most valuable pieces in the collection and had followed him out to the beach expressly for the purpose of robbing him. In either case, the perpetrator would have had to be an insider: someone who knew that Paul would be at the party, and that he would be carrying the cigarette case.

They were still sitting in the interrogation room, Maureen behind the desk and Charlotte in the chair that had been vacated by the uniformed policeman, whom the detective had dismissed.

Maureen continued. "I'm just a girl from da Bronx. I don't know a *minaudiére* from a minivan. But you travel in these social circles. And you've had experience in detective work."

Charlotte nodded.

"I'm not asking you to do any active investigating," she said as she handed Charlotte her card. "But if you see or hear anything that raises your suspicions, I'd appreciate it if you'd give me a call."

"I'll be glad to," Charlotte said.

The funeral was on Wednesday at Bethesda-by-the-Sea Episcopal Church, an elegant turn-of-the century gray stone Gothic building with a soaring bell tower set in the center of a perfectly manicured green lawn. It looked as if it belonged in Greenwich rather than Palm Beach. It was the Smiths' church and the most socially prominent house of worship in Palm Beach. It was only a few blocks from Charlotte's hotel (if she had been asked to assign a Manhattan address to it, she would have called it East Sixty-seventh) and she declined Connie and Spalding's offer to drive her there. Though cool by Florida standards, it was a gorgeous morning, and she preferred to walk. She arrived a few minutes early, and, following a sign through a cloister surrounding a courtyard with a velvety green lawn, wandered out to a charming meditation garden at the rear of the church grounds. She was strolling among the English-style flower beds, looking at the colorful plantings lining a reflecting pool, when a familiar figure entered the garden. It was Dede, looking stunning in a fitted black suit. Her hair was done up in a French twist topped by a fetching black pillbox hat with a black veil.

She was a far cry from the gawky teenager of only a few years ago whose taste in fashion had leaned toward the streetwalker look: skintight shorts and skimpy halter tops worn with extra high heels. In some ways, Dede now had a better fashion sense than her mother, the famous designer. At least she had a more conservative fashion sense. Nowadays she always looked elegant and appropriately dressed, unlike Marianne, whose get-ups often ran to ridiculous extremes.

Catching sight of Charlotte, Dede headed down the path and joined her in front of a bed of begonias. "This is one of my favorite places in Palm Beach," she said after they had exchanged greetings. "Do you have a minute to talk?"

Charlotte checked her watch. The funeral service wouldn't begin for fifteen minutes. "Yes," she replied. "Would you like to sit down?" she asked, nodding at a nearby garden bench.

"I was going to call you today," Dede said once

they were seated. She sat quietly, her fingers fidgeting in her lap. "I wanted to thank you for getting Mother out of trouble."

Charlotte waved a dismissive hand. "They would have learned eventually that the cigarette case was missing."

"Nana said the police now think that the killer might have taken the cigarette case in order to make it look like the murder was committed during the course of a jewel theft."

"That's one theory," Charlotte said.

Dede lifted her veil and looked at Charlotte with her big, pale green eyes with their flecks of gold. "I think I know who might have murdered Paul," she said softly. "I've found something out."

Charlotte was stunned. "What is it?" she asked.

Dede let out a deep sigh. "I didn't know who to tell, and I didn't know if what I found out warranted my going to the police." She rested her forehead in her hands. "I'm so glad you're here."

After a moment, she continued. "It's about the preservation association. As you know, Paul was the treasurer. It was a volunteer position. It's mostly a volunteer organization: the only paid employees are Lydia and myself and a secretary. Though we contract out a lot of work."

Where on earth was this leading? Charlotte wondered.

"But Paul worked at it very hard. He was very devoted to the organization. He hated to see the old Spanish colonial gems being torn down, as we all do. It was like a part-time job for him. He spent, I'd say, twenty hours or more a week at it. He kept a desk at the association's office."

A few people had wandered into the garden and were strolling down the path. Dede waited for them to pass and then went on.

"After his death I took it upon myself to clean out his office space. I was the natural one to do it. The estate lawyers had asked me to take care of the house. They're Nana and Spalding's lawyers too, so I knew them. I figured I'd move everything over there, and let the lawyers figure out what to do with it."

"Are you still living at the guest house?"

"For the time being. I'm taking care of Lady Astor, who I guess I've inherited. I don't know what will happen to the house. I don't think Paul has any heirs in this country. He does have a great-nephew in Paris, who manages the Feder store there. I imagine the house will be sold eventually."

Charlotte nodded. The fantasy passed briefly through her mind that she might be the one to buy it.

"Also, we shared an office," Dede said, going on with her story, "and I didn't want to keep looking at his things. He collected lead soldiers, and he had one on his desk, a knight of Muscovy. He specialized in pre-Revolutionary Russian soldiers. I was packing it up in its box when it became detached from its base." She paused before continuing. "Hidden in the base was a little key. I had been wanting to clean his files out, but the cabinet they were in was locked. When the key fell out, I recognized it as a filing cabinet key and tried it on the locked cabinet."

"And it worked?" Charlotte prompted.

Dede nodded. "The cabinet was full of files. I was at the office till all hours last night trying to figure out what they were about."

Charlotte noticed there were black circles under her

eyes.

"But eventually I did. He was building a case against Lydia Collins." She looked over at Charlotte. "For embezzlement."

"Embezzlement!"

Dede nodded. "She's been embezzling money from the preservation association. As near as I can tell, she's embezzled about three hundred thousand dollars."

"Whew!" exclaimed Charlotte, shaking her head.

"That's what I said." A half-smile crossed Dede's anxious face. "But my language wasn't as polite."

"Over how long a period?"

"About two and a half years. Maybe it's even more money that that: it looked as if Paul was still assembling the case against her."

"I thought she had money. The widow of the bumper king and all that."

"That's what I thought too. And maybe she did have money—once. But money has a way of evaporating around here: it's a very expensive lifestyle to keep up. I know a lot of trust fund babies who're suffering from chronic cases of 'the shorts.' Including myself," she added, with a rueful smile.

"But still . . ." Charlotte mused. "To steal three hundred thousand dollars!"

"She wanted to keep up with the Joneses. Socially insecure people like Lydia are desperate to be accepted, but it takes more than just money. You also need to have social cachet. I've been thinking a lot about it. I think Lydia saw Villa Normandie as giving her that something extra."

"Her vehicle for climbing the social ladder," said Charlotte, who was always amazed at the lengths to which people would go for social acceptance.

"Exactly," Dede said. "That's how she got her job at the preservation association, which is a status job. She was hired because of what she'd done to restore Villa Normandie. Villa Normandie was out of the ordinary. Anybody can have fine French furniture . . ."

Anybody in Palm Beach, that is, Charlotte thought.

". . . but only Lydia Collins had original art from the *Normandie* and the ideal art deco house to display it in."

"And you think the money went into the house?" Charlotte asked.

"I'm sure of it. She spent a fortune on that place."

"Why hasn't anyone discovered her crime before this?"

"She was very clever about it. She knew what she was doing. The contributions would come in, and she would funnel them into her personal accounts at banks where the association also had accounts. I felt sick when I finally figured it out—sick at her greed and selfishness."

Charlotte was impressed that Dede *had* figured it out. It struck her that she had her mother's smarts and her grandmother's charm, without the brashness of the former or the flakiness of the latter.

"Weren't there outside auditors?"

"Yes, but she was the one who prepared the books. Her title is Executive Officer for Administration and Finance. She wears two hats: administrator and finance officer. It's like what they say about computers: garbage in, garbage out. If the information she gave them was phony, how were they to know?"

"But something tipped Paul off."

"Yes. As I said, she was very clever. She worked with small amounts in order not to attract suspicion.

110

She kept the money moving from account to account. Until last October, when she transferred a hundred thousand dollars directly from one of the association's operating accounts into one of her own."

Charlotte raised an eyebrow in her signature expression.

"It was as if she wanted to get caught," Dede said.

"What date was that?"

"October ninth. I'm sure that transfer is what tipped Paul off. In retrospect, it all makes sense. We've had so many successful fundraising functions, plus we get a lot of donations and bequests. I could never understand why we were always short."

"Things like that always make sense in retrospect," Charlotte said.

"I had the feeling something wasn't right, but who was I to raise questions? It was my first real job."

"Have you told anyone about this?"

Dede shook her head. "I didn't want to upset Nana, and I haven't been on good enough terms with Mother lately to confide in her."

"I wonder why Paul kept his files at the office, where she might come across him working on them, instead of at his home."

"There was a lot of work involved. Asset tracing, they call it. Figuring out where the money went. I imagine it was easier for him to work on the records there, where they were kept, when Lydia wasn't around, than to risk her seeing him carrying them in and out."

Charlotte nodded.

"But now I'm thinking that maybe she did find out, either indirectly or directly. He may simply have confronted her with the evidence."

"Whereupon she decided to kill him."

Dede nodded. "I don't think Lydia could have done it herself. I don't think she had the opportunity to leave the party. But she could have set him up to be murdered by a hired killer." She looked over at Charlotte. "It's a motive, anyway."

"A very good one," Charlotte said. "do you have any thoughts about where you want to take it from here?"

"I'm leaving that up to you." For the first time that morning, a smile broke out on Dede's lovely face.

"Thanks," Charlotte said.

What she would do with Dede's findings, Charlotte decided as the two of them headed back to the church, was turn them over to the police. Whether or not Lydia had set Paul up to be murdered, she had committed a felony and stood to be prosecuted for that. Charlotte had recently read in the newspapers about the head of a national charitable organization who had been caught with his hand in the till to the tune of close to a million dollars and had been sentenced to six years in prison, a sentence that was reported as being unusually harsh for a white collar criminal. But she guessed that Lydia could expect to spend at least some time in jail. Actually, Charlotte was surprised there wasn't more embezzlement in a place like Palm Beach, where charitable giving was a way of life. Maybe there was, but nobody was aware of it. Connie had told her that over a hundred charitable organizations had held fundraising events in Palm Beach last season—so many that there was even a catalogue of them. Charlotte suspected that many of these were run just as the preservation association was: by a handful of paid employees with access to large amounts of money, and only a part-time board of volunteers to oversee them. What's more, she suspected that few of those volunteers possessed Paul's dedication and financial acumen.

Arriving at the entrance to the church with Dede a few minutes later, Charlotte noticed that the street was now lined with cars. She had once read that Palm Beach was the Rolls Royce capital of the world, and there were now half a dozen of the luxury automobiles parked in front, with a couple of Jaguars and Bentleys thrown in for good measure among the more ordinary Cadillacs and Mercedes Benzes. They were greeted at the door by an usher who Charlotte recognized as the young man to whom she had returned her necklace at Feder Jewelers. He escorted Charlotte and Dede to seats about midway down the long, soaring nave. The church was rapidly filling up. Paul may not have had any immediate family, but it looked as if the entire Palm Beach social community had turned out to see him to his maker.

The beautiful church was filled with the best-dressed group of funeral attendees Charlotte had ever encountered. In most places, Charlotte's penchant for hats would have been considered something of an affection, though one that was easily forgiven in an actress, but it was the norm in Palm Beach. The millinery industry was doing a land-office business here. Hardly a woman in the congregation was without a black hat, and the styles reflected the many ways in which one could acquire money: the older woman immediately in front of Charlotte wore a shabby velveteen number that would have been outdated in 1956. Undoubtedly, she was a bastion of the old guard. Then there were the safely stylish picture hats of the newly rich, and the daring ventures of the self-consciously arty, the most outstanding example of which was the foot-high turban worthy of Carmen Miranda that was worn by Marianne. Finally there were the timeless classics, a category to which Charlotte's own signature fedora belonged. One of the few hatless attendees was Maureen White, who was recognizable from the back by her starched denim shirt and long, honey-colored braid.

The black cloche worn by the newest suspect, Lydia Collins, fell somewhere between categories four and three: on the classic side, befitting her position as a community leader, but with the artistic flair expected of a woman who had amassed an outstanding collection of art deco works. The admiral stood beside her: tall, handsome, patrician. Quite a catch for the widow of the bumper king. Seeing him, Charlotte thought back to the night of the benefit. She hadn't seen Lydia go out to the beach, and, like Dede, she had concluded that it would have been virtually impossible for her to have left, but she had seen the admiral go out there, alone. Could he have killed Paul on Lydia's behalf? It struck Charlotte as unlikely. Admirals didn't do that sort of thing. Unless their relationship was a grand passion, which she doubted. But she made a mental note to check it out. Admiral-type people were very good at concealing grand passions. Perhaps he himself was in on the scam. Which was a possibility, albeit remote. But who would have thought Lydia to be an embezzler? Charlotte made another mental note, to check out the admiral's financial situation.

The funeral service had begun. Unfortunately, it

was a rite with which Charlotte was becoming increasingly familiar. So many of her old friends seemed to be dying off: a great era in Hollywood history was marching to its grave.

The casket was like Paul himself: polished and elegant. It was borne by the usher who had escorted Charlotte to her seat and five other young men whom she presumed to be affiliated with Paul's Worth Avenue store. As the pallbearers slowly carried the coffin up the aisle behind the priest, Charlotte found herself pondering that single $100,000 diversion of funds: a large and evident withdrawal following a series of small and well-concealed withdrawals. And probably the withdrawal that had tipped Paul off. Why would Lydia have risked detection by breaking her pattern? It was possible that she had simply become more brazen as time went on, that she had been driven by that feeling of infallibility that was said to affect criminals who go without getting caught. Or she could have been desperate for the money. If the latter were the case, Charlotte could think of only two things for which Lydia would have desperately needed money. One was art and the other was to pay a hit man.

If Paul had indeed been killed because he'd discovered that Lydia was embezzling association funds, and if neither Lydia nor the admiral had killed him, that meant that he had to have been murdered by a hired killer. Also, the neatness of the killing would seem to point to a professional; a direct-in-and-out thrust, Maureen had said. No defense wounds. Charlotte had no idea how much a hit cost, but she suspected that the price was higher in Palm Beach. There was no reason why a hired assassin should be exempt from the soak-the-rich philosophy espoused by the providers of other services to Palm Beach residents. She did know that she'd always been amazed at how cheap a hit was when she'd read about them in the newspapers. She would have thought the price of taking a human life to be in the millions, and instead it often ended up being only twenty or thirty thousand. Triple the going rate for Palm Beach, and the price would be, say, almost $100,000—which was the amount that had been diverted in that final transaction.

Thinking it unseemly to be considering the economics of a professional killing while a funeral service was in progress, Charlotte turned her attention to the rites, which included a choir singing the Psalms and the Canticles. Like everything else about Palm Beach, the service was tasteful and elegant.

Fifty minutes later, the service was concluded, and Paul was received into the glorious company of the saints. After exiting the church, Charlotte waited for Maureen, who emerged a few minutes later.

After informing the detective that there was a new development, she made an appointment with her for later that afternoon.

She had put off speaking with Maureen immediately because there was something she wanted to look into first. She had a friend who was fond of quoting in Latin the principle known as Occam's Razor. Charlotte often teased him about his habit of quoting Latin axioms, suggesting that it was the only use he could find for his Ivy League education in the classics, apart from reading the inscriptions on the pediments of banks and public buildings. But she found Occam's

Razor helpful to bear in mind. She didn't remember the Latin, but the translation was "all unnecessary constituents in the subject being analyzed should be eliminated." In the subject currently under consideration, there was one constituent that might very well be unnecessary: the notion that Lydia had used the $100,000 she had embezzled from the preservation association to buy art. And Charlotte knew how it could easily be eliminated.

7

AFTER THE FUNERAL CHARLOTTE HEADED OVER TO the Society of the Four Arts, which was on Royal Palm Way, Palm Beach's equivalent of Forty-second Street. She had read in a tourist brochure that Addison Mizner had left his collection of art books to the society's library. Over the years the society had added to the collection, with the result that it now had one of the finest collections of art books in the country. The library was located in a Spanish-style building in a complex overlooking Lake Worth. She entered through a triple-arched loggia flanked by a pair of panther sculptures. The inside wall of the loggia was adorned with a mural of maidens in classical dress symbolizing Art, Drama, Literature, and Music. Once inside, she was directed by a librarian to a revolving magazine rack at one side of the room. There she found exactly what she was looking for: a collection of recent auction catalogues from Christie's Park Avenue salesroom.

According to Dede, Lydia had diverted the

117

$100,000 from one of the preservation association's operating accounts on October 9. If she'd used the money to buy art, it must have been subsequent to that date. Sifting through the catalogues, Charlotte eliminated those dated prior to October. About halfway down the rack, she found the one she was looking for. The cover bore a reproduction of a section of one of the Dupas panels from the *Normandie,* showing the legs of a golden sea nymph floating on silver waves. The title was *Ocean Liner Decorative Art and Furnishings.* The date was October 30, 1992.

The Dupas panels, listed as Lots No. 155 through 166, were obviously the choicest pieces of the sale. The description read:

> Twelve "verre eglomise" panels, designed by Jean Dupas, the glass executed by Jacques Charles Champigneulle for the Grand Salon of the SS *Normandie* circa 1934, the rectangular panels painted in gold and silver leaf and grisaille, depicting mythological figures, the tail of a sea monster, and a partial view of ocean waves—49 x 32 inches each.

A lengthy footnote in fine print explained how the panels comprised part of one of the four murals that Dupas had been commissioned to design for the corners of the Grand Salon, and described his *verre eglomise* technique of painting the reverse side of a glass panel with gold or silver. The footnote was followed by derailed descriptions of each panel. The low/high price estimate for each panel was $7,000 to $12,000, or a total $84,000 to $144,000—a range that bracketed the $100,000 that Lydia had diverted.

The police could easily find out who had bought the panels, but Charlotte was positive it was Lydia, using the money she had embezzled just three weeks before. As she herself had said, "I just *had* to have them." Which meant that she wouldn't have had any money left over to hire a hit man. An unnecessary constituent in the subject being analyzed had been eliminated. Charlotte could now conclude that: (A) Lydia hadn't killed Paul; (B) she had done it herself, which was highly unlikely; or (C) someone she knew had done it for her.

Which brought Charlotte back to Admiral John W. McLean III (USN, retired).

An hour and a half later, Charlotte found herself climbing the winding staircase to the third floor of Villa Normandie for the second time that week, this time in the company of Maureen and one of the policemen on her team. They were escorted by a housekeeper into the Grand Salon, where they were to meet with Lydia. Presented with the evidence from the Christie's catalogue, Maureen had also concluded that Lydia had used the $100,000 she had misappropriated in October to buy the Dupas panels, hence ruling out the idea that she had used that money to pay a professional assassin. But Maureen raised a possibility that hadn't occurred to Charlotte, which was that Lydia could have directed a professional killer to steal the cigarette case in order to make Paul's murder look like a jewel theft, and then sold the case in order to pay him off. Or had the assassin sell it off himself. At an estimated value of $200,000, the case would have been more than enough to pay for a hit, even if the seller received much less than retail value

119

for it. Maureen's team would be contacting their informants in the underworld to find out if anyone had ordered a hit. They would also be checking pawnshops and fences in the area to see if anyone had brought in the cigarette case, as well as issuing a notice of the theft to other police departments. The records from the preservation association's offices would be confiscated, including those in Paul's files. But before doing anything else, Maureen wanted to talk with Lydia to see if she could get a sense of whether the society matron was just an embezzler, or an embezzler who had committed murder to cover up the financial irregularities.

Lydia was waiting for them in the Grand Salon. By day, it looked less like the real thing than it had by night. The crowns of the palms that could be glimpsed through the tall windows were a reminder that this was an earthbound vessel. Their suspect sat facing Lake Worth on one of the salmon-colored tapestry couches from the *Normandie,* holding her silky terrier, Song Song, in her lap. She was dressed in a black turtleneck sweater, worn with a heavy gold chain necklace, and black slacks with a gold belt.

A man whom Charlotte presumed to be her lawyer sat in an armchair at one side of the couch. His open briefcase rested on the round salmon-colored lacquer game table before him, which also looked to be from the *Normandie.*

At their arrival, Lydia and her lawyer stood up, and introductions were made. When everyone was seated again, the group's attention turned to Maureen.

"I assume you know why I'm here," the detective said to Lydia.

Lydia nodded. Though her face was brightened by

red lipstick, she appeared drawn, and she puffed nervously on a cigarette.

The lawyer spoke first. He was a bald, portly young man with big, sad-looking brown eyes, under which the flesh hung in folds despite his youth. "I've instructed Mrs. Collins to be completely forthright with the police."

Maureen leaned toward Lydia. "Why don't you tell us about it?" she said. She spoke softly and with as much sympathy as a police officer could offer. "In your own way, taking your time. This isn't a formal police investigation."

Like hell it's not, Charlotte thought as Lydia looked up hopefully.

Maureen continued. "It's just a chance for you to tell us in your own words what happened. Take it step by step," she urged. "How did it start? What was it that made you take the money that very first time?"

There was silence for a moment as Lydia rubbed the silky terrier's neck with fingernails that would have been the envy of the Dragon Lady. She stared out the tall windows, with their views of the palm-fringed lake. Then she heaved a deep sigh and started to speak:

"As I've already told Miss Graham, it started with an egg cup," she said, speaking with the flat vowels of a Great Lakes accent. "A silver-plated Christofle egg cup. I paid three dollars for it at an antique shop in Detroit. The owner had no idea what it was. Today you couldn't touch it for three hundred." She shifted her gaze to Charlotte and Maureen. "I'll never forget that egg cup. You know, when you're being pushed, the first taste is always free."

"Collecting was an addiction for you, then?" asked

121

Maureen.

"Yes. After the egg cup, my husband and I would go out looking for other pieces. Only occasionally at first. But it ended up being nearly every weekend. At the beginning, we only collected silver and porcelain. Finding it was such a thrill. Once in a while, we'd purchase items that came up for sale at auction or at an antique shop. But we preferred scouring the flea markets and antique fairs."

"How long ago was this?" asked Maureen.

The lawyer had started taking notes.

"Oh, a long time ago. Fifteen years, maybe. We wouldn't find something every time. That's what made it so much fun. If you ran across something every time, you'd get bored. If you never found anything, you'd get discouraged. We'd turn something up every fifth, sixth, seventh time—just enough to keep it interesting. I have a cousin who's a psychiatrist, and she told me there's a name for this: it's called intermittent reinforcement."

She looked over at her lawyer, who nodded his encouragement.

"Anyway, it was still a recreational habit at that point. What turned it into an addiction was the furniture." Lydia ran her fingers over the delicate gilt-wood arm of the couch. "We found it at a junk shop in Brooklyn, of all places. Talk about treasure amid the trash! We'd never seen anything like it: it was the combination of the Old-World elegance of the Aubusson-style tapestry and the modernity of the lines that intrigued us.

"We knew the furniture was from the Grand Salon, of course," she continued. "We bought it all. It had come from a Catholic church in Brooklyn, which had purchased it at a *Normandie* auction in 1945." She looked around at the room. "That's when we decided to turn this room into a replica of the Grand Salon. We started with the light towers. Harley commissioned a glass artist to make replicas of the Lalique originals."

They all turned to look at the magnificent ruffled glass light towers.

"Then, as luck would have it, the Dupas panels came up for sale at an antique dealer with whom we did business. We bought twenty-six in 1977, and another twelve in 1984. Then Harley died."

"Is that when your financial problems began?" Maureen asked.

Lydia closed her eyes for a moment, as if she were damping down the pain of the memory. "Harley had made a number of bad investments. Or, I should say, he'd made one bad investment. An acquaintance here in Palm Beach convinced him to invest most of his fortune in an enterprise that went sour. Or," she amended. "maybe it was sour to begin with."

Maureen mentioned the name of a company, and Lydia nodded.

"You're not alone," Maureen told her.

"I know. But being one of many doesn't make it any better. Nor does the fact that the principals went to jail for fraud."

Charlotte considered how one set of financial transgressions had led directly to another, in a cycle of monetary greed.

"I didn't know anything about it until after Harley died," Lydia continued. "I was shocked to find out after his death that there was very little money left. I quickly figured out that I could make enough to cover my overhead by renting out the house. I would leave for a couple of months a year and stay in a cheap pension in Italy. To everyone here, I was traveling abroad. But I couldn't rent for any longer than that without people suspecting that I did it because I needed the money."

"Which would have meant sacrificing your social position," Maureen said.

Lydia nodded. "We had worked so hard to get here," she said, her eyes darting around the room, with its opulent furnishings. "It meant so much. It was everything that Flint wasn't, you know?"

Charlotte knew. The grace of Palm Beach had worked its magic on Lydia too, but she hadn't had the resources to pay for it.

Lydia continued. "The rental income covered the real estate taxes and the utility bills, but that was about it. Fortunately the job at the preservation association came along. But even with my salary from that, I didn't have nearly enough. Not to support myself and my addiction. The misappropriation of funds started in small amounts—just enough to cover my latest fix: another piece of furniture, another piece of silver."

Setting the dog down, Lydia reached forward and stubbed out her cigarette. Then she stood up and walked over to the window. From the back, she looked like a girl, so petite was her figure. "Why did I do it?" she said, asking the question that was on everyone's mind.

"Yes," Maureen said. "Why did you do it?"

Lydia turned around. "It's like asking a drug addict why he does crack. I needed the money to play the game. Several times, when I had to convince a dealer

124

to let me have a piece on credit, I felt like one of those addicts who's always reassuring his dealer that he's good for the money. By the way," she added with a bitter chuckle, "it's no coincidence that they're called dealers in the antiques trade, too. Then I'd take the money from the preservation association's accounts."

"I kept thinking I'd get caught," she continued as she turned back to the view. "In a way, I think I was hoping I *would* get caught. Then the missing panels came up for sale at Christie's." Her eyes shifted to the bottom of the huge glass mural that dominated one end of the room. Then she looked over at her lawyer. "Ron?" she said.

Reaching forward, the lawyer removed a letter from his briefcase and passed it to Maureen. "This is a letter from Mrs. Collins to the president of the preservation association. In it, she offers to transfer ownership of all fifty of the Dupas panels to the preservation association."

Maureen gave the letter a cursory glance and then passed it back to the lawyer. "Restitution is a matter between Mrs. Collins and the preservation association," she said. "It has nothing to do with the police."

"The panels are worth between seven and twelve thousand each," Lydia said. "Or between three hundred fifty and six hundred thousand for the fifty. That should more than make up for. . ." Her voice trailed off.

Maureen shrugged. "I'm sure that the preservation association will be delighted to recover the money that's been lost, but your offer to make restitution doesn't negate the fact that you've committed a crime. If you're expecting to avoid prosecution, I think

125

you're operating under a delusion."

Lydia looked questioningly at her lawyer, who nodded agreement. Then she resumed her seat on the couch, with Song Song on her lap. With her fingernails, she carefully combed the dog's fur out of its eyes.

Maureen leaned forward in her chair. "Mrs. Collins, we need to know the answer to one very important question."

Lydia nodded.

The detective fixed Lydia with her gaze. "When did you learn from Mr. Feder that he was aware that you had misappropriated funds from the preservation association's accounts?"

Lydia stared at her blankly. "When did I learn that from Paul?"

"Yes," said Maureen.

"I never discussed it with Paul. The first I knew that he had found out was when I talked with you a short while ago." Then it dawned on her. She spoke as much to herself as to them: "You think that I killed Paul as part of a cover-up?" She leaned against the back of the couch and raised her red-lacquered fingertips to her forehead "Oh, my God."

"I'm not drawing any conclusions," Maureen said. "But Mr. Feder's discovery that you embezzled the funds does provide you with a motive for his murder. Were you at the party for the entire evening?"

"Yes. Of course I was. I was the chairman. The first I knew that Paul had been murdered was when my caterer, René Dubord of Château Albert, informed me of it at the beginning of the soup course."

"You didn't go out to the beach?"

Lydia stiffened her spine and carefully lifted a wave

126

of fried, dyed hair away from her temple. Then she summoned every measure of dignity that society afforded the widow of a bumper king.

"I may have had an addiction that I couldn't control," she said, "but I am *not* a murderess."

Charlotte pulled up in the Smiths' circular driveway at five-thirty the next evening. She would be meeting Eddie at Château Albert at seven, but she had arranged to have cocktails beforehand with Connie and Spalding. The Smiths' house was just around the corner from Villa Normandie: a big, rambling place in the Tudor style (what they used to call "stockbroker Tudor" in Connecticut) complete with half timbers, undulating slate roof, mullioned windows, and dovecote. Charlotte would have been willing to bet that it was the only Tudor in Palm Beach. It was a serious house and a far cry from most of the homes in Palm Beach, which had a fantasy element to their architecture that befitted the playground of millionaires. It was the type of house that one might expect to find clinging to a windswept Dorset cliff or overlooking a misty Scottish moor. It was, in fact, very similar to the Smiths' house on the Cliff Walk in Newport. But then, so were Connie and Spalding out of sync with the local scene. That's why she loved them. They could always be relied upon to react in an utterly predictable manner. They were prehistoric relics of another era.

The door was answered by Marianne, who was wearing a voluminous orange silk kimono that Charlotte remembered from her Kabuki collection of a few years back, and which was the product of Marianne's liaison with a Japanese actor. Now that

Charlotte thought about it, maybe that's where her subconscious had come up with the image of the orange life vest.

Marianne was holding a leaf of Belgian endive heaped with dip. "Come in, dear Aunt Charlotte," she said, gesturing with the endive, and proceeded to escort Charlotte through the center hallway into the living room, where Connie and Spalding were sitting with their cocktails.

Like Connie and Spalding, the room was predictable: tastefully and elegantly furnished with beautiful antiques, many of them family heirlooms from Spalding's side of the family, who could trace their Rhode Island roots back to the founding of the state.

"Charlotte, you look lovely," said Connie, rising to greet her with the obligatory kiss to the air on either side of her cheeks. "Is this the night of your date with Eddie?" she asked.

"Yes, it is," Charlotte said as Spalding handed her a drink: her usual Manhattan, straight up. In a Manhattan glass, with a cherry.

"Ready and waiting, and just the way you like it, I hope."

"Thank you," she replied as she seated herself on the couch. Then she took a sip and looked up at Spalding. "Exactly the way I like it." She turned to Connie. "Spalding's arranged for us to eat at Château Albert for Normandy night, which I think is very fitting." She turned to her host. "Thank you, Spalding."

"Anything I can do for the sake of romance," he said.

Marianne, who had vanished into the adjoining

library, now reappeared with a rectangular box, elegantly wrapped in silver paper. She presented it to Charlotte: "This is to thank you for getting me out of a tight spot."

Charlotte looked up, surprised.

"Don't say you didn't do anything," Marianne warned as she sat down next to Charlotte.

"But I didn't," Charlotte protested. Setting down her drink, she proceeded to open the present. "Someone would have thought of the jewelry angle eventually. Besides, if that hadn't done the trick, the new information provided by your daughter certainly would have."

"Meanwhile I would have been rotting away in jail," Marianne said, adding, "It's not the first scrape you've gotten me out of."

"Nor will it be the last," Spalding interjected cynically.

Marianne shot him a dirty look.

Charlotte removed the wrapping paper to reveal a box from Feder Jewelers She looked at Marianne. "Whatever it is, you shouldn't have done it." Then she opened the blue calfskin lid. Inside was the cloisonné *minaudiére* that Marianne had been carrying the night of the benefit, before she dropped it in the sand.

"I got it back from the police," Marianne said, her deep-set brown eyes smiling. "Fresh from the evidence locker. I thought you ought to have it. Or rather, Mother did. It was her idea."

"We're very grateful, Charlotte," Connie said.

"Oh, Marianne," Charlotte exclaimed as she removed it from the satin lining of the box and examined the multiple compartments. "I love it," she said, adding, "You shouldn't have."

"But I did, so there," Marianne said, sticking out her tongue. "Now we want to hear the latest. Dede's only told us the basics. Lydia Collins turns out to be an embezzler! I don't know her, but Mother and Spalding do."

"I'm shocked," Connie said, shaking her head in disbelief. "I can't believe that someone would betray a public trust like that."

Connie belonged to the old school, and still believed that anyone who would devote their energies to the public interest could do no wrong.

"Historic preservation," Marianne snorted. "Lydia preservation is more like it. What did she need the money for? I thought she was married to the bumper king of Flint, Michigan."

Charlotte related what she had discovered about Lydia's purchase of the Dupas panels coming just after the date of her biggest raid on the coffers of the preservation association. "But it turned out that she needed money in general. Apparently her late husband had made some bad investments."

"That explains why she puts the house up for rent," Connie said. "She lists it every season with Barclay's, for thirty thousand a month. When she originally told us about it, she made it sound as if it made no difference to her. But I wondered. Who would rent unless they had to?"

"She admitted that's why she rents it," Charlotte said.

"She's rented to the same person every year: a German industrialist, who's actually very nice. But we were worried. After all, she *is* our next door neighbor." Connie looked over at her daughter. "Do you remember what happened a few years ago on Jungle Road?"

"Oh, Mother," said Marianne dismissively.

"What happened?" Charlotte asked.

Marianne explained. "An heiress whose money was tight rented her house to a porn magazine publisher who used the grounds to shoot nude photo layouts. The town was outraged. They live in never-never land here," she added.

"That's the way we like it," said Connie. "We don't want our precious island turned into another Forty-second Street."

"Then why did every little old lady in Palm Beach go out and buy the magazine when it came out?" Marianne asked. "Including you, Mother dear." She explained to Charlotte: "Main Street News was sold out."

"I was just curious," Connie said defensively. She turned to Charlotte. "You were saying?"

"It turns out that Lydia owes money all over town," said Charlotte, conveying the latest, which she had found out from Maureen just that morning. "Including to Feder Jewelers, which may have been what tipped Paul off."

"As if embezzling a hundred thousand dollars in a single shot wasn't enough all by itself," said Marianne. "What do you think of Dede's theory that Lydia killed Paul to prevent him from exposing her as an embezzler?"

"I think it's a good theory," Charlotte said. "But I don't think she could have done it herself. No one saw her leave the premises. Someone would have had to do it for her." She turned to Connie and Spalding. "Which is why I wanted to talk with you, as a matter

131

of fact."

"Why?" asked Connie, puzzled.

"I wanted to ask you about the admiral. At the time of the murder, I was out on the deck with Eddie. We saw him go out to the beach."

"But what would his motive have been?" Connie asked.

"A grand passion?" Charlotte suggested.

"For Lydia Collins?" exclaimed Connie incredulously. "Charlotte, there's nothing between him and Lydia. He's a walker: he's with a different woman at a different party every night of the week. I've even been out with him a couple of times myself when Spalding's been away."

"What's he like?" Charlotte asked.

"Very charming, very gracious. Though I'd have to say that he's guarded. He doesn't reveal much about himself. He's a widower. He had a distinguished career in the Navy, from what I understand."

"He was awarded the Navy Cross during the Korean War," offered Spalding.

"He's a very good dancer," added Connie.

"Could he have done it because he needed the money?" Charlotte asked.

Connie shook her head. "I think he probably has enough money. He lives fairly modestly. He has a condo down by the Brazilian Docks. He does have a fishing boat, the *Sea Witch*, that he docks there. I imagine it must be quite expensive to maintain, but what else would he need money for?"

"To cover the high cost of living in Palm Beach?"

"Charlotte, a man like that—charming, handsome, accomplished, available—wants for *nothing* in Palm Beach. There are rich widows by the dozens who are

132

happy to pay his way for the pleasure of not having to go out alone."

"And hostesses by the dozens who are looking to balance their unevenly balanced dinner tables," added Marianne.

"The only thing a man of polish like Jack McLean needs to spend money on in Palm Beach is a well-cut tuxedo. Once he's done that, it's a free ride for the rest of his life." Connie paused for a moment, and then said, "I'm making him sound more calculating than I think he is."

"What do you mean?" Charlotte asked.

"I think he and the other men like him here enjoy the life. They aren't squiring rich widows around because it's a free ride, but because they enjoy the company of attractive, sophisticated older women." Connie straightened up and batted her cornflower blue eyes.

"Women such as ourselves, you mean?" Charlotte teased.

"Exactly. Paul was another man who lived that way," Connie went on. "But for him it was good business as well: getting to know prospective customers."

"Well, I know how I'll get by if you kick the bucket before I do," said Spalding with a good-natured chuckle.

"You'd have to take lessons at Arthur Murray first, dear," Connie twitted, then turned back to Charlotte. "Have we demolished your theory of Jack McLean as a murderer?"

"Totally," Charlotte said.

"Now what?"

"I don't know," she replied.

* * *

After thanking Marianne for the *minaudiére* and saying goodbye to the Smiths, Charlotte got back into her rental car and headed for Château Albert, where she was to meet Eddie. She was as nervous as a schoolgirl on her first date and at the same time oddly calm. She had the feeling that the whole scenario was being orchestrated by a *deus ex machina,* one with an ironic—if not to say somewhat cruel—sense of humor. Charlotte had met Eddie when her marriage to her first husband was breaking up, a casualty of her sudden ascent to stardom. Her second husband, whom she had loved very much in an affectionate sort of way, had died prematurely of a heart attack. Then had come her notorious affair with the cowboy actor, Linc Crawford, who had been the love of her life. He had also died of an apparent heart attack. After a number of other love affairs, she had made the mistake of marrying her third husband, a drunkard and a womanizer, from whom she had been divorced only six months later. Finally she had married for the fourth time, a man she had thought to possess all the old-fashioned virtues, but who had turned out instead to be just plain boring. It was as if this god with the cruel sense of humor were saying, After doling out a lifetime's worth of pain and anguish with regard to men, we're now going to set you up with a wonderful guy whom you could have been with all along, had the timing been a little different.

Or maybe she was just building castles in the air.

On her way to Château Albert, Charlotte took a detour past the admiral's condominium. By Palm Beach standards, it was modest, just as Connie had said. His fishing boat, the *Sea Witch,* was docked across the street. It was good-sized—Charlotte would have put it at fifty feet or more—and it certainly hadn't come cheap. The docking fees must also cost a pretty penny. But the boat appeared to be the only indulgence in an otherwise unpretentious lifestyle, and surely the financial resources of a retired rear admiral would be sufficient to support a boat. Another argument against the admiral dismissed, she thought as she drove on.

Ten minutes later, she arrived at Château Albert, which was located in a charming off-street plaza of quaint offices and apartments across the road from the police station. As she pulled up in front of the club, Charlotte was greeted by a tanned young valet, who promptly whisked her car away. Where did they park all the cars? she wondered, imagining them all lined up in some gigantic parking lot in West Palm Beach. A minute later, she had passed through the opening in the tall ficus hedges that shielded the club from the plaza, and was immediately transported to Normandy, France.

The building was in the style of a Norman country inn, with a first-floor façade worked in a complex pattern of brick and stone, and a second floor façade of half-timbered oak. The roof was steeply pitched and broken up with dormers, turrets, and overhangs. Carefully grouped pots of red geraniums rested on the sills of the tall windows on the first floor, and the tricolor flew from a flagpole in the cobble-stoned entrance courtyard.

It had *beaucoup de charme,* as the French would say.

As Charlotte understood it, the Château was an exclusive private dining club, membership in which was convenient for paying off social obligations for

135

those, like the Smiths, who didn't keep a full-time cook on staff.

Charlotte was greeted at the door by René himself, whose manner, as always, was smooth and debonair. After touching his lips to her hand, he informed her that Eddie had already arrived. Then he escorted her through a stone-paved center hallway past a staircase with a massive hand-carved oak balustrade into a small barroom.

Eddie was sitting at the bar in a room that was empty except for the bartender. Charlotte had wondered if she would feel differently upon seeing him again, if her feelings would have lessened after the novelty of seeing him for the first time. But there he was, and her heart did a little loop de loop.

He greeted her with a kiss on the cheek.

"Here is Miss Graham," René announced, as he pulled out a stool for her.

"You make it sound as if you arranged all of this, René," Eddie commented.

"Who knows?" said René, his dark eyebrows lifting. "Maybe I have powers you're not aware of." He pantomimed Cupid shooting his arrow, then, moving around behind the bar, he removed two small glasses from an overhead rack and pulled out a bottle, which he set on the top of the bar.

"This is Calvados, the specialty of Normandy," he told them. "We say in Normandy: 'Calvados is to the apple what cognac is to the grape.' This is my finest: Calvados du Pays d'Auge." He winked. "I think we have a very special occasion to celebrate here," he said as he removed the cork.

Standing up, Eddie removed another of the small stemmed glasses from the overhead rack and set it on the bar. "Please, René," he said, gesturing at the third glass. "Won't you join us?"

"I would be delighted," René said. After dismissing the bartender, he poured the apple brandy into the three glasses, and they raised a toast to the memory of the *Normandie*.

"Tell me," said Charlotte, looking around at the enormous old oak Calvados casks behind the bar, the heavy beams on the ceiling overhead, and the half-timbered walls, "is this an old Norman inn that you disassembled and had shipped over here, or did you build it from scratch in the Norman style?"

"I renovated it in the Norman style," René told her. "There was a restaurant here before. I imported Norman workmen. Everything is authentic." He laid his hand on the bar. "The bar is a slab from the trunk of a three-hundred-year-old tree, the curtains are Alençon lace, the dinnerware is Norman faience."

"It's lovely," said Charlotte.

"Have some Norman cheese," René said. Reaching under the bar, he produced a tray of cheese and crackers, which he set in front of them as a concession to the American custom of serving cheese before the meal. "Tonight is our Normandy night. We are serving only authentic Norman cuisine."

Charlotte and Eddie helped themselves as René pointed out the various kinds of soft, full-flavored cheeses that were native to that province of France: camembert, pont-l'évêque, pavé d'auge.

"And was the building modeled after a real Château Albert?" Charlotte asked, as she spread some of the rich pont-l'évêque on a cracker.

"No," he said. "This building is modeled after a modest country house. But there *is* a real Château

Albert. It's there," René said, pointing to a photograph hanging on the wall. It showed a big old French château made of red brick and limestone, with a steeply pitched slate roof.

"What's the significance of it?" Charlotte asked, studying the photo of the tall, elegant building, with its formal *allée* of preached lindens lining the drive to the front entrance.

"It's where I grew up," he said. "My family estate. Louis the thirteenth, built in the early seventeenth century. I'm originally from Normandy, you see. That's another reason why the ship meant so much to me." He paused, and then said: "I imagine that you're wondering why I'm here"—he nodded at the photo—"and not there."

Charlotte smiled. "Well, as a matter of fact. . ." She passed a cheese-topped cracker to Eddie and spread another cracker with cheese for herself.

"An American millionaire owns it now. My father lost his fortune—and the château as a result of debts he incurred in Deauville's high-stakes gambling salons, and what he didn't lose gambling, he squandered on his racehorses. That was when I was fourteen. He died not long after, a ruined man."

"How tragic," Charlotte said.

René nodded. "After his death, my mother and I lived in our former bakehouse. We were reduced to the status of tenants on our own estate," he added bitterly. "I think that's another reason why *Normandie* always meant so much to me. She was a substitute"—he waved at the photo—"for all of that."

"Then you lost the *Normandie*, too," said Charlotte.

René nodded and downed his shot of Calvados in a single swig. "You have to drink this all at once," he explained. "To make a *trou Normand*."

"*Trou?*" asked Charlotte, whose French was pretty lame.

"A hole for the food," he explained.

Charlotte complied. The smooth brandy warmed her stomach. "You never finished your story the other night," she said. "Of how you ended up here."

"Ah, as I told you, it is a very long story. I think you have better things to talk about tonight, eh?" he said with a wink.

"Please, I'd like to hear the rest of it," said Charlotte. She turned back to Eddie. "After the *Normandie* burned, René went back to France and joined the Resistance. He stopped his story just as he was captured." She noticed that he was again wearing the red and black rosette of the Résistance in his lapel.

"I think the telling of this story will take some more Calvados," René said and proceeded to pour another round. Then he continued with the story he had started at the party at Villa Normandie:

"As you said, I was captured. I was put in a prison for political prisoners in Fresnes, outside of Paris. Cell eighty-five. All my life, I will remember that number. We were crowded seven and eight into a cell that was meant for one. But I was lucky to be alive."

He paused, and Charlotte asked what he meant.

"The guests didn't stay long in that hotel," he explained. "The Gestapo would order regular clean-outs. Prisoners were either executed, or, if they were lucky, shipped out to Buchenwald. I was there eight months—long enough that it was time for them to get rid of me."

Charlotte and Eddie listened as they sipped their Calvados. René once again downed his in a single swig.

"Then came D-Day. As the Americans drew near Paris in June of 1944, the executions were stepped up. I thought for sure that I would be put to death. But as you can see"—he patted his belly—"I lived to tell the tale. There were only eight hundred of us left when the prison was finally liberated."

"And after that?" Eddie asked as he picked up his glass with a burn-scarred hand. Charlotte noticed that he hadn't volunteered the information that he had been part of the Navy crew in charge of the *Normandie* conversion.

"I had been planning to go back to my village," René answered. "Its name was Oradour-sur-Glane. Does that mean anything to you?"

"It sounds vaguely familiar," Eddie said.

"The Oradour massacre. In June, 1944. One of the most notorious Nazi atrocities of the war. Every man, woman, and child in the village was murdered by the SS. Six hundred and forty-two people, including my mother, my aunts and uncles, my cousins. They shot the men and locked the women and children in the church, and then burned it down."

His mother burned alive! Charlotte was horrified. "But why?" she asked.

"Supposedly in reprisal for a Résistance attack on a military formation moving toward the Normandy beachhead." René shrugged. "But the Germans didn't need an excuse to behave like butchers, as we well know."

For a moment, there was silence.

"I'm sorry," Eddie said.

René shrugged. "There was nothing to go back to," he continued. "so I signed on again with the French

Line. I was the dining room steward on the *Ile de France* for twelve years. But the *Ile* wasn't *Normandie*. Nothing could have been *Normandie*. She had been my life, my love. I loved her with the kind of passion that is usually reserved for a beloved mistress."

"I'll drink to that," said Eddie.

Charlotte and Eddie drained their glasses, and René poured another round.

"Eventually I left the French Line and came to New York. I was drawn there the way one is drawn to the final resting place of a loved one. The East Side restaurant that the *Normandie* crew used to frequent when the ship was interned was still in business, and I used to go there often. One day the owner asked me if I wanted to buy him out, so I did. I had saved up quite a bit."

According to gossip, the dining room steward aboard the *Normandie* earned more than the captain, thanks to the generous tips of the passengers, and Charlotte suspected that much the same was true aboard the *Ile de France*.

René continued: "Before, the restaurant had been only marginally profitable. People from the neighborhood, a regular clientele of French emigrés. I turned it into a very successful bistro."

Charlotte wasn't surprised. With his impeccable manners, infallible memory for names, and polished diplomatic skills, René was a natural restaurateur. "What was it called?" she asked.

René cited the name and address, and she nodded in recognition.

"I first came down here with a lady friend fifteen years ago."

That was another thing that hadn't changed,
141

Charlotte thought: René's penchant for rich American women, and theirs for him.

"An acquaintance took us to the Club Parisienne, as this place was then called. While we were here, I got into a discussion with the owner—naturally we both shared an interest in French cuisine—and learned that he was about to retire. The idea of moving south sounded good to me . . ."

"And the rest is history," Eddie broke in.'

"Pretty much," René agreed. "Another acquaintance suggested that I turn the restaurant into a private dining club. So I sold the bistro in New York, and set to work. The renovations took two years."

A noisy group of four had come in and taken seats at one of the tables at the back of the room.

René downed his glass, and then said: "And that, *madame et monsieur,* is how René Dubord ended up in Palm Beach, Florida."

"It's quite a story," Eddie said.

"I warned you that it would take more than one shot of Calvados," René reminded him. "And now," he said, gesturing in the direction of the dining room, "would you like to sample the cuisine of Normandy?"

8

THE DINING ROOM AS CHARACTERIZED BY THE SAME sense of rustic elegance as the rest of the building, with a floor of quarry tile, a beamed ceiling, high-backed runged chairs with rush seats, and windows with lace curtains. René showed them to a table in a private nook by a huge fieldstone fireplace hung with old copper pots. It was a romantic setting for a romantic event. As René pulled out her chair, Charlotte was reminded of those late-night suppers with Eddie in the intimate Café-Grill aboard the *Normandie*, and it struck her that the course of life tended to express itself in geometric patterns. Sometimes it felt as if it were traveling in a circle, sometimes as if it were doubling back on itself, sometimes as if it were traveling at an upward or a downward angle, or in a zigzag path. Sometimes it ran at cross purposes to itself or meandered in a wavy line. Maybe it was the art deco influence, but right now she felt as if the dominant geometric motif in her life was a spiral. Ever since her arrival in Palm Beach, it seemed as if she kept coming back to the same places she had been before, but on a different plane. First there had been René, then the *Normandie*, then Eddie—all coming back into her life after fifty-three years. Everything the same, and everything so different.

Charlotte hadn't seen Eddie since the night of the *Normandie* benefit, and she filled him in now on the investigation into Paul's death, and Dede's discovery that Lydia Collins was an embezzler—it was an easy way for a nervous date to launch a conversation. When he learned how much Lydia had stolen from the preservation association, Eddie's first reaction was to wonder if he was ever going to get paid for his gig at the party. Charlotte then went on to tell him her theory that McLean might have murdered Paul on Lydia's behalf, and asked him if he thought the admiral could have done it. "He was your commanding officer, right?" she asked.

"Yes," Eddie replied, "but I haven't seen him in fifty years." He shook his head. "But I don't think he could have done it. He was one of the most upstanding men I've ever known. Big Jack, we used to call him. It was a nickname from his Yale days. He played football there."

"Then I guess I'll abandon that theory," Charlotte said. "I don't seem to be getting anywhere with it."

A waiter appeared at their table with a dark bottle of *cidre bouche,* which he described as the sparkling cider that was native to Normandy, and a plate of hors d'oeuvres, which included dry-cured duck sausage, a duck galantine, a *pâté de campagne* of pork and veal, and pickled vegetables. He also brought menus, which listed four more courses, as well as red and white dinner wines, a dessert wine, and a sampling of Normandy's fruit brandies.

The Calvados had already gone to Charlotte's head, and being in Eddie's company had heightened the giddy sensation. She could just imagine how she would feel before the evening was over. Moreover, all three entree selections were cooked in Calvados.

The choice of main courses included veal chops in a Calvados and cream sauce, chicken sauteed with apples in a Calvados and cream sauce, or filet of sole cooked in butter, cream, cider, white wine, and Calvados. "Not exactly *cuisine minceur,*" she said as she scanned the menu.

"Nope," Eddie agreed. "Good thing I don't have a cholesterol problem."

Charlotte entered that snippet of information on the credit side of the Eddie ledger; these things were important at their age.

"Charlotte," he said, after they had finished making their selections, "I know you've helped out with criminal investigations before. That's why the Smiths asked you to look into Feder's murder, right?" He sat across from her, drumming his fingers on the table and looking uncharacteristically serious.

She nodded.

"I want you to help me with something," he announced.

"Of course," she said, wondering what it was that could possibly require her help.

They were interrupted by the reappearance of the waiter, who took their orders—steamed shrimp and mussels marinated in onions, vinegar, and butter to begin with, and the veal chops for the main course.

"First, I have to tell you a story," Eddie said after the waiter had gone. Picking up the bottle of fermented cider, he filled their glasses. "If you think René had a whopper of a story, wait until you hear mine. Oddly enough, it's tied into the same event as part of René's: the *Normandie* fire."

Charlotte sipped her cider, which was delicious, and waited.

Eddie also sampled the cider. Then he began: "As you know, I enlisted in the Navy right after Pearl Harbor. I was an assistant to McLean, who was the District Materiel Officer in charge of the conversion. It was a hell of a job. There were only nine of us supervising the conversion, ten counting McLean, and we were under orders to convert the *Normandie* to a troopship in five weeks. I had almost no free time, but whenever I did have a few minutes, I used to spend them at the piano in the Grand Salon."

Charlotte smiled, remembering how he had played that piano on the *Normandie's* last voyage.

"There was one song that I played a lot. It was 'Just One of Those Things.' I can't count how many times

145

in my life I've played that song—our song." He grasped Charlotte's hand and held it in both of his. "I was still a lovesick young puppy, Charlotte. All I thought about was that crossing—and you."

Once again, Charlotte noticed the terrible scars on the back of his hand.

"On that day, I had gone there after lunch. I was there—in the Grand Salon—when the fire broke out. I was just sitting there, thinking of how the room had looked on that crossing. The salon was in the process of being converted into an officers' lounge. It looked a lot different. The furniture and the carpet had been put into storage, the windows were painted black, the murals had been removed. There were two crews working in the room: a welding crew that was cutting down the metal stanchions that had supported the light fountains—the glass had already been removed—and a crew from the carpet company that was laying linoleum over the parquet floor."

Charlotte shook her head. The thought of linoleum being laid over that beautiful parquet floor—the floor that was was a reproduction of the one in the throne room at Fontainebleau—was heartbreaking.

"That's my last memory," Eddie continued. "Of that moment in time: sitting at the piano, looking out at the room where we had danced the night away. Thinking of how beautiful it had been before they took out the murals and the furniture and the light fountains. At that point, the welding crew had taken down three of the metal stanchions, and they were working on the fourth. Two weeks later, I woke up at Bellevue with my hands in bandages and a terrible headache. I have no memory of anything that happened in between."

146

"Not a thing?" Charlotte asked.

"I shouldn't say that. I get flashbacks from time to time. About trying to find my way out—feeling my way along that long, smoky, dark corridor. The stream of cold air rushing in. . ." His voice trailed off, and he shook his head. "Traumatic amnesia, they call it," he explained. "It's very common in cases where there's a head injury, as there was in mine."

He paused to heap two crackers with the pâté. He passed one to Charlotte and ate the other himself. Then he went on. "Even though I can't remember anything, it's an event that's haunted me all of my life. A day doesn't go by that I don't think about it. It's right here in front of me, all the time." He held out his hands, with their terrible scars. "Oddly enough, it's also what made me what I am. If it weren't for the burns, I'd still be playing piano. It was because I wasn't able to play for so long that I went into arranging and ultimately into conducting."

"Your hands were too stiff?"

He nodded. "It took years of therapy before I got the full range of motion back in my fingers. To continue," he said, "I had no memory of the events that occurred between that moment and when I woke up at Bellevue. Until two and a half weeks ago."

"What happened two and a half weeks ago?"

"I went to a dinner party at Villa Normandie. I had met Lydia Collins when I first came down here last spring to talk with the chairman of the Big Band Hall of Fame Ball," he said. "Lydia very kindly volunteered to throw a dinner party in my honor when I returned. Which she did—two and a half weeks ago."

"Out of her own good will?" Charlotte asked. Such

147

a friendly gesture didn't strike her as being Lydia's style.

"To tell you the truth, she was chasing me," Eddie admitted with a trace of embarrassment. "A healthy widower with a fair amount of change in the bank is like the ring on the merry-go-round in this town."

Charlotte nodded. "So I'm finding out. The admiral also fits that category. The Smiths told me that he's out every night of the week." She smiled. "But I'm told that you have to be able to dance."

Eddie laughed. "Yes, that's true," he agreed. "Anyway, they'd had a grease fire in the kitchen just before I arrived. It was no big deal; they'd put it out right away. But the smell of the smoke was still in the air. Do you remember your first impression when you walked in?"

Charlotte nodded. "So like the Grand Salon on the *Normandie*. All the memories came rushing back in a flood."

"Exactly. At the moment I walked in, it also happened that someone was playing our song on the piano. Lydia had hired the guy who plays the piano at the bar in your hotel for the evening."

Charlotte nodded again. "I heard him play just the other night."

"It was something about hearing the song, smelling the smoke in the air. It was as if someone took a key and unlocked the door to the compartment in my brain that had been locked up since February ninth, 1942. The memory of what happened that afternoon rose up from somewhere in the depths of my brain. It was like watching something float to the surface of a murky pond. I still couldn't remember it all, of course, though a lot of it has since drifted back in bits and pieces. But I remembered the most important part."

"Which was what?" prompted Charlotte, who was still wondering what this fascinating story had to do with him needing her help.

"Do you remember the conclusion of the New York Attorney General's investigation into the *Normandie* fire?" he asked.

"Yes. It was that the fire was started accidentally by the welders who were taking down the light stanchions. That a spark from a welding torch accidentally ignited a bale of life preservers stored in the Grand Salon."

"The wording was 'There is no evidence of sabotage. Carelessness has served the enemy with equal effectiveness.' Or something to that general effect, anyway," Eddie said.

"I remember," Charlotte said as she put some hors d'oeuvres on Eddie's plate and some on her own.

"Wrong," he said. "I saw it with my own eyes. The memory of that second in time is what came back to me two and a half weeks ago at Lydia's party."

She looked up at him. "It *was* sabotage?"

He lifted a finger, then set the salt and pepper shakers on either side of Charlotte's octagonal faience plate. "Here are the welders." He pointed to the salt shaker on her left. "And here are the linoleum installers." He pointed to the pepper shaker on her right. "And here, in between, is a head-high pile of kapok-filled life preservers—Mae Wests," he said, pointing to the plate.

"And where are you?"

"On the bandstand at the forward end of the room," he said, moving the flower vase with its spray

149

of pink orchids into position to the right of the pepper shaker representing the linoleum workers. "The only one with a bird's-eye view. The spark supposedly went from the welding torch to the pile of life preservers." He moved his finger in an arc from the salt shaker to her plate.

"Didn't they use some kind of shield?"

"They did. A sheet of scrap metal. But it didn't matter. Because the ignition source wasn't the welding torch. The fire was started with an incendiary device that was tossed into the pile of life preservers by one of the workmen who were gluing the linoleum down here," he said, pointing to the pepper shaker on her right, and then moving his finger in an arc from that shaker to the left-hand side of her plate, next to the salt shaker."

"Whew!" said Charlotte, letting out a deep breath.

"There were two guys. One slightly older than the other. The younger one was about twenty, I'd guess. Before the younger guy threw the device, the older-man gave him an order, in German. The order was *jetzt*. Do you know what *jetzt* means in German?"

She shook her head.

"I looked it up. It means *now*. After the younger guy threw the device, he looked around. That's when he saw me. We locked eyes. I remember it now as clearly as if it took place yesterday. He had very clear, gray eyes. I don't think he realized until then that I was there. They had their backs to me. I hadn't started playing, and the room wasn't brightly lit. I also think they were the ones who conked me on the head."

"Conked you on the head!"

"My concussion was from a blow to the head. The

doctors thought I must have fallen in an attempt to escape. But to get back to that moment: after the fire broke out, we all tried to extinguish it. The life preservers were packed in burlap-covered bales, and the flames raced from bale to bale. It was like watching a fire spread across a field of dry grass. We beat at it with coats, sweaters, pieces of linoleum—our bare hands. That's how I got burned. After that . . . I still don't remember." He ran his fingers through his close-cropped white hair. "One of the rescue workers found me in a corridor in tourist-class and carried me out. I have no idea how I got down there."

"That would have been one deck down," Charlotte observed.

He nodded. "I think those guys cold-cocked me, dragged me down there, and left me for dead. They probably would have stowed me in the cargo hold if they thought they could have done that and still got out in time themselves."

"I'll say this is a story!" Charlotte exclaimed. "Have you told Jack McLean?"

He shook his head. "I wanted to wait. Once I remembered what had happened, I was determined to find out who those guys were. They had tried to kill me, after all. I also felt a patriotic duty to expose them, as it were. You see, it was the Navy that took the blame."

"Carelessness," Charlotte commented.

Eddie nodded. "The fire may have spread because of carelessness, but it didn't start because of carelessness. There are a lot of guys who have been carrying the *Normandie* fire on their consciences for a lot of years—Jack McLean among them, I suspect. He was the scapegoat. He took the heat for the higher-

151

ups. Never complained about it either," he added.

"Odd that you should have run into him down here."

Eddie shrugged. "Life is full of odd coincidences." He reached out and grasped her hand. "Some of them have a lot more significance than others, like meeting up again with your girl after fifty-three years." He smiled, and Charlotte melted.

"Did you find out who they were?" she asked.

"Yes. It was difficult, but not as difficult as I would have thought. I started with the Attorney General's report, which listed the names of everyone who was aboard at the time of the fire. That was over three thousand people: mostly workmen and prospective Navy crew members. Then I narrowed the list down to the employees of the Tri-Boro Carpet Company. They were a subcontractor to the Robins Dry Dock Company, which had been hired to do the conversion work."

"And who the linoleum layers presumably worked for," said Charlotte.

Eddie nodded.

"That limited it to nineteen. But that's where I got stuck. So I made up a possible scenario. Since I had heard the one guy speaking German, I figured that he might be a member of the German-American Bund, a German fifth columnist."

"Didn't the contractor conduct security checks?" asked Charlotte. "It would seem as if having all those workmen aboard was asking for trouble."

"McLean had asked Robins to provide him with a list of all its foreign employees, which was checked out by Naval Intelligence. But for some reason he never asked for a similar list from the subcontractors.

He probably didn't have the time. Tri-Boro Carpet was one of thirty-five subcontractors. On the day the fire broke out, there were over two thousand workmen on board, and only ten of us to supervise them. The Navy was desperately short of men: hundreds of new ships were coming into service, and it was hard-pressed to crew them."

Charlotte leaned back and let out a deep sigh.

"We were well aware that security was a mess," Eddie went on. "There were simply too many of them and too few of us. The Chief of Naval Operations and the Commandant of the Third Naval District had both asked the White House for more time. But Roosevelt was determined to have the ship ready to take on troops by January thirty-first—no ifs, ands, or buts—and we'd already had to ask for one extension, to February fourteenth."

They were interrupted by the arrival of their appetizers, which looked delicious.

"As I said, I assumed he was a Bund member," Eddie continued after the waiter had left. "I asked myself, 'What would a member of the Bund have done for the duration of the war?' I came up with two possible answers: One, he would have stayed in the United States to commit other acts of sabotage, or two, he would have gone back to Germany."

Charlotte nodded, and started on her plump, spicy mussels.

"Since no other major acts of sabotage occurred, I figured the answer must be number two. I also figured that he would probably have wanted to get out of the country after the fire. Then I asked myself, 'What would he have done in Germany?' And the answer was 'Become a Nazi.' Finally I asked myself, 'How

153

does one locate former Nazis?' And the answer was the Jewish Documentation Center in Los Angeles, the Nazi-hunting organization."

"Did you ever think about a second career as a private eye in your retirement?"

He shook his head. "I'm not retired yet, and I'm not planning to retire."

Charlotte nodded again. It was reassuring to hear that Eddie thought the same way she did. Slow down maybe, but retire? Never.

"I have to admit that I was pretty proud of myself," he continued as he took a bite of his appetizer. "I figured that if these Nazi hunters could track down Eichmann and Mengele, they might be able to track down my guy too."

"And were they able to?"

Eddie leaned forward. "Charlotte, it was a snap. That's where I've been for the past couple of days—out in L.A. They have a worldwide network of sources and informants, and all their information is computerized. I gave them the names on the carpet company roster, and they checked them against their archives. The whole process took twenty minutes. I figured that the names on the list were probably aliases, but that they might have used the same aliases on their passports or some other documents, and that the center might have a record of the aliases."

"And did they?" asked Charlotte.

He nodded. "One of the names on the roster was Bill Roe. Sounds like the soul of Ireland, doesn't it? Well, there wasn't a Bill Roe in the center's archives, but there was a Wilhelm Roehrer. I can't take the credit for spotting the similarity in the names. That goes to one of their staff people—they're old hands at

154

that sort of thing. He had been a minor Nazi, an SS *oberscharführer* or technical sergeant. A small fish, not worth going after for them. He had worked as a prison warden. After the war, he escaped over the Alps into Austria, and from there into Italy, where he booked passage to the United States out of Genoa. He was carrying a fake International Red Cross passport."

"Why America?" she asked.

"Why not? It was his former home; he spoke fluent English. Where else would he have gone? He wasn't going to hang around Germany and risk being prosecuted. They told me at the center that a lot of former Nazis were among those who flooded into the U.S. after the war."

"How do you know Bill Roe and Wilhelm Roehrer are the same person?"

"I don't. But I have a sense that they are. Isn't that the way an investigation works? You follow your nose?"

"Very much so," Charlotte concurred. She had always thought that an investigation was not so much a matter of drawing a conclusion from the facts, but of marshaling the facts to support a conclusion. In other words, verifying the intuition instead of dismissing it. "How do we find out?"

"That's where you come in. They gave me his address. He retired to Florida from Richmond Hill, Queens, where he worked as a heavy-machinery mechanic. He lives in Clearwater, which is near Tampa. I want you to go there with me. I figure that we can pose as investigators for the OSI, the Office of Special Investigations. It's a unit of the Justice Department that's assigned to investigating Nazis who entered the United States illegally. But I'm not good

155

at that kind of stuff. You're the one who's the actress."

"Have you thought of taking your findings to the authorities?"

He shook his head. "Two reasons. First, this is my baby. As I said, I've been obsessed with this for fifty years. It's not something that I trust someone else to get to the bottom of. Second, who would I go to? The OSI tracks down ex-Nazis; it wouldn't prosecute a sabotage case. The New York Attorney General's office? Do you think they're going to care about a lead on a fifty-year-old case? The people who worked on the original investigation are probably all dead by now. For that matter, maybe this guy Bill Roe is dead."

He had a point, Charlotte thought.

"But if I were to present the authorities—the FBI, or whoever—with some concrete evidence, it might be different. I don't have to reel the fish in hook, line, and sinker, but I at least ought to be able to show them that I have something on the line."

It took Charlotte only a minute to make up her mind. Paul's murder was now in the hands of the police, and shopping was something that held only limited appeal for her. Plus, a trip to the west coast of Florida offered the prospect of spending more time with Eddie.

"Sure," she said.

They left early the next morning after a hearty breakfast at Charlotte's hotel. It was a five-hour drive. They spent the first part of the trip making plans: Charlotte, with her acting skills, would pose as the OSI investigator, and Eddie would pose as her assistant. Their strategy would be to offer Roe an ultimatum: either admit to sabotaging the *Normandie* or face extradition to Germany. That was, *if* there was any evidence that Bill Roe, as he called himself, was in fact a former Nazi, and not an innocent retiree. They had no idea what form this evidence might take. As Eddie pointed out, it wasn't as if he was going to have a swastika hanging in his living room. A German accent, perhaps; a clear expression of recognition when addressed by his German name; a strong reaction to being confronted with his past misdeeds. There was even the remote chance that Eddie might recognize him. Their secondary goal would be to induce him to implicate the others who were involved in the plot. They knew for a fact that there was an accomplice, but those two, in turn, must have been taking directions from a higher-up. They hoped that Roe would be induced to confess by the threat of extradition. But if the intimidation ploy didn't work, they were prepared to resort to the age-old method of eliciting information: buying it.

They spent the second part of the trip riding in silence—there wasn't even anything worth listening to on the radio—and watching the flat, yellow scrubland of central Florida roll by. They were skirting the northern boundary of the Everglades, and the land had been drained and diked to create fields for sugar, rice, cattle—even the occasional alligator farm. Charlotte knew there were people who enjoyed this kind of country. Spalding and Connie had acquaintances who owned cattle ranches in central Florida, and she had known others who liked to hunt here. But it held absolutely no appeal for her. However, she did enjoy riding with Eddie, feeling his presence, looking at his profile. She was reminded of her first reaction to him fifty-three years ago. It had been as if they were connected by the blue-violet arc of a surging electric current: thrilling, but also a little frightening. They had spent much of the previous evening reminiscing about those four wonderful days. Now it was different. It was as if they shared the same glowing cocoon, a cocoon that was bathed in the same blue-violet light, but now the light was gentler and more subdued, tempered by the years. Comfortable.

After a little more than three hours of driving across the central Florida savanna, they came to Fort Myers and then headed north along the densely developed coastal strip. At noon, they crossed the Sunshine Skyway Bridge, the long, high bridge over Tampa Bay, which deposited them in St. Petersburg, just south of Clearwater. They had no trouble locating Roe's home, which was only a few blocks from the Gulf to Bay Boulevard, the main east-west highway. It was a small, neat, Spanish-style bungalow on a culs-de-sac at the end of a street lined with similar bungalows. A neatly clipped hibiscus hedge lined the foundation, and a cluster of palm trees were planted in the center of the small front yard.

It appeared that someone was at home: a car was parked in the carport.

They parked on the street and walked up the path to the arched entryway. Charlotte was carrying a briefcase in order to appear more official, and she had worn her reading glasses and a skirt-and-sweater outfit that was suitably conservative. Eddie wore a golf cap over his short white hair. In addition to looking like investigators, they also wanted to disguise themselves: their well-known faces could easily give them away.

Glancing at white-haired Eddie, Charlotte had to smile. "The senior citizen investigators," she joked as she rang the bell. Though they both looked considerably younger than their real ages, they were still pretty old for Justice Department investigators. But she supposed they wouldn't stand out as much in a state full of retirees as they might elsewhere.

A large-boned woman with a stern mouth and blond hair going to gray answered the door. She wore an apron that was dusted with flour.

"We're here to see Mr. Roe," Charlotte said. "Are you Mrs. Roe?"

The woman nodded.

She looked to be in her mid-fifties to early sixties, considerably younger than her husband, whom they had figured to be at least seventy.

"He's very sick," she told them, speaking with a heavy German accent, which was an encouraging sign.

"We're from the Office of Special Investigations," Charlotte said and quickly flashed her Actor's Equity card. What the hell—the woman's eyesight couldn't have been that good. Whose was after fifty?

The woman's glance shifted from Charlotte to Eddie, who was standing just behind her on the doorstep, and then back to Charlotte.

Then she opened the door and escorted them through a small, neatly furnished living room and down a hall to a bedroom, where a pale, unshaven man with an oxygen tube in his nose was sitting up in bed watching a television game show. He had a long face that was still fleshy despite his illness, and full lips. His dark gray hair was combed straight back from his forehead.

The room was spotlessly clean, but it smelled of sickness. Framed photographs of family members hung on the wall, and more of them stood on the dresser top. A crucifix hung over the headboard, and there was one small window, which overlooked a concrete patio at the rear of the house. The oxygen pump made an eerie whooshing sound.

Mrs. Roe took a seat on the edge of the bed. "They've come back," she said. "But it's different ones this time."

Charlotte and Eddie exchanged puzzled looks. What was she talking about? they wondered. Had someone else been here asking questions?

Then the woman said something in German, of which Charlotte caught only the word *geld*. She didn't know German, but she'd picked up enough Yiddish over the years to know what *geld* meant.

The man nodded. "I'm dying," he whispered.

On a hunch, Charlotte decided to play it straight. If he was dying, he didn't have anything to lose. "Are you *Oberscharführer* Wilhelm Roehrer?"

He nodded wearily.

Charlotte wondered if Eddie recognized him, or vice versa. She tried to imagine how Eddie must be feeling—face to face with the man who had almost killed him.

"We came here to find out about the *Normandie* fire," she said, then turned to his wife. "What's wrong with him?" she asked. Realizing that Roe was too weak to say much himself, Charlotte wanted him to save his energies for the questions that were to come.

"Cancer in the blood," the wife replied, shrugging in apology for not knowing the correct term in

160

English.

Charlotte turned back to Roe. "Then you must have a lot of medical bills," she said. She nodded at Eddie, who stepped forward with the briefcase, and opened it to display the cash. "Maybe this will help you with some of your expenses."

"How much?" asked Mrs. Roe directly.

"Two thousand," Eddie replied.

The man closed his eyes in visible relief, and Eddie closed the briefcase and handed it to Mrs. Roe.

"We want to know the name of the man who was giving you your orders," Charlotte said. "Who was your boss for the *Normandie* operation?"

"The other man asked that too," Roe said. He spoke in a hoarse whisper, with great effort. He also had an accent, but it was slight by comparison with his wife's. With every exhalation, he made a wheezing sound.

"What other man?" said Charlotte.

"Isn't he connected with you?" Roe asked. "He was here two weeks ago, asking questions. He came back two days later," he added, the implication being that he returned the second time with the *geld.*

Charlotte exchanged looks with Eddie. Someone else was also onto the fact that this ailing Nazi had been involved in the sabotage of the *Normandie.* "Who was this other man?" she asked.

"I don't know," Roe replied.

"And what did you tell him?"

"I told him I didn't know my contact's name," he replied. "Just his code name, which was the Fox, and his number, *Abwehr* F473."

The *Abwehr* was the German secret service.

"The code name for the *Normandie* operation was

161

Unternehmen Goldene Vogel," Roe continued. "It means Operation Golden Bird. It's from the title of a Grimm Brothers fairy tale. The golden bird was the *Normandie.* The fox was a character in the fairy tale."

"How did you communicate with him?"

"By mail," Roe said "He sent the directions to me in the care of a member of the New York Bund."

"Did you know anything about him?"

"Only that he must have had some pull. He arranged for us to get the jobs with Tri-Boro Carpet, and he made sure that we were assigned to the Grand Salon on the day the welding crew was taking down the light stanchions."

"How did he recruit you?"

"My friend and I lived in the same neighborhood in Queens. It was mostly a Russian neighborhood. We had gone to summer camp together: a Russian fascist summer camp in Connecticut. The *Abwehr* agent had gotten our names through someone at the camp. He contacted us through a local Bund leader."

"But the Bund leader wasn't directly involved?"

Roe shook his head.

"And the man you ordered to throw the bomb—he was your friend?"

He nodded. "It was actually an incendiary pencil, it generated a heat of three thousand degrees. We picked it up in a locker on the ship. Our instructions were to throw it into the pile of life preservers when the welders were working nearby. He wanted us to make it look like an accident."

So, Charlotte thought, Eddie's memory—the memory that had been resurrected at Lydia's dinner party—was accurate. It had been perfectly embalmed for fifty years.

162

Roe continued: "They weren't supposed to be able to put the fire out," he said. "But in the end, it didn't matter that they succeeded in putting it out. The *Normandie* was finished anyway." He said it with the air of a man who was talking about a deed well done.

Charlotte remembered how the fire hoses hadn't worked, the fire alarm hadn't gone off, the blaze hadn't been called into the fire department until it was well underway. Those events had been blamed on carelessness, but maybe it had been deliberately orchestrated carelessness.

"And the name of your accomplice, the friend who you ordered to throw the incendiary pencil?" she asked.

Roe's voice had become weaker. "He was a Russian, a member of the Russian Fascist United Front. The Russian fascists were our allies. We had the same goal: to defeat the Bolsheviks. But their reasons were different; they wanted to restore the Romanovs to the Russian throne."

"His name?" Charlotte prompted.

"His alias was Paul Fahey Another Irishman, like me." He chuckled weakly at the irony. "But his real name was Paul . . ." Roe gasped for air. "Paul Feder . . ." His voice trailed off.

Charlotte sucked in her breath.

Then he finished saying the name: "Paul Federov."

"Whew!" said Charlotte once they were back in the car, which had been baking in the sun. She leaned back against the hot seat and took a deep breath. "Where can we go to talk?" she said. "We have to think this one out."

Eddie turned the key in the ignition and then raised

163

his fists in an expression of triumph. He turned to Charlotte. "I think that information was well worth two grand," he said with a big grin. "What do you think?"

"Definitely," she said. "The question is, What do we do with it?"

"There was a chicken wings place back on the highway," he said. "Are you hungry?" He checked his watch. "It's already past one."

"Very," she said.

9

IT WAS THE PATTERN THEORY OF LIFE AGAIN, Charlotte thought as they headed back out to the highway. Here she was, back in the loop, but on a different plane. There had been the René spiral and the *Normandie* spiral and the Eddie spiral, and now there was the Paul spiral. The difference was that this was a much more complicated pattern. The earlier patterns had been like sofa springs: life simply coming around again. The Paul pattern was like a double helix that was held together by molecular building blocks in a structure so complex it would take a Nobel laureate to decipher it. They had come to Clearwater to investigate the sabotage of an ocean liner fifty years ago and had instead uncovered a possible clue to a murder that had occurred only last week. The only thing that all these spirals had in common was the *Normandie:* it was as if Lydia's decision to create a replica of the Grand Salon on the third floor of her art deco house had caused a chain reaction that sent streamers shooting off in all directions, like the streamers that departing passengers throw from the deck of an ocean liner.

She would be relieved when the pattern of life returned to something less complicated. Her life had never come even close to traveling in a straight and steady line, but a gentle arabesque might be nice.

A few minutes later, they were sitting on barstools at a high wooden table chowing down on chicken wings with Chernobyl sauce (the sauce came in mild, medium, and Chernobyl) at a highway establishment called Hooter's that was named after the ample endowments of its skimpily clad waitresses and possibly for the utterances emitted by the clientele in appreciation thereof.

Yes, they were in the South, Charlotte thought.

"Very attractive personnel," said Eddie, with a sideways glance at the shapely young woman who had just set down their mugs of beer. She wore a tight orange T-shirt bearing a cartoon of an owl, the Hooter's logo, and black short-shorts with slits up the sides.

"Aren't you too old to be gawking like a teenager?" Charlotte teased.

"You're never too old," Eddie replied with a grin. He picked up his mug and took a long swig. "Well, what do you think?" he asked.

"I don't know what to think."

"The first question is, Are Paul Federov and Paul Feder one and the same?" he said, reaching into the serving bowl for another chicken wing.

"I think they must be," Charlotte replied and proceeded to tell him what the Smiths had said about Paul's White Russian background, and what Dede

165

had said about his lead soldier collection specializing in figures of the Imperial Russian Army. "But it should be easy enough to find out."

Eddie nodded. "So what now?" he asked as he munched.

"Okay, let's take this one step at a time," Charlotte said. "Paul Federov, or Paul Feder as we know him, grows up in a Russian neighborhood in Queens where he becomes friends with a German named Wilhelm Roehrer, who has fascist sympathies. By the way, did you recognize Roehrer?"

"I don't know," Eddie replied. "He was the same type as the guy on the *Normandie:* the full, fleshy face. But I couldn't say for sure. I didn't see him that well at the time. He was looking down at the roll of linoleum."

"What about Feder? Do you remember him from the party?" Charlotte called up a mental picture of Paul. "He was very tall—six foot three or four—with very pale gray eyes, just like the eyes you remembered Roehrer's accomplice as having."

Eddie shook his head. "I didn't meet him, though I did see the photo in the newspaper. I couldn't tell; it wasn't a very good picture."

"That's okay. We can get a better one from the police." Charlotte remembered those same gray eyes, staring lifelessly up from the beach. "Okay, to continue. Roehrer and Federov attend a fascist summer camp in Connecticut, where, unbeknownst to them, they are singled out by an *Abwehr* agent, code name the Fox, to be operatives in a plot to sabotage the *Normandie:* Operation Golden Bird. The agent contacts a Bund member back in Queens, who recruits them for the sabotage caper. Have I got it right?"

"As I understand it."

"The Fox makes arrangements for them to work for the company that is laying the linoleum. He provides them with an incendiary device and sets up the circumstances in which they are to detonate it, namely the removal of the light stanchions in the vicinity of a stack of inflammable life preservers. Fifty years later, a man shows up on Roehrer's doorstep and wants to know who his accomplice was. Roehrer, who is dying, and is concerned about his wife's financial security, tells him to come back with money."

"Which he does, two days later," Eddie added as he took another swig of his beer. "This sauce is really hot," he said.

Charlotte also took a swig of the cold beer, and then continued: "The next week, Paul Feder is murdered. The murder takes place on the fiftieth anniversary of the *Normandie* fire. Since the congruence of the dates is too improbable to be written off to coincidence, I think we have to work under the assumption that Feder's murder was related to Operation Golden Bird. Especially since someone had just visited Roehrer the week before seeking to discover the identity of his accomplice."

"I agree," Eddie said.

"Which means that we can eliminate Lydia and the admiral as suspects," Charlotte added. She thought of Occam's Razor again: another unnecessary element in the subject being analyzed had been eliminated.

It was odd how all the players in the drama had assembled in Florida, Charlotte thought. But then, Florida was a place where old warhorses came to die, if they weren't dead already or living in California.

167

She remembered once reading a quote to the effect that Palm Beach was a place where few things begin but many things end.

Eddie looked up from his plate of chicken wings. "And from there?"

Charlotte shrugged. "I don't know. Do you have any ideas?"

"Only one," he replied. "This is how it goes: the whole sabotage idea lies dormant for all these years. Then one day my memory decides to kick into gear, and I start looking into what happened on the *Normandie* fifty years ago. By coincidence, somebody else starts looking into the same event at the same time—somebody who wants the information badly enough to pay for it."

"Maybe the authorities are more interested in the *Normandie* fire than you thought," Charlotte suggested.

"For argument's sake, let's call the other party the FBI. I think this is what may have happened. I think Feder knew who the Fox was. I think the Fox got wind of the reopening of the investigation and killed Feder to prevent him from revealing his identity to whoever was looking into the case."

"Rubbing out the witness. But why wouldn't the Fox have killed Roehrer? Wouldn't he have assumed that Roehrer knew too?"

"Not necessarily," said Eddie.

"What about the significance of the date—the fiftieth anniversary?"

"Maybe the Fox is a murderer with a sense of style. Maybe he liked the irony of killing the person who might expose him on the anniversary of his act of sabotage. Or maybe he's just a neat freak: someone

168

who likes to have all his ducks lined up in a row."

Charlotte nodded thoughtfully. "How can we find out who the Fox is?" She asked, then went on to answer her own question. "I know! We could track down the party that was making the inquiries—the FBI, or whoever—and find out if they have any information about him."

"How would we do that?"

"Contact the Jewish Documentation Center. Ask if anyone else has been inquiring about *Oberscharführer* Wilhelm Roerher. If that's how you found Roehrer, it might be how someone else found him too. Eddie?" she said. But his attention was elsewhere.

"I'm thinking about the Fox," he said.

"Yes?" Charlotte prompted.

"He would have to be an American with a reputation to protect. If he was a former Nazi living in a foreign country, it seems unlikely that he would have gotten wind of the fact that investigators had reopened the *Normandie* case."

"Nor would he probably have cared," Charlotte offered. "How likely is it that they would come after him after all these years?"

Eddie nodded and then continued. "He would also have to have been one of the ten Navy officers supervising the conversion or an official with the Robins Drydock Company, in order to have arranged the circumstances as he did."

"Like Jack McLean?"

"Or me. Or probably dozens of others."

"You said the Attorney General's report gave the names of all the people who were aboard at the time of the fire," she said. "We might be able to select a list of possible suspects from that."

169

"Here's a possibility," Eddie said as he tossed a chicken bone into the rapidly filling discard bucket.

"Yes?"

"Roehrer said that he and Federov came to the attention of the Fox through a Russian fascist summer camp in Connecticut. It shouldn't be hard to find out more about this camp. Then we could see if any of the people on the list had a connection with the camp, or with the area."

Charlotte was munching on her chicken wings.

"Charlotte?" Eddie said. He waited a minute for her reply, and then said, "Charlotte, are you there?" He waved a hand in front of her face.

"Yes, I'm here."

"Well, what do you think?"

She looked up at him. "Do you remember describing what happened to you when you walked into the Grand Salon at Villa Normandie? How the combination of the smell of the smoke, the song the piano player was playing, and the way it looked unleashed a flood of memories?"

He nodded.

"Well, something of the same sort has just happened to me. Except that the memories weren't buried as the result of a head trauma. The door was just closed, the memories forgotten."

Eddie looked at her, puzzled.

"What you just said about the summer camp triggered a memory," she said. "Eddie, I *know* that camp."

She told him the story in-between naps on the long ride back across the desolate scrubland of central Florida, which lay baking under the tropical sun. The main character in the story was Aleksandr Andreivich Koproski, or as he had been known in the small town of Hadfield, Connecticut, "the count." A minor Russian nobleman, he had fought with the anti-Bolshevik Volunteer Army in the Ukraine, where he was injured. After the collapse of the Whites, he escaped to Constantinople. From there he eventually made his way to Paris, where he met an American Red Cross nurse, Dorothy Welland, who was serving with the relief forces. She was an heiress, twenty years older than he. Captivated by the romance of helping a tragic, titled Russian aristocrat, she took him under her wing and nursed him back to health. Then she brought him back to Connecticut and introduced him into New England society. Eventually she married him, and they set up housekeeping at a dairy farm in Hadfield, High Gate Farm, that had been purchased for them by her father. The farm became the gathering place for White Russian emigrés, including Prince Theodore, who was a nephew of the czar and a pretender to the Russian throne.

As Charlotte told the story, she found that she remembered more of the details with each sentence. It had been years since she had even thought about the count and his eccentric entourage.

"Charlotte," said Eddie, interrupting the flow of her story, "how do you know all this?"

"I was a neighbor of sorts: a student at a finishing school in Hadfield, Miss Walker's School for Girls. My father paid to send me there, which was about his only contribution to my upbringing. It's no longer there, in part because of the count. But that's another story. It was right next door to High Gate Farm." She resumed her story: "But the count quickly became

171

bored with the life of a country squire, and became involved in Russian monarchist politics. Eventually he founded a political organization whose goal was to overthrow the Soviet regime and restore the Romanovs to the throne. The organization was headquartered at the farm and funded by his wife's money."

"Was that the Russian Fascist United Front that Roehrer talked about?"

"I don't remember the name, but it must have been," she said, and then continued: "At first he was fairly rational about his mission, but as time went on he began to suffer from delusions of grandeur. He saw himself as the future White Russian führer. At one point, he even had postage stamps printed up with his image on them. He liked to think of himself as part of a world trio—Hitler, Mussolini, and Koprosky—who were destined to shape twentieth-century history."

"Was this guy for real?" Eddie said incredulously.

Charlotte nodded. "He sounds crazier than he really was. A lot of what he did, he did in jest: he was a showman, a buffoon, an incorrigible romantic."

"In other words, a real character."

"To say the least," she agreed. "He liked to dress up in storm trooper regalia: brown shirt, Sam Browne belt, jackboots, swagger stick, swastika armbands. Very Erich von Stroheim. He'd drive around Hadfield in one of his Pierce Arrows with swastika pennants flying from the fenders. He turned one of the cow barns into a shooting gallery. He would invite guests to take pot shots at photographs of Stalin and other Communist leaders. I managed to hit Stalin right on the nose once," she added proudly.

"What did the town think of this guy?"

"Well, it was a pretty sleepy little town, and I think a lot of people appreciated the fact that he livened it up. As my housemother once commented, 'He stands out in Hadfield like a Hottentot at a meeting of the DAR.' I think they were amused more than anything else. New Englanders have always had a high tolerance for eccentricity. Also, he was a charming man and very well-liked. People thought of him as a romantic—a quixotic figure with the impossible dream of restoring the Russian monarchy."

"In jackboots?"

"You've got to remember, this was early on. Hitler still wasn't perceived as being the threat he later became. Also, despite the swastikas, Alex—"

"Alex?" interrupted Eddie.

Charlotte smiled. "We were on a first-name basis. That's yet another story, which I'll tell you sometime. Anyway, despite the swastikas, Alex forswore any Nazi associations. He would say over and over again that just because he was anti-Communist didn't mean that he was pro-Nazi. It was the enemy-of-my-enemy-is-my-ally philosophy."

"What did his wife's family think of him?" Eddie asked.

"They detested him. He was an embarrassment to them. Once he came to a party they were throwing at the Waldorf Astoria in his storm trooper garb. But their politics were almost as extreme, though more subtly expressed."

"What do you mean?"

"It may have been Alex who was parading around in jackboots, but the Wellands also had fascist sympathies," Charlotte explained. "They were like a lot of wealthy families at that time. They respected
173

Hitler for solving Germany's unemployment problems and Mussolini for making the trains run on time. But to get back to Alex: as time went on, he became more and more deluded. He started gathering arms in preparation for the coming struggle against the Reds, and he started training troops. He converted his chicken coops into dormitories for a summer camp for Russian youths from New York."

"Youths like Paul Federov?"

"Exactly. He looked on these young men as the nucleus of a volunteer army that would some day reclaim Russia from Stalin's grip. You could think of them in terms of Hitler Youth."

"Koprosky Youth," said Eddie.

"Exactly. Loyal and obedient fighters willing to risk everything to advance the cause. I don't remember much about the camp, actually, since I wasn't at school in the summer. But there was a small coterie of these young men who lived at the farm year-round."

"Are you suggesting that he's the Fox?"

She shook her head. "He was arrested in January, 1942."

"For what?"

"Espionage. I thought the charges were ridiculous, as did everyone who knew him. But it was right after Pearl Harbor; people were convinced there were spies under every bed. One of the Russian fascist satellite organizations to which he had sent money—Dorothy's money, of course—had a remote connection with the Bund. He was prosecuted by a politician who was trying to make a name for himself. He served five years in a federal penitentiary."

"But someone who was associated with him could be the Fox."

"I think it's a good bet. Someone who observed Roehrer and Federov, and thought they would make likely recruits for Operation Golden Bird. The question is, How do we find out who? Dorothy died in the fifties, and Alex died twelve years ago. But there must still be people in Hadfield who might remember Alex's associates. Do you still have the list of the names of those who were aboard the ship at the time of the fire?"

Eddie nodded. "It's at my hotel."

"Then maybe we could take it up to Hadfield and show it around."

Eddie shivered. "Brr," he said. "I'm a California boy. I'm not sure my blood's thick enough for Connecticut in February."

"C'mon," Charlotte chided him. "But first we have to make sure that Paul Federov and Paul Feder are the same person."

They got back to Palm Beach just after seven and headed directly for Château en Espagne in search of concrete evidence that Federov and Feder were one and the same. After parking on the street in front of the house, they opened the wrought-iron gate and walked down the path to the jungle-enclosed courtyard that had so intrigued Charlotte on her earlier visit, and which set the house apart from its carefully manicured neighborhood. On this visit, she noticed little things that she had missed the first time. The wood of the front door was pitted and old, and its cast-iron hinges looked as if they had been scavenged from a European monastery. Moss-covered statues were tucked away in niches that had been carved out of the lush tropical foliage at the edges of the courtyard, and old urns were planted with gardenias, whose sweet scent perfumed the air. The house had lost none of its appeal. If anything, the romantic quality that had captivated her on her earlier visit was enhanced by the fact that the house was no longer occupied. In the violet twilight, it had the air of an abandoned farmhouse in the Tuscan countryside.

"Nice place," said Eddie, looking up at the tower. He was clearly charmed as well. "I wonder what's going to happen to it now."

"Dede says it will probably be put up for sale." As Charlotte spoke, the thought passed through her mind again that she might buy it, and as it did, she felt a pang of nervousness. Was she ready to commit to the life of the lotus-eaters? she wondered. After all, she was at heart a Yankee ascetic, as at home as a puffin on the rock-bound coast of Maine, where her summer house was located.

Putting the thought out of her head for the moment, she headed toward a gate in the stucco wall of the courtyard, over which snaked a lush bougainvillea in full flower. Like the front door, the door in the gate was made out of the native pecky cypress, which had aged to a silver sheen. "I think we get to Dede's through here," she said.

"No security system?" asked Eddie.

"There's one for the house, but none for the grounds, or at least there wasn't when I was here with Connie and Spalding for dinner. Palm Beach has a low crime rate; it's hard for burglars to get off the island without getting caught."

Opening the gate, they found themselves at the pool. Like the rest of the house, the pool was just right. Lined with colorful Spanish tiles and surrounded by lush vegetation, it was as inviting as a natural pool in the rain forest of a tropical paradise.

As Charlotte surveyed their jungly surroundings, it struck her why she was drawn to this life. It was because the elaborate social ritual offered a camouflage that shielded one from the outside world as thoroughly as the lush vegetation shielded Château en Espagne from the street. By living amid it, but not partaking of it, she could be left to live her life in peace and quiet. There was something fundamentally soothing about the endless round of charity benefits—the same people doing the same things over and over again. They were like bake sales on a grander scale: inflated to monstrous proportions, but still basically small-town at heart.

She could enjoy it, that was, as long as she wasn't the one who had to bake the cookies. She had already gone that route out in Minneapolis.

Skirting the pool, they followed a path through a garden of citrus trees hung with pots of orchid plants, and emerged at the guest cottage at the back of the house. It was a small two-story stucco structure with a latticework-enclosed veranda that was pierced with Moorish arches and blanketed with flame vines. Passing under one of the arches, they rang the doorbell.

Dede answered the door.

"Aunt Charlotte!" she exclaimed, kissing her on the cheek. "What a surprise! And Mr. Norwood," she added, reaching out to shake Eddie's hand. "Please, come in."

She was dressed in a flowing, caftanlike dress that went perfectly with the decor, which was Moorish in style, with low couches covered in exotic fabrics and

177

heaped with pillows, and tables of polished brass. Ornate carved screens over the windows created the darkened atmosphere of a seraglio.

"I feel like I'm in Fez," Charlotte said.

"The woman who owned the house before Paul decorated the guest cottage like this," Dede explained. "I just stuck with the style. I like it very much. It's well-suited to the climate."

"I'm glad we found you in," Charlotte said. "I'm sorry we didn't call first, but we were on our way back from Clearwater, and we thought we'd drop in to see if you were here."

"I just came from the preservation association office," Dede said. "What were you doing in Clearwater?"

Charlotte proceeded to tell her the whole story, from the official explanation for the *Normandie* fire to Eddie's sudden recovery of his lost memories to their encounter with Roehrer and their theory that Paul was his accomplice "What do you know about his background?" she asked.

"Not much," Dede replied. She nodded at one of the low-slung sofas. "Please," she said. "Have a seat." Then she took one herself. "I do know his parents were White Russians. They came to this country from Paris when he was eight."

"To Queens?" Charlotte asked as she sat down.

Dede shrugged. "I have no idea. He went back to Paris after the war to be apprenticed to a relative who was a jeweler. That's where he learned the jewelry trade. From there, he went to Fouquet."

"Ah!" said Charlotte recognizing the name of the famous art deco jewelry designer.

"Eventually he opened his own shop in Paris, and

178

then one in New York and one in Palm Beach. . .”
Dede went on.

There was a long pause.

“What is it?” asked Charlotte. Dede seemed disturbed by their conversation.

“It’s just that I can’t believe Paul would do something like this,” she replied, shaking her head in disbelief.” He was so”—she grasped for a word— “solid. The preservation association was just one of the organizations he was active in. He was also the backbone of the civic association.”

“Maybe that’s why he was so solid,” Charlotte said “If he was inveigled as a youth into doing something that he later came to regret, perhaps he spent the rest of his life trying to make amends. If he was as upstanding as you say, the lives that were lost and the injuries”—she glanced over at Eddie’s hands—“must have weighed heavily on his conscience.”

She thought of the mood of his house: quiet, meditative, almost monastic. Maybe his life of public service had been an act of penance. As was, perhaps, his role in Marianne’s *Normandie* collection. “How old was he?”

“His obituary said he was sixty-nine.”

“Which would have made him nineteen in 1942,” Charlotte said. “Young enough to be easily influenced. Especially if his parents were devoted to the Russian fascist cause.”

“I suppose so,” Dede concurred.

“We’re pretty sure that Paul Federov and Paul Feder are the same person, but we want to be positive before we go any further,” Charlotte went on. “We were wondering if we could look through his papers. Maybe there are letters or scrapbooks or something.”

179

Dede looked hesitant.

"I know the estate lawyers have entrusted you to look after the house," Charlotte added in an effort to reassure her. "We would expect you to stay there with us. After all, you don't want us pinching the silver or anything."

Dede smiled. "I don't see why not," she said finally, her doubts allayed. She rose, and, after fetching the keys from her tiny kitchen, led them to the door. "His personal papers would all be in his office in the tower."

After stopping to greet the dog, Lady Astor, who was tethered to a shelter that had been built against the garage wall, Dede led them into the house and through the kitchen to the tile-paved entry hall.

"Have you found out yet what's going to happen to the house?" Charlotte asked as they climbed the stairs to the second floor.

"Paul's great-nephew—his brother's grandson—is coming from Paris to take care of the estate. But from what I understand, he's not interested in the house. I imagine he'll put it up for sale. I hope that whoever buys it lets me stay on. I love my little nest."

"And the business?" asked Charlotte.

"The great-nephew is going to take over the business. He already manages the Paris store, so he's the natural successor."

From the head of the stairs, they walked down a hall and then up a spiral staircase punctuated by small, stepped, arched windows, to the tower room. Looking up, Charlotte was intrigued by the view into the center of the narrowing spiral, with a spoked pecky cypress ceiling at its eye.

Noticing Charlotte's glance, Dede asked, "Do you

know the story of why the exterior tower became a signature of a Mizner design?"

"No," Charlotte said. "But I'd like to hear it."

Dede proceeded to tell the story: "Mizner had no formal architectural training. As a result, he sometimes made technical mistakes. After forgetting a staircase in one house, he later added it in the form of an exterior tower. People liked it so much that they began asking for a 'Mizner mistake.' "

"That's very interesting," Charlotte commented.

"I don't know if it's true, but it makes for a good story," Dede said as they came to the top of Mizner's mistake.

If Charlotte had been in love with the house before, she was all the more in love with it once she had seen the tower room. By contrast with the rest of the house, which was sparsely and elegantly furnished, the tower room appeared to be where Paul had actually spent his time.

It was filled with books, papers, and comfortable chairs in which to sit and look out at the beautiful view, which was especially so at this time of day. To the north one could see downtown Palm Beach, with its barrel-tiled roofs of various heights and pitches and in various shades of terra cotta; to the south was the clear green expanse of the golf course, to the west the lake and the twinkling skyline of West Palm Beach, and to the east a view of the Atlantic Ocean.

I could live here, Charlotte thought as she wandered around the room, looking out of the windows.

"Terrific views," commented Eddie, who was doing the same.

"Yes," Dede agreed. "This is the best part of the

house. It's also where Paul spent his time when he wasn't at the store. Here's the lead soldier collection that I was telling Aunt Charlotte about the other day," she said, leading them over to a glass-fronted bookcase.

The bookcase appeared to have been custom-made, and stood on legs that raised the shelves to eye level. Dede flipped a switch that illuminated the interior. The soldiers were three or four inches high and rested on wooden pedestals of the kind in which Dede had found the filing cabinet key. They were wonderfully detailed, each with individual expressions. On the front of each pedestal was a label, which was handwritten in an elegant script.

Leaning over, Charlotte read some of the labels aloud: "Palace Grenadier, 1913; Subaltern, His Imperial Majesty's Lancer Regiment, 1909-13; Private, His Imperial Majesty's Cossack Regiment, 1812; Private, Kubordinsky Infantry Regiment, 1914-17."

"As you can see, they're all Russian," said Dede. "This is the one in which I found the key." She pointed to a knight of Muscovy mounted on a horse. "I thought it would be best to put it in here with the others."

Straightening up, Charlotte's glance landed on a manikin wearing a military greatcoat and a military cap.

"A Russian military uniform," Dede offered by way of explanation. "I think Paul inherited it from his father."

Next to the manikin was a small table on which stood a photograph in an elegant frame of chased silver. Charlotte picked it up. It showed a sad-eyed

Nicholas tightly clasping his hemophiliac son. He was surrounded by Empress Alexandra and their four daughters.

"What is it?" asked Eddie, peering over her shoulder.

"The Russian imperial family," she said. "I think we're on the right track," she added as she set the photograph back down.

"What are we looking for first?" Dede asked as she scanned the bookshelves lining the room. "Scrapbooks or photograph albums?"

"Either," Charlotte replied.

It took only a minute to find them: a row of old photograph albums with bindings of crumbling leather. "Here they are," said Charlotte. Pulling three off a shelf, she sat down with one in a leather armchair next to a computer desk and passed the other two to Dede and Eddie.

The yellowing photographs were clearly mementoes of Paul's days in Paris as a jeweler's apprentice. They showed him against familiar Parisian backdrops, usually with a group of young men, sometimes with a girl. He had been strikingly good-looking: tall and straight, with those penetrating gray eyes.

Charlotte passed her album over to Eddie, who was sitting at the computer. "Is this the man you saw throw the incendiary pencil in the Grand Salon on the *Normandie?*"

Eddie studied the photographs for a moment. Then he tapped a scarred forefinger on a photo of Paul sitting on the steps at Montmartre. "Yes," he said. "That's him. I remember those eyes."

With that confirmation, they continued looking for

evidence that would link Paul with the camp in Connecticut.

"I think I've got something," said Eddie after a few minutes.

Setting her album aside, Charlotte got up and looked over Eddie's shoulder at the album that lay open on his lap.

It was a five-by-seven portrait of the same young man. He sat with his arms folded across his chest, staring out at the camera through pale eyes, his blond hair worn *en brosse*. He was wearing a dark shirt with long sleeves, each of which bore a red armband with a black swastika in a white circle.

"It's Paul!" Dede cried. She studied the photograph, and then said: "He looks like a poster boy for Hitler youth."

"Russian fascist youth," corrected Charlotte. "There was a difference. Though with all the storm trooper garb, it was often hard to tell. I wonder if there are any pictures of the camp?"

Eddie turned back to the preceding page, where a photo showed a group of youths posed in front of a building.

"That's it!" said Charlotte. "That's High Gate Farm. Those are the chicken coops that Alex converted into barracks for his Russian fascist youth. And that's the armory," she said, pointing to the old stone silo that rose in the background. "It's where Alex stored his guns and his ammunition."

"What did he use them for?" asked Dede.

"To take potshots at photographs of Stalin and other Soviet leaders. Also, to defend himself from the impending Red menace. I wonder if any of these others could be Roehrer." She pointed to a young man with a full face and a scowling expression. "This looks like him, don't you think?" she asked Eddie.

"Could be," said Eddie. "He has more hair here."

Charlotte turned to Dede. "Do you think we could borrow this photograph and the portrait of Paul? We promise to bring them back. Scout's honor."

"I suppose so," Dede agreed reluctantly. "These photographs wouldn't mean anything to anyone else now, anyway. Not even to Paul's great-nephew. Just don't tell the estate lawyers you took them."

As Charlotte proceeded to remove the camp photograph from the cardboard corners with which it was fastened to the page, she noticed that Paul was holding an attack dog on a leash: a German shepherd. The dog strained at the tightly drawn chain as if it were about to lunge at the viewer.

If there was any doubt left in Charlotte's mind that Paul Federov and Paul Feder were one and the same, it evaporated in that instant. She remembered the dog in the picture as clearly as if she had seen it the day before.

"The dog!" she exclaimed, staring at the photograph she now gripped in her hands. "I'd completely forgotten about the dog."

"What about the dog?" asked Eddie.

"Her name was Lady Astor!"

10

AFTER LEAVING DEDE'S, CHARLOTTE AND EDDIE stopped at a travel agency and reserved seats on a flight to Boston for early the next morning. Then they strolled down Worth Avenue to Tab-oó, a legendary Palm Beach bistro, which had once claimed to be, along with Harry's American Bar in Paris and "21" in Manhattan, one of the three most famous bars in the world. They had devoted the day to work; the evening would be reserved for romance. Having spent much of their time together reminiscing about their affair on the *Normandie,* they now moved on to fresh territory. They were still in the getting-to-know-you (again) stage of their relationship, and their dinner table conversation was largely a matter of filling in the blanks: finding out what had happened to each other over the course of fifty-three years, what they had sought from life and what life had delivered, and what they expected from here on out. Except for the fact that Eddie didn't like raw oysters, they discovered that their attitudes toward almost everything were strangely similar. Like Charlotte, Eddie had been a workaholic who had sacrificed his personal life to his career. Like her, he was flirting with the idea of taking it easy: willing at last to let up on the ambition that had propelled him to the top, but wary of what might happen if he did. Like her, he was keenly aware that there wasn't much time left. They departed around ten when the stares and whispers of the other diners indicated a growing awareness of the couple's celebrity status and headed down Worth Avenue toward the Colony Hotel.

The Colony was a small, exclusive hotel at the end of Worth Avenue, a block from the ocean. Its Polo Cocktail Lounge was a Palm Beach institution, a place where the elite met to drink and dance, where people like Charlotte and Eddie could go and not be stared at. As they entered, Charlotte noticed that a few handsome middle-aged men were standing at the bar, eyeing the single older women. But their approach struck Charlotte as being more restrained and mannerly than that of their sycophantic counterparts in similar enclaves of the rich. She had once asked Connie why Palm Beach seemed to be relatively free of this particularly noxious (at least for single older women who weren't interested) brand of human parasite. "It's because Palm Beach is so much more sophisticated," Connie had told her. "You have to be smart to play the game here. Your typical Miami gigolo wouldn't make the grade."

One representative of this species—a short, tanned, fit-looking man in a raw silk sports jacket—was making a play for a diamond-bedecked woman with a bouffant blond hairdo who was seated at the bar, opposite the door. Charlotte was observing his modus operandi when she realized that the object of his attentions was Lydia Collins. She was dressed in a tight-fitting orange jump suit, and she looked thin, chic, and miserable. Also perhaps, a little drunk. Had Charlotte been a career counselor, she would have advised Lydia's would-be swain that this would be only a temporary position at best, that for long-term security he had better look elsewhere.

Eddie and Charlotte were seated by an officious maître d' at a table near the bar, overlooking the dance floor. The band appeared to be on break.

"There was something I wanted to ask you earlier," Eddie said after they had ordered their drinks. "Why was the dog named Lady Astor?"

"I presumed it was because of the Cliveden Set," Charlotte replied. She went on in response to Eddie's puzzled expression: "They were a group of British

187

fascists led by Lady Astor, who lived at an estate called Cliveden, which is why they were called the Cliveden Set."

"I remember now. Nancy Astor. She was an American, from Virginia."

Charlotte nodded. "I always thought the dog's name was a political statement," she said. "The way hippies in the sixties named their dogs Mao. Or maybe the dog really *was* named after Lady Astor. I know that Dorothy's family—the Wellands—socialized with the British upper crust."

The waitress had arrived with their drinks: a Manhattan for Charlotte and a martini for Eddie.

"Maybe Paul's dog is a descendant of the original Lady Astor," Charlotte continued after the waitress had left. "Or maybe she was just named after her. She was the mascot of High Gate Farm. Whenever anyone arrived, Lady Astor would come running out to greet them." It was odd, Charlotte thought, how a life that had changed as completely as Paul's could still harbor this one relic from a previous existence. Then one day life turns in on itself again, and that relic suddenly takes on new meaning, like the Fortuny gown that had hung in her guest room closet all those years.

"You never did tell me about your relationship with the count," Eddie teased, his green eyes dancing.

"Do I have to?" she said. "It's kind of embarrassing."

"Yes," he said firmly.

"Well, okay," she conceded. "He had a sort of clubhouse at the farm, a hexagonal stone building with a big stone fireplace and a bar. The count's clubhouse became the neighborhood hangout. The champagne was always flowing, at Dorothy's expense I might add, though she was never there."

"Where was she?" Eddie asked.

"I don't know. But she didn't seem to mind. She treated Alex like her spoiled little boy. He actually called her Mother. Anyway, Alex liked women, and he especially liked young women, of which there was a liberal supply at Miss Walker's School for Girls, right next door."

"And you were part of the supply."

She nodded. "The school was like a prison. It even looked like a prison—a big, ugly, red brick Victorian monstrosity. I hated everything about it: the building, the teachers, the other girls. Alex's clubhouse was everything the school was not: sophisticated, fun, lighthearted."

"And Alex?" he asked.

"He was designed to be the heartthrob of every teenaged girl. Which was basically because he was a perpetual sixteen himself. He was very, very handsome, and very charming, and, of course, dashing."

"Those jackboots," Eddie said.

Charlotte laughed. "The Pierce Arrows helped too. When the school authorities learned that the girls were hanging out at Alex's clubhouse, they declared the farm off-limits. But that didn't stop us. We would sneak out of the dorm at night. Until we got caught."

"What happened then?"

"I was expelled," she said with a smile.

Eddie gave her a look of mock horror.

"Along with half a dozen others," she added. "It was actually all very innocent, as far as I was concerned anyway. We would drink, dance, smoke cigarettes. Flirt a little, occasionally take pot shots at

Stalin—that was about it. But our expulsions caused a full-blown scandal. A lot of the parents withdrew their daughters. The next year there was another scandal. Some of the girls got caught at a co-ed skinny-dipping party at the pond on the farm. There was a fire at the school right after that, and it was never rebuilt."

Charlotte took a sip of her Manhattan, which wasn't as good as the ones Spalding made. "I remember reading a newspaper account in which 'the satyric depredations' of the count were cited as a reason for the school's demise," she continued. "I always loved that phrase: satyric depredations.'"

"What happened to you after that?"

"My mother more or less railroaded me into marrying my first husband," she said. "I guess she figured it was one way of keeping me out of trouble. We moved to New York, and I enrolled in acting school and took a job as a cigarette girl at the Versailles Nightclub."

Eddie clicked his tongue. "How risqué," he said.

"My husband didn't like it much, I can tell you that," she said, and then continued: "In those days, every schoolgirl wanted to be a Powers and Conover model, so I decided to give it a try. I signed on and became the Jantzen bathing suit girl of 1938."

"I remember those ads," Eddie said, raising his eyebrows.

"As fate would have it, the movie director Howard Weiss saw one of the bathing suit ads and invited me out to Hollywood for a screen test. And that was the beginning of my Hollywood career."

"In other words, if you hadn't been corrupted by the count, you would have led a respectable life as a

Connecticut matron, and I never would have met you."

"Basically, yes," she said. She raised her glass: "Here's to Count Alex Koprosky and his satyric depredations."

The band had taken their places on the bandstand and had started to play. The song was "La Cumparsita." It was a obviously a band that catered to the musical tastes of Charlotte and Eddie's generation. For a moment, they watched as the couples drifted out to the dance floor. Then Eddie asked her to dance, and they followed Lydia and her tanned swain down the aisle between the tables.

If Lydia recognized Charlotte, she gave no indication of it.

The song was a tango. Charlotte had forgotten what a good dancer Eddie was, how beautifully they danced together. Doing the tango always made her feel as if they should be hangers-on at a baroque middle European hotel, awaiting the last train out before the tanks came rumbling down the boulevard. In other words, as if they were all alone, surrounded by a hostile world.

"I'm glad we met up, Charlotte," Eddie whispered in her ear as he held her close. "I never thought I would feel this way again."

"Nor did I," she said, thinking that maybe her life was going to travel in gentle arabesques after all. "Happy Valentine's Day," she whispered back. "It's February fourteenth."

Eddie looked surprised. "And so it is," he said.

Afterward, they took a walk on the moonlit beach. Though they had been up since dawn, neither of them was tired. Unlike the night that Paul had been murdered, which was the last time Charlotte had been on the beach, there wasn't the stiff breeze that sometimes gave tropical nights an eerie feeling. Instead, the air was sweet and balmy, and the surf as gentle as a lake. They walked hand in hand down the beach, carrying their shoes, feeling the cool sand squish between their toes. From town they could hear strains of music from the cocktail lounges of the brightly lit hotels along the beach.

On their way back, Charlotte bent down to pick out a glistening shell from the center of a tangled mat of dark brown seaweed. Its bands circled the opalescent body like ringlets of fine, glossy brown curls.

"What kind of shell is it?" Eddie asked.

"It's a tulip shell," Charlotte said as she brushed off the sand. "It's spiraled," she added, tracing the pattern of the brown bands with her forefinger. "Always moving upward and onward, but always coming hack to the same place." She looked over at Eddie. "Kind of like us."

Eddie pointed to the flat base of the cone-shaped shell. "If I understand you, you're saying that we were here, and now"—he pointed to the tip of the cone—"we're here."

"That's right. Fifty-three annual rotations later." She touched a finger to the tip. "The peak."

"I hope not," Eddie said. "I think I'm good for a few more go-rounds."

They arose early the next morning for their flight to Boston, and immediately upon landing set off for Hadfield in their rental car, stopping briefly at a sporting goods store along the way to buy some winter clothes for Eddie, who, coming from California, was ill-equipped for a northeastern winter. (Though Charlotte hadn't brought any winter clothes to Florida, she at least had the suit and coat she had worn on the flight down.) Hadfield was located in the northeastern corner of Connecticut—"the quiet corner," their map called it—about an hour and a half from Boston. The drive was lovely. It was a perfect February day: sunny and in the forties, with a cloudless blue sky. There had been a light snowfall the day before, and the snow-clad fields sparkled in the morning sun. Charlotte had forgotten how picture-postcard-perfect this part of Connecticut was. The rural country road that took them on the last leg of their journey wound its way past elegant old farmhouses and stately old barns—all of them prosperous-looking and picturesque. There was hardly a split level to be seen, much less any of the mobile homes that were a blight on many another rural landscape. But then, this corner of Connecticut only pretended to an agrarian economy: what appeared to be working farms had for generations been the elegant country retreats of wealthy families from Boston, Providence, and New York who preferred a quieter lifestyle than that offered by the more social summer resorts of Newport or Southampton.

Looking out at the snow-blanketed hills and fields, Charlotte felt an overwhelming sense of being home. As enamored as she was with the land of the lotus-eaters, it was this landscape that was part of her soul.

Once they left the highway, she found her sense of the geography coming back, and she pointed out various sights to Eddie: the pond where she used to ice skate, the house where the headmistress had lived, the office of the female physician who had tended to the students' ailments. Just before entering Hadfield, they passed the boys' prep school that had been their brother school. Unlike Miss Walker's, it was still thriving. Seeing the ivy-covered walls, Charlotte was reminded of the formal mixers: the crystal bowls of fruit juice punch, the stern glances of the chaperones, and the boys themselves—gangly, pimply-faced, awkward. No wonder the high-living Alex had been so enticing.

They arrived at the outskirts of Hadfield five minutes later. One always knew when one had entered Hadfield by the stone walls lining the roads, most of which had been built by Italian stonemasons at the direction of Dorothy Welland's father, whose summer estate had comprised several hundred acres at the center of town. Other summer residents had followed suit, with the resultant miles of stone walls giving the landscape of Hadfield a visual consistency and elegance that was lacking in the neighboring towns. A few minutes later, they passed the site of Miss Walker's. A modern garden apartment complex now occupied the grounds, which was identified by a sign as "Hadfield Hills Apartments." All that was left of the former school was a stone wall that had once enclosed a sunken rose garden.

Gazing out at the apartment buildings, Charlotte felt absolutely no sorrow at the loss of her school. If ever there was an institution that deserved to be consigned to oblivion, it was Miss Walker's School for Girls.

A moment later, they pulled into the driveway of High Gate Fitness Camp, as the former High Gate

194

Farm was now known.

The farm had been called High Gate because it stood on a ridge overlooking the rolling countryside, and because of the elegant white wooden gate in the stone wall that ran past the front door. In those days it had been one of the most picturesque farmsteads in a valley of picturesque farmsteads, and it remained so today. A parking lot had been added, but beyond that it looked much the same. After parking the car, they headed into the office, which was located in the count's old hexagonal stone clubhouse. Entering, Charlotte was struck by how much smaller the clubhouse looked than it had years before to an impressionable teenaged girl. Smaller, and more ordinary. Of course it was an office now, but even the great arched stone fireplace that had been the centerpiece of so many of the count's parties no longer looked as glamorous as it had then. With a roaring fire, the hunting trophies hanging on the walls, and the collection of antique guns and knives, the clubhouse had appeared to her then like a Hollywood movie set, and the count like a leading man on the silver screen. Little had she known what glamorous movie sets lay only a short distance in her future.

Approaching the front desk, Charlotte introduced herself to the receptionist as Mrs. Lundstrom, which had been her married name, and Eddie simply as Mr. Norwood. She was counting on the receptionist being young enough not to make the connection with Eddie Norwood, the famous bandleader. Though Charlotte was tolerant of the celebrity business—it was her bread and butter, after all—she didn't want to be bothered with it now. After she explained that she was

195

looking for the manager, the receptionist disappeared into an inner office and returned in the company of a man who introduced himself as Tony Pardo.

He was a short, stocky man with bulging biceps and a pleasant manner who listened patiently as Charlotte explained that they were seeking information about two young men who had been associates of the count, and then inquired if he could refer them to someone who had worked at the farm.

"I think your best bet would be Clara Johnstone," he said. "She worked in the main house as a housekeeper for Dorothy and the count, but she took a motherly interest in those young men. She still lives in the same house." He pointed down the road. "The third house down on the right—a red Cape."

"Thank you very much," said Charlotte. As she was turning to leave, she noticed that Pardo had leaned back against the edge of the desk and crossed his arms. She had forgotten: business couldn't be dispensed with this quickly in rural Connecticut. She turned back. "How long have you lived here?" she asked.

"My wife and I bought the farm in '75. We run it as a camp for kids in the summer and as a fitness center for adults during the rest of the year. It's been rough going, but we're making it. We never knew the count of course, but we hear stories." He looked at Charlotte. "Did you know him?"

Charlotte nodded. "I was a student at Miss Walker's.'"

"One of those, eh?" he said with a smile.

She held up her hands in mock denial. "I wasn't at the notorious skinny-dipping party, if that's what you're implying."

"If you were, I wouldn't hold it against you," he said. "I'll tell you one thing: there isn't a woman of a certain age around here who doesn't swoon when the count's name comes up in conversation" He laughed. "He must have been quite a guy."

"He was," Charlotte said, exchanging looks with Eddie. "At least to an impressionable girl of seventeen."

"I'll tell you another thing," Tony went on, "that in spite of all his carryings-on, the people around here thought very highly of him. Everybody always thought he had been imprisoned unjustly. A lot of the local people even testified on his behalf, though it didn't do him much good."

"The country was still reeling from Pearl Harbor," Charlotte explained. "People were convinced there were spies everywhere. The prosecution couldn't see him for what he really was—an innocent dreamer. But that's why everybody loved him. They loved him the way people love a poet or a balladeer."

"Aren't you gilding the lily a little, Charlotte?" Eddie asked.

"Maybe," she said.

"It must have been something to see him driving those Pierce Arrows around town," Tony continued. "speaking of dreamers, did you know that he was going to make football the national sport of Russia?"

"This is after the Romanovs were restored to the throne?" Eddie said.

"Of course," Tony replied. "With Count Aleksandr Koprosky installed as president of a new constitutional monarchy."

"I didn't know that, but it sounds like him," Charlotte said. "I do know that he loved football. I

197

once attended a Brown game with him. He thought the team played so well that he bought the goal post from the college." She nodded at the far wall. "He used to have it standing right over there."

They all looked over at the blank stone wall.

"He said he wanted it as a symbol of what a small, dedicated group could do," she explained.

"As if restoring the Romanovs to the throne was on the same level as winning a football game," said Eddie. "I'll say he was a dreamer."

"All that stuff was sold at auction before we came here, including the swastika banners," Tony said. The phone had started to ring and he turned to pick it up. "Good luck with Clara," he said over his shoulder.

They thanked him and headed out.

Clara Johnstone's house was a small Cape Cod that must have dated back to the early 1800's. It stood sideways to the road, which was lined by a row of old sugar maples and a stone wall. A big old barn, connected to the house via a shed, stood at the back, and an English setter was chained to a woodpile in the yard. They parked in the driveway, which encircled a gnarled old apple tree, and walked up a flagstone path to the front door, setting off a chorus of barks from the dog. Since puffs of smoke could be seen coming out of the chimney, they assumed that Clara Johnstone was at home.

Their knock was answered by Mrs. Johnstone herself, a tall woman with blue eyes and hair as white as the fresh coat of snow covering her yard. Charlotte guessed her to be in her mid-eighties.

Charlotte had concocted an elaborate explanation for their visit, but it turned out that none was needed.

At the mention of Tony's name, Mrs. Johnstone escorted them into a comfortable parlor where a cast-iron wood stove was thumping away. The aroma of baking bread wafted in from the kitchen.

"We're here to inquire about two young men who were associated with Count Koprosky," Charlotte said as they sat down on a couch that was covered with a hand-knitted afghan throw. "We were wondering if you could identify them from their pictures and tell us a little bit about them."

"I'll do my best," Mrs. Johnstone said cheerfully. "I knew most of them." She lifted the reading glasses that hung from around her neck and set them on the bridge of her nose.

Opening her handbag, Charlotte withdrew the photo of Paul Feder wearing the swastika armbands, and handed it to her.

"Why, this one's easy. That's Paul Federov. He was . . . How shall I put it? The teacher's pet, I guess you'd say. He was a favorite of the count's. Which was a bit of a surprise, since they were so different. Paul was very quiet, artistic. But very devoted to the count."

"Then the count would have been a kind of father figure?" Charlotte asked.'

"Very much so," Clara agreed.

Which might explain why Paul was drawn into the sabotage scheme. He might have thought that it was something the count would approve of. Charlotte handed Mrs. Johnstone the other photo and pointed to the young man whom they believed to be Wilhelm Roehrer. "And this one?"

"That's Wilhelm." She paused. "His last name began with an R."

199

"Roehrer?" suggested Charlotte.

"That's it. He was very good friends with Paul, although he was a few years older. They came from the same neighborhood in New York. I could never warm to the boy, to tell you the truth." She looked at the picture again. "And there's Lady Astor," she said with a smile of recognition.

"Lady Astor?" said Charlotte, feigning ignorance.

"The German shepherd," said Mrs. Johnstone. She handed the photograph back to Charlotte, who returned it to her purse. "Paul and that dog were inseparable," she continued. "He doted on her, and she on him. I wonder what ever happened to those boys?"

Charlotte didn't reply. Instead, she said, "We're also trying to identify another man," she continued. "He would have been acquainted with the two young men, but perhaps only remotely. We have a list of names. We were wondering if you would look it over to see if any of the names sound familiar."

"Anything I can do to help Tony," Mrs. Johnstone said. "He and Pat have been so good to me. They even shovel me out in the winter."

The list that Charlotte withdrew from her purse had been cut from a thousand names to fewer than a hundred. The only names left were those of Navy and Coast Guard officers and managers from the Robins Dry Dock Company: the men who would have been in a position to give orders.

Again Mrs. Johnstone donned her reading glasses.

The only sounds were the ticking of the grandfather clock in the corner and the sound of melting snow dripping from the icicles that hung like a glistening fringe from the eaves above the windows.

"I only recognize one name," she said as she passed the list back. "But he wasn't associated with the farm, although he did play golf with the count occasionally. He was associated more with the Welland family—that was the family of the count's wife, Dorothy."

"And who was that?" Charlotte asked.

"Jack McLean," she replied.

The decorated rear admiral a Nazi saboteur! For a moment, Charlotte was shocked speechless. Once she had regained her composure, she looked over at Eddie, who sat with his mouth hanging open.

"They used to call him Big Jack McLean," Mrs. Johnstone went on. "He had been a football star at Yale. He was very friendly with Freddie Welland, Dorothy's brother. They spent their summers together in Hadfield as boys. He used to help Freddie's uncle with that paper he put out."

"What paper was that?" Charlotte asked. Her mind was teeming with questions. Foremost among them was the question of how McLean had been recruited: one didn't go from Ivy League football star to enemy agent just like that.

"Let me think," Mrs. Johnstone said. She took off her glasses and stared at the ceiling. "*The Yankee Patriot,*" she finally answered.

"Do you know of anyone who could tell us more about Jack McLean and his association with the Welland family?" Charlotte asked, hastily adding, "Does the Welland family's house even still exist?"

Clara nodded. "It does. But it's a monastery now: the Benedictines. The Welland descendants—what was left of them—moved away long ago. I'm afraid I couldn't help you there. But you could check with Jeannie."

201

Jeannie Stavola was the president of the Hadfield Historical Society and a former Associated Press reporter from Boston who had moved to Hadfield with her writer husband when their children were born. She had straight, shoulder-length brown hair, parted in the center, and a round, earnest, old-fashioned kind of face. Starved for news she could dig into, Jeannie had turned her reportorial talents to the small town of Hadfield, and had made it her business to know everything that had transpired in Hadfield and vicinity since the town was settled in 1693. Since her big old Greek Revival house fronted directly on the village common, she had become the town's major conduit for information. As she put it: "I often have the feeling that people have been tracing the same paths between houses for the last three hundred years."

They met her at the Hadfield Inn, an historic inn that also fronted directly on the common, catty-corner from Jeannie's house and next door to a steepled Congregational Church that looked as if it belonged in a tourist brochure for New England. The inn had once served travelers on the major north-south and east-west stage routes. According to Jeannie, the fact that Hadfield was situated at the confluence of these routes had once made it the most prosperous rural village in Connecticut.

The inn billed itself as the oldest continuously operated inn in the country, but since Charlotte had been a guest at half a dozen inns that made the identical claim, she was skeptical. Nevertheless it was very old, with a wide plank floor that had settled unevenly over the years, and a low ceiling lined with

with hand-hewn beams.

Jeannie told them what she knew about Big Jack McLean over club sandwiches and steaming cups of New England clam chowder.

"He was a fascist!" she said. "They were all fascists. We had a regular little nest of them here. Of course, it was the count who took all the heat, but Koprosky was an innocent compared to the rest of them."

She spoke fast, with a staccato delivery. Charlotte had the impression of a wire machine tapping out its copy.

"He was of the Virginia McLeans. One of the FFV's."

"FFV's?" said Charlotte.

"First Families of Virginia."

Charlotte remembered his charming hint of a southern accent.

"The McLeans made their summer home here because the family patriarch had rheumatism. Didn't want anything to do with the damp air of any of those seaside places like Newport. Also, they had horses. They needed barns and fields. Newport isn't very horsey. I understand that Jack McLean is now a decorated rear admiral. But we can all attest to the political lapses of our youth." She smiled. "Spoken by a former member of the Students for a Democratic Society. Actually, I only attended a couple of meetings, but it once gave me a lot of status in some circles."

"Like the Weather Underground?" teased Charlotte.

Ignoring her, Jeannie continued with her story: "Actually, it was Freddie Welland who dragged Jack McLean into fascist politics. Freddie had also gone to

203

Yale, where he got in with the America Firsters. Yale was a hotbed of the America First movement," she said.

"I didn't know that," Charlotte commented.

"Oh, yes," Jeannie said. "The sons of all those rich Midwestern industrialists. But it was Freddie's uncle Walter who was the real fascist. He was an eccentric. An elderly bachelor. He had a small round head, with a fuzzy growth of white hair. Like those professor characters on *Sesame Street*."

Charlotte had no idea who she was talking about. The world of children was terra incognita to her.

"Anyway, Uncle Walter was a Roosevelt hater of the first order. The old traitor-to-his-class bit. He wouldn't even use Roosevelt dimes. He put out a fascist newspaper called *The Yankee Patriot*."

"What did Yankees have to do with it?" Charlotte asked. As a diehard Yankee herself, she took umbrage at a fascist's use of the term.

"His idea was that the country had gone slack. What it needed was government by an elite who were representative of the old-fashioned Yankee virtues of self-sacrifice, hard work, and so on. Instead of National Socialism, he called his political philosophy Yankee-ism."

"He didn't like the Nazi identification?" Charlotte asked.

"*Mezza, mezza*," said Jeannie, holding her hand out palm down and tilting it from side to side. "He thought the country needed a dictator like Hitler to whip it into shape, but he disassociated himself from the more distasteful aspects of Nazism—the anti-Semitism, the shock troops."

"A refined fascist," Charlotte noted dryly.

Jeannie nodded. "He was in good company: Yeats, Pound, Lawrence, Shaw. Anyway, his politics also grew out of the hallowed Yankee tradition of hating the British. In a sense, he was still fighting the War of Independence. If you can picture the Minutemen as storm troopers, you've got the basic idea."

"Did he have any actual connection with the Nazis?"

"Oh, yes. He went to Germany in 1938 and was wined and dined by Hitler. Basically, he got the same sell as Lindbergh."

Charlotte nodded. One question answered, she thought. If McLean *was* the Fox, he could have hooked up with the *Abwehr* through Uncle Walter. "And what was Jack McLean's connection with Uncle Walter?" she asked.

"Clara Johnstone told us that he worked on Walter's paper."

She nodded. "He was one of the editors. They printed it right here in Hadfield. The printing presses were in Uncle Walter's barn. It had a pretty decent circulation too—thirty or forty thousand, if I remember right."

"And what about the count?" Charlotte pressed. "What was his relationship with the members of this little group?"

"They all knew one another. Hadfield isn't exactly a metropolis. I'm not sure how close Uncle Walter was to Koprosky. He probably considered the count to be kind of a joke, like all the older generation of Wellands. But I know Freddie and Jack socialized with him. They were closer to him in age."

"Socialized?" said Charlotte.

"Played golf, mostly," Jeannie explained. "The

count was very into golf. They also hung out at his clubhouse."

Which would explain how McLean might have come into contact with Roehrer and Federov, Charlotte thought. "About this newspaper," she continued. "Is there any way we could see it? Any old issues on file at the local library?"

"That can be easily arranged. We have boxes of old issues at the historical society office. It's on the other side of the common." She signaled the waitress for the check, and within minutes they were crossing the common, which was dotted with stately old Dutch elms that had survived the blight.

The historical society office was located in the old Town Hall, a jewel of Greek Revival architecture, complete with pediment and Ionic columns. After unlocking the front door, Jeannie led them through the unheated hall, which was lined with deacon's benches, and still decorated for Christmas.

"We have our annual Christmas pageant here every year," Jeannie explained, nodding at the decorated stage. "Everyone in town participates. We all do whatever it is we feel like doing, and somehow it works out perfectly. Then we all go out to the common with lighted candles to sing Christmas carols."

"It must be lovely," Charlotte said.

"It is," Jeannie agreed. She had led them to a small room at the back of the hall, which was filled with cardboard boxes. "This is just our temporary home, which is why it's such a mess," she said. "We're going to move into the old library as soon as the new one's finished."

After rummaging around among the boxes, she

located the one she was looking for, slid it out, and opened it up. She handed Charlotte a sample issue of *The Yankee Patriot*.

The term newspaper was misleading; it was more like a newsletter, but was nevertheless quite professionally produced. This issue described a rally for "Yankee patriots" that was to be held in Concord, Massachusetts, on July 4th. Charlotte read aloud from the story:

" 'The Yankee Patriot Party is fighting to preserve true Americanism. To be a Yankee patriot is to be for the U.S.A. one hundred percent. This rally is our last chance to get together on a plan of action before our traitorous administration succeeds in selling out our noble country to the Bolsheviks.' "

"What's the date?" asked Eddie, who was standing by the door, looking uncomfortably cold in his new windbreaker.

"May, 1942," she said.

"Bad enough that they were spouting this claptrap in the thirties; even worse that they were still spouting it after the country had gone to war," said Jeannie, who was riffling through the contents of the box.

Charlotte checked the masthead on the inside column of the second page. The editor-in-chief was Walter Welland and the assistant editor was Frederick C. Welland. "There's no mention here of Jack McLean, but he would already have joined the Navy. "Do you have any earlier issues?" she asked.

"Let's see if we can find one from the late thirties," said Jeannie. Digging down to the bottom of the box, she produced an issue from 1938. "He's listed here: 'John W. McLean the third, Contributing Editor.' There's also an article by him on the front page," she added, handing the issue to Charlotte.

The article was well-written, and more moderate in tone than the article in the 1942 issue. Liberally sprinkled with quotes from Lindbergh and other America Firsters, it basically advocated that the Europeans fight it out for themselves. "May we keep this?" Charlotte asked.

"Yes," said Jeannie. "On one condition."

"What's that?" Charlotte asked.

"That you tell me what a famous American actress and a big bandleader are interested in Jack McLean for." Jeannie's cheeks dimpled in a smile.

"Ah," Charlotte said. "You're on to us."

"You'd have to be deaf, dumb, and blind not to be," Jeannie said. "And not have watched any television for the last thirty years to boot. I was on to you from the moment I first saw you."

"Well then, the others we've talked to here must be deaf, dumb, and blind, because they hadn't a clue."

Jeannie waved her hand dismissively. "They're in their own little world," she said. "With rare exceptions—Walter Welland being one of them— they're not concerned with what happens outside the perimeters of Hadfield. But I'm from a different gene pool."

"I'm afraid we can't tell you yet," Charlotte replied, "but we promise that we'll let you know why we're looking into Jack McLean just as soon as we can. Can we still have the copy of *The Yankee Patriot?*"

"I suppose so," said Jeannie. "We only have about three hundred copies of each issue to preserve for posterity." After replacing the box, she led Charlotte and Eddie out through the hall and then locked the door behind them. A light snow had started to fall. "Spies," Jeannie said, as they headed back toward the common.

"What?" asked Charlotte.

"Spies," she repeated. "I'm getting spy vibes." She looked intently into Charlotte's eyes. "I'm right, aren't I?" Then she proceeded to jump up and down on the snowy sidewalk. "Oh goody, spies!" she exclaimed, arms flapping. "As you can see," she added, "we're a little starved for excitement around here."

Charlotte didn't say a word. The woman certainly hadn't lost her nose for a good story.

11

THE COUNTRY INN WHERE THEY WERE TO SPEND the night, Foxhollow Manor, had once been the summer retreat of a Providence industrialist and his family. A thirty-room Georgian manor built on a sixty-acre estate in the 1920's, it had been turned into an inn when the descendants of the original owner could no longer afford to keep it up. Now it was run by a hotel chain that made a specialty of inns catering to bridal parties and couples seeking a romantic weekend getaway. This inn also catered to equestrians since the property included an elegant stable and miles of riding paths. Charlotte had booked a room there because it was the only available lodging that was located right in Hadfield, but she hadn't overlooked the appeal of the complimentary bottle of champagne, the king-sized four-poster bed facing a working

209

fireplace, and the "romantic brunch," served in the room. (Though her imagination didn't carry her quite so far as the candlelit bubble bath *à deux,* which was a special offering for the Valentine's Day weekend). When she'd called to make the reservations early that morning, she'd been informed that there were only two rooms left: a luxury suite—the Thoroughbred Suite—and a smaller, connecting room, the Palomino Room. She'd reserved both, but she had a feeling they wouldn't be needing the Palomino Room. At least, she *hoped* they wouldn't be needing it.

They got to the room at four and, with their bottle of champagne, promptly settled into the two leather wing chairs that stood before the fireplace. The Thoroughbred Suite was decorated like an English club, with dark green paisley wallpaper and matching bedspread, an antique Oriental carpet, British hunting prints, and a brass hunting horn on the mantel. There was even a saddle and a pair of old riding boots standing in a corner, and a collection of books on the desk with titles such as *Lameness in the Horse, Productive Horse Husbandry,* and *Diseases of the Horse's Foot.* The books seemed to Charlotte to be carrying the English country squire illusion just a little too far, but the room was pleasant and cozy nonetheless. The view was of a broad expanse of lawn that was now covered with snow. Behind the leafless trees at the far edge of the lawn, an orange sun was setting in an overcast violet sky. The light snow that had started falling earlier that afternoon had become heavier.

As she felt the warm glow from the champagne stealing over her, Charlotte was struck by the thought that they might be snowed in. The driveway leading to the inn was half a mile long, and couldn't have been

210

easy to plow. It wasn't an unpleasant thought. As Eddie had said, "You're never too old."

"It seems unreal, doesn't it?" she remarked, looking over at his handsome, tanned face in the chair next to hers. "We meet six days ago in Palm Beach, and here we are at a country inn in Connecticut on Valentine's Day weekend."

Eddie nodded. "With a nor'easter on the way."

"Do you think so?" she asked.

"It looks that way to me. But what do I know? I'm from Pasadena. I haven't experienced a snowstorm in years. Not counting airports, that is. Maybe we'll be snowed in," he speculated, and looking over at her, he added, "I wouldn't mind."

"Nor would I," she agreed.

It was dinnertime before they got around to Jack McLean. Perhaps they hadn't discussed him earlier because they were both still trying to make sense of the wild card they'd been dealt. Or perhaps it was because they'd been otherwise engaged. They were seated at a candlelit table in the dining room of the inn—more hunting prints and hunting horns—before a roaring fire, watching the snow fall through the French doors that led to a terrace overlooking the lawn. It was a gentle snow—there was no wind to rattle the windows—but it had that determined quality that's so often a sign of a big storm: the flakes were big and they fell quickly and steadily. According to their attentive young waiter, the weatherman had predicted ten to twelve inches. It was their fourteenth storm of the season, he added. Charlotte had gone to Palm Beach to get away from the winter, and here she was in the middle of it again. But somehow she didn't

211

mind. Being with Eddie probably had more than a little to do with it. In any case, they wouldn't have to deal with it for long. They were scheduled to return the next day. Eddie had to start rehearsing for the Big Band Hall of Fame Ball, which was only a week away, and his subsequent tour. The ball was the big annual fundraiser for the organization, which hoped to raise enough money to find a permanent home for their collection of Big Band memorabilia.

But until then, they had nothing to do but enjoy each other's company and try to figure out what had happened in February of 1942 that had resulted in the murder of Paul Feder on a Florida beach fifty years later.

"So," said Eddie once they were served their plates of ordinary old prime rib (the menu was a far cry from Château Albert), "Jack McLean was the Fox. I never would have thunk it was him." He shook his head as he cut into his meat. "I still can't believe it."

"It's disturbing," Charlotte agreed. As an actor, she prided herself on being a judge of human character, and she never would have pegged McLean for a spy. But then, playing games with mirrors was the spy's specialty. "Why can't you believe it?" she asked, curious.

Eddie thought for a moment.

"Is it because of the social credentials, the Ivy League education, the impressive career?" Charlotte probed.

"I suppose that's a lot of it, yes," he said thoughtfully.

"There's nothing about being a member of the establishment that precludes one's being a spy," she commented, thinking aloud. "Look at his namesake:

Donald McLean. Part of the most devastating spy ring of the twentieth century. He was from the right background, but he still betrayed his legacy."

"Betraying his legacy I can more or less understand," Eddie said. "Even betraying his country. In either case, he would have been committing himself to an impersonal ideal. But to risk the lives of the men under his command . . ."

Charlotte nodded. As hard as it was for her to fathom, it must have been many times harder for a man who had looked up to McLean as a leader and then been critically injured as a result of his treachery.

"He sure pulled the wool over my eyes, and over the eyes of all the men under his command," Eddie said bitterly. "We thought he was the next thing to God." He gestured emphatically with his fork. "If it does turn out that he's the Fox, I'm going to revel in the fact that I played a role in exposing him."

Charlotte was surprised to see a glint of anger in his smiling eyes; she had never seen him angry before.

For a moment they sat, eating their dinners, soaking up the heat from the fireplace, watching the flakes come down through the snow-dusted windowpanes.

Then Charlotte said, "I want to go over this McLean business again, from start to finish. Tell me if I leave anything out or if I say anything that doesn't sound right to you."

Eddie nodded.

"Okay," she began. "He's from a distinguished family, has a privileged upbringing. He's a childhood friend of Freddie Welland, who's involved with the America First movement at Yale. Through Freddie, he meets Freddie's Uncle Walter, an admirer of Hitler who heads a fascist organization called the Yankee Patriots. At some point, he's recruited by the *Abwehr*, probably through Uncle Walter's Nazi connections. The United States enters the war, and he joins the Navy. He's assigned to oversee the conversion of the *Normandie* to a troopship, an assignment that is viewed by the *Abwehr* as a perfect setup for sabotage."

"Sounds good to me," Eddie said.

"Through his connection with Alex Koprosky, he becomes acquainted with two of the count's young fascist protégés, and recruits them for Operation Golden Bird through a Bund leader in New York. He arranges for them to work for the carpet company that's been hired to lay the linoleum in the Grand Salon."

"I'll bet that's why he never ordered security checks on the employees of the subcontractors," Eddie interjected.

"Good point," Charlotte said, and then continued. "He supplies his operatives with an incendiary device and sets up the conditions for the fire, namely the stack of burlap-covered life jackets stored near the welders who are taking down the metal light stanchions."

"What he didn't count on," Eddie said, "was the young Navy lieutenant who just happened to be sitting at the piano that afternoon, dreaming of his ladylove."

Charlotte smiled. "The war goes on. McLean has a change of heart and renounces his previous fascist associations. Writes them off to youthful folly, as Jeannie did her attendance at SDS meetings during her college days. Or maybe he just sees the handwriting on the wall."

"That seems more likely to me," Eddie offered. "Who wants to stay on the losing team if you can switch sides without anyone ever knowing?"

Charlotte nodded. "He goes on to a distinguished career, and his previous fascist associations become a potential source of embarrassment, to say nothing of his role in Operation Golden Bird. The past is buried, until one day he gets wind of the fact that someone has visited Roehrer and is asking questions."

"How would he have gotten wind of that?" Eddie asked.

"Maybe through Roehrer himself. Roehrer said he didn't know who the Fox was, but maybe he was lying."

"I doubt it. That's how intelligence organizations protect their members—by insulating one level from the next."

"Okay," she agreed. "We don't know how he found out. If there is some sort of reinvestigation of the *Normandie* fire going on, it could even be that the authorities questioned McLean himself. In any case, he decides that Federov has to be eliminated to prevent his exposure."

"Even if Federov didn't know his identity?"

"If the authorities could prove that a sabotage plot existed, then they could carry the investigation further. Perhaps they could even find out about McLean through *Abwehr* records. But if they can't prove there was a sabotage plot, then there would be no investigation to carry forward."

Eddie nodded. "Okay," he said. "I'll buy it."

"By a twist of fate, Federov and McLean both end up in the same town. When McLean finds out that questions are being asked, he decides to kill Federov and picks the preservation association's benefit as the place to do it."

Eddie interrupted. "Two questions," he said. "One: how would McLean have found out that Federov and Feder were one and the same? And two: why would he have killed Feder? Why not kill the person who was looking into the fire, and nip the investigation in the bud?"

"The answer to number one is, I don't know. The answer to number two might be that he didn't want to call attention to himself. If an investigator was killed, the authorities conducting the investigation might have come looking for him. Whereas Feder was once removed, so to speak."

Eddie nodded.

"To continue," she said. "Seeing Feder head out to the beach, he follows him and waits for a convenient moment to stab him. Having learned from the newspaper, or from Lydia, how valuable the cigarette case is, he takes it in order to make it look like a jewel theft."

"How long would you estimate he was out there?" Eddie asked.

"I have to admit that my attention was elsewhere," she replied with a smile. "But I'd guess twenty to thirty minutes. We could check with Maureen. She would have the statements from him and from the other guests."

"In any case, long enough to do the job."

"Yes," Charlotte agreed, then shrugged. "End of story," she said. "At least, what we know of it. Are we ready to take it to the police?"

"I don't see why not."

They landed at West Palm Beach International Airport late the next afternoon. The predicted storm had fizzled out. In New England parlance, it was just a duster. Only four inches of snow had fallen, much to their disappointment, since their room had been very comfortable (and they had needed only the one). As they drove back to Palm Beach along Okeechobee Boulevard, Charlotte was struck by the contrast between the snow and cold of the small, pristine New England village and the tropical climate and glitzy atmosphere of Florida's Gold Coast. It was like seeing a movie in color on a large screen after watching it in black and white on a tiny television set. Or maybe it was just being back in Palm Beach with Eddie. In any case, when they drove across the arched stone bridge that connected the island to the mainland, she had the feeling that they were entering a fairy-tale city. It was an impression that was enhanced by the sight that met them on the other side of the bridge: a wide boulevard lined by four rows of columnar royal palms, with a median of boxwood-edged flower gardens filled with colorful plantings of impatiens and geraniums. Such was the effect of this magnificent approach that she half expected to be greeted by a a trumpet fanfare.

As they drove down Royal Palm Way, Charlotte realized that she felt happier and more youthful than she had in years. She wondered what was going to happen now. Were she and Eddie really as compatible as they seemed? Was she ready for a full-fledged relationship or even marriage—her fifth? On the one hand, her mind was racing with questions like these. On the other, she didn't much care. She had reached the point in life where *now* was what mattered. Because the next day, the next week, the next year, either or both of them might not be around. Maybe this was what Ponce de Leon had discovered when he'd come to Florida seeking the fountain of youth, and Mizner and Singer after him. That only by coming to terms with death can you really find life.

She dropped Eddie off at the Breakers, where he would be meeting with his band to start rehearsals, and then proceeded on to the police station. She found Maureen in her office, showed her the copy of *The Yankee Patriot,* and told her the whole story.

"This is great," Maureen said when Charlotte had finished, relieved to have a new angle to pursue. "We weren't getting anywhere with the jewelry angle. We've leaned on every fence in Florida. We've called in every IOU from our street contacts." She set the copy of *The Yankee Patriot* aside.

"How about the weapon?" Charlotte asked.

"It still hasn't turned up. But we know more about it from the autopsy. A dagger, which is unusual. We don't often run across double-edge blades here. It's not like in Spanish Harlem or Little Italy, where the stiletto is a favorite weapon. With a six-inch blade. Apart from that, nothing."

"What are you going to do now?"

"First, I'm going to find out more about Jack McLean. I have some contacts at the CIA," Maureen said. "I feel as if I need more definitive proof before I can accuse a decorated rear admiral of treason."

"And if you find it?"

"We'll conduct a search. Look for the dagger and the cigarette case. Meanwhile, I'd appreciate it if you wouldn't mention this to anybody."

"Of course," Charlotte agreed. "Call me if you hear anything."

It was just after seven the next morning when Charlotte heard from Maureen. Her message was brief. "Meet me at Villa Normandie as soon as possible," she said. "Go right past the house to to the back—by the lake. I'll tell them to let you through." In ten minutes, Charlotte was on her way downtown in her rental car. As she drove, she pondered the significance of Maureen's statement: "Tell *them* to let you through." *Them* must be Maureen's underlings. *To let her through* implied some sort of barrier, which in turn implied that a crime had taken place. Maybe even another murder. Why else would Maureen have summoned her to a crime scene at seven on a Monday morning? The fact that the event—whatever it was—had taken place at Villa Normandie implied that Lydia was involved. Which also implied that their sabotage theory as a motive for Paul's murder was shot to hell. Whoa! she warned herself. Slow down! She was jumping from one conclusion to the next like an Olympic gymnast, without a shred of evidence to support any of them.

She arrived at Villa Normandie ten minutes later. The tricolor was still flying from the deck on the second story, but there was a Barclay's International Realty "For Sale" sign on the front lawn. She was stopped just inside the entrance gates by a policeman.

"Charlotte Graham," she said. "Detective Maureen White said I should go right on through to the back."

The policeman nodded in recognition of her name and gave her a once-over—curious, Charlotte supposed, to see how the old warhorse was holding up. Then he directed her to drive past the swimming pool to the parking area in front of the garage.

219

At the parking area, she was directed by another policeman to a path through a dense stand of low, leafy palms that led to a lawn overlooking the Lake Trail, which was a footpath that ran along the shore of Lake Worth.

Emerging into the open a few minutes later, she could see a cluster of policemen gathered around a huge tropical tree at the edge of the Lake Trail. She walked down to the foot of the Bermuda grass lawn, where she joined Maureen at the edge of the trail. "What's up?" she asked.

"Good morning," Maureen said. "I thought I owed you. We've got another body." She nodded in the direction of the tree.

Charlotte raised an arched eyebrow in her signature expression.

"He's over here," said the detective, leading Charlotte toward the tree, whose enormous gray roots formed buttresses that were four or five feet high. A moment later, they were standing in front of a wedge-shaped enclosure created by the buttresslike roots.

Lying on its side between the walls of the roots was the body of Admiral John W. McLean III. He was casually dressed in tan chinos, a white knit shirt, and a navy blue cardigan golf sweater. In the center of his upper chest was a neat, round stab wound ringed by a circle of fresh blood.

"The wound appears to be identical to the one in Feder's chest," Maureen said.

Charlotte was stunned. McLean was the last person she expected to be the victim. "I don't know what to say," she told Maureen, nonplused.

"That makes two of us," the detective said.

Charlotte looked down again at the body. What

impressed her about it was its sheer size and stateliness. In death, Big Jack McLean was as tragic as a mighty felled oak. "I guess this means our theory that McLean killed Feder to protect his reputation is out the window."

"Not necessarily," Maureen replied. "If it's true that McLean was involved in the sabotage plot, then both murders might be tied to that. We're waiting for the medical examiner now, but it certainly looks like the same weapon."

"Yes, it does," Charlotte agreed.

"It also looks like a professional hit to me. That was my biggest problem with Marianne Montgomery as a suspect in Feder's murder. It was too neat: it's rare that a knife is thrust directly into a body at the right angle, and then pulled directly out again."

"In other words, the murderer was a person who knew what he was doing."

Maureen nodded. "Had to have done it before. Probably more than just once. Also, there aren't any defense wounds, which means that the victim was taken by surprise. As was the case with Feder."

Charlotte looked up from the spot where the body lay to the asphalt-paved trail. At this point, the trail curved to accommodate the spreading roots of the giant tree, which must have been thirty feet in circumference. "Was he walking on the trail?" she asked.

"We think so," Maureen said. Turning away from the body, she led Charlotte out to the trail.

Here the trail overlooked a narrow stretch of the Intracoastal Waterway which was dotted with uninhabited islands that were used as bird sanctuaries. The morning sun had tinted the still waters a pale pink. The vegetation was damp with dew, and the mourning doves cooed plaintively.

It was hard to believe that a murder had taken place in such a tranquil setting, Charlotte thought as they stood there.

The trail had been cordoned off to the north and to the south, and she could see policemen turning away early-morning joggers, dog walkers, cyclists, and roller bladers. A few of the more curious were hanging around on the other side of the yellow tape to see what was going on.

"We think the perpetrator hid behind the roots of the tree," Maureen said. "I just walked about a hundred feet in either direction; it's the only place along this stretch of the trail where he could have concealed himself."

"It's quite a tree," Charlotte said. She'd noticed plaque on the trunk that said "Mysore Fig, *Ficus Mysorensis,* 1932."

"Yes. It's one of our historic specimen trees. The garden club puts up those plaques. It also makes a very good hiding place."

"For the killer and for the body," Charlotte commented.

Maureen nodded. "There's a lot of traffic on the trail, as you can see," she said, nodding toward a couple on a bicycle built for two who were being turned away by the police. "If he hadn't hidden the body, it would've been discovered right away, which might not have given him enough time to get away."

"Who did discover it?"

"A dog walker," Maureen said. "The dog led him over there. You'd be amazed at how many bodies are discovered by dogs."

"Any clues?"

"There are footprints. We're going to have casts made. But that's it. We're looking for the weapon now." She nodded at the policemen who were scouring the edges of the trail. "But I doubt we'll find anything."

"What was McLean doing here?" Charlotte asked.

"I don't know," Maureen said. "His car's parked in front of Lydia Collins's garage. I'm going to talk with her now. Do you want to sit in?"

Charlotte said she would.

Leaving the crime-scene unit to their work, they made their way back up the lawn. The house loomed ahead of them with its three increasingly narrow stories. Charlotte half expected to see stacks rising from the flat roof, so much did it resemble an ocean liner. At the head of the lawn was the swimming pool, which occupied a terrace at the rear of the house. It was surrounded by a tall hedge that shielded it from passersby on the Lake Trail. Passing the pool, they continued around to the patio at the side of the house and mounted the gangway that led to the front door. "She's expecting you," said the policeman who was posted at the door. "She's upstairs," he added as he opened the door for them. Crossing the hallway, they climbed the spiral staircase to the Grand Salon on the third floor.

The exquisite Dupas mural was still there: it had not yet been handed over to the preservation association as restitution for the stolen money. Looking at it now, Charlotte remembered Lydia recounting her delight at having located the twelve missing panels. How it must have irked her that her magnificent reproduction of the Grand Salon was complete save for those panels. Without them, the mural must have looked like a row of teeth with three or four missing, and the room unfinished. Their absence had annoyed Lydia enough that she had been prompted to steal to buy them. If she was willing to steal, would she also have been willing to kill? Maybe it was she who had killed Paul, slipping away for a few minutes without detection. Then she'd gone on to kill McLean because he'd found out that she'd murdered Paul. A few years in jail for embezzlement was one thing, but going to the electric chair for murder was quite another. Or maybe she'd gotten the admiral to kill Paul for her, and then killed him in turn to keep him quiet.

But upon reconsideration, Charlotte dismissed her speculations as ridiculous. Grasping at straws, in fact. Lydia hardly came up to Jack McLean's chest. He could easily have overpowered her. Nor did she fit the picture of a professional killer that Maureen had drawn.

They didn't see Lydia at first. She was slouched at the far side of the room on a settee surrounding one of the crystal light fountains. She was smoking a cigarette and staring out at the ocean through sunglasses with round, white frames the size of cocktail coasters. The tiny silky terrier sat in her lap. Maureen announced their arrival, and they crossed the room and sat down in two of the sleek needlepoint-covered *Normandie* armchairs.

Seeing Lydia in the morning light that streamed through the porthole-shaped windows, Charlotte was reminded of the film *Lost Horizon,* in which one of the characters ages a hundred years when she leaves the

224

paradise of Shangri-La. Lydia Collins had gone from a well-preserved society matron to an old lady overnight. Her unkempt hair was growing out gray. Her face, devoid of makeup, looked old and haggard. Her pink silk dressing gown was stained, and her talonlike nails were cracked and chipped. Even the dog lacked the usual ribbon in its topknot.

"I assume the police officer told you that Admiral McLean has been murdered and that his body was found on your property," Maureen said.

Lydia nodded, and flicked the ash of her cigarette into a bisque-colored ashtray that said SS *Normandie.*

"Had he been here first?" Maureen asked.

Lydia shook her head. "I haven't seen him since Friday."

Friday was the day that the news of Lydia's transgressions had hit the local papers, along with the fact that she was being questioned in connection with Paul Feder's murder. It looked as if Jack had been shunning her.

"Then what was he doing here?" asked Maureen.

"He liked to walk on the Lake Trail early in the morning," Lydia replied. Her voice was low and flat, stripped of emotion. "But as you know, there's a parking problem."

Parking on South Ocean Boulevard was strictly controlled. It was a way of keeping the undesirable element—namely anyone who didn't live in Palm Beach—off the town's beaches. In fact, the town had very cleverly arranged it so that the only place one *could* park was in front of a store.

"I had told him he could park by my garage and walk down to the Lake Trail from there," she said. "He's been coming here to walk in the mornings three

225

or four times a week for months now."

"Did he always come on the same days of the week?" Maureen asked.

"Not always, but usually. He usually came on Monday, Wednesday, and Friday. He took his boat, the *Sea Witch*, out on the other days. Or sometimes he'd play golf. He was a man of habit," she added.

Which meant, Charlotte reasoned, that anyone who wanted to kill him would only have had to tail him for a few days to find out his routine.

"What time did he arrive and leave?"

"He walked for an hour. He usually arrived at six-thirty and left at seven-thirty. Or so he told me. I'm not usually up at that hour."

"Were you up this morning!" Maureen asked.

Lydia slid her sunglasses down her nose and looked at Maureen over the tops as if to say, Are you kidding? At that ungodly hour?

Like Charlotte, Maureen must not have considered Lydia to be a serious suspect because when Lydia went on to say that she was asleep, Maureen didn't pursue it. She certainly didn't look like someone who had gotten up at the crack of dawn to commit a murder.

"Do you know of anyone who might have wanted to kill him?"

Lydia shook her head.

They left after Maureen had asked a few more routine questions.

"I was shocked at how she looked," Charlotte said as they walked back down the spiral staircase. "What's happening with her case now?"

"The preservation association has hired a law firm

that specializes in fraud to conduct an investigation. They'll also be taking title to the Dupas panels," Maureen said. "Since the panels have a value of half a million or more, they should more than make up for her debt."

"Is the U.S. Attorney's office going to prosecute?" Charlotte asked, referring to the speculations that had been in the newspapers.

"I don't know," Maureen replied. "There's an element on the board of the association that's applying pressure to keep it in the family, so to speak, but I don't think it's going to work."

"How could it work?" said Charlotte "She's committed a crime."

Maureen gave her one of those How-can-you-be-so-naive? looks. "For one thing, the board has a lot of powerful members who are quite capable of pulling strings. For another, they could make the argument that she embezzled the money because she was mentally unbalanced."

"On what grounds?" Charlotte asked.

"She claims that she was driven to take the money because of a psychological breakdown brought on by discrimination on the part of Palm Beach's old guard society that resulted in her being excluded because of her social background, or lack thereof."

Charlotte rolled her eyes. "If you don't try to get in, they aren't going to exclude you," she pointed out.

Maureen shrugged, as if to say that the behavior of social climbers was beyond her. "Actually, I don't think public pressure will allow them to let her off. It would be an open invitation to embezzlers, which would be the wrong message to send in a town where so much money is raised for charities."

Charlotte nodded.

"Also, the more they dig, the more they turn up. Vacations, phone calls, limos, dinners—all charged to the association's accounts. She claims that she charged her personal expenses only for the sake of convenience, that she intended to pay the money back, but. . ."

"In other words, not just a few events that might have resulted from a mental breakdown, but a systematic pattern of abuse."

Maureen nodded. "Actually, you're right about her not being able to avoid prosecution, though. Because its's not only the preservation association that has something to say about it. The IRS is conducting its own investigation, as is the insurance company through which she was bonded."

"What you're saying is that they *will* prosecute, even if the preservation association won't."

"Right. I think this is one former society woman who's going to spend a lot of time behind bars. Who knows? Maybe they need somebody to organize fundraisers for the prisoners."

The policeman at the door was just signing off his walkie-talkie when they reached him. "It's Roberts down at the lake," he told Maureen. "He wants you to go right on down there."

"Did he say why?"

"He thinks he's found the weapon."

Roberts met them at the far side of the pool and led them down to the Lake Trail. He was very young—why was it, Charlotte wondered, that lately it seemed as if the world was being run by kids?—and very excited at what was probably his first contribution to a major investigation. He was tanned, fit, and good-looking, and wore the uniform of the Palm Beach police—a brown shirt and khaki Bermuda shorts. To Charlotte, it looked like an outfit that Ernest Hemingway would have worn on safari in Africa, but who would expect the Palm Beach police to dress like policemen? This was never-never land, after all. At the Lake Trail, they headed north to a spot that Charlotte recognized as being at the end of the cross street on which the Smiths' house was situated. Here Roberts turned off the trail and led them down to the shore of the lake, which at this point was lined with coconut palms. He stopped at the edge of the water, at a place where the coral that formed the bedrock of the island was exposed.

Resting in a niche in the coral was a cylindrical structure made of brick with an opening in the front. Except for the fact that it had a cast-iron lid, it might have been a colonial-era beehive oven

"What have we got here?" asked Maureen.'

"It's an old manhole. It used to provide access to a storm drain that drained that road." Roberts gestured toward the Smiths' street. "The soil surrounding it has eroded away, and part of the brick has fallen off," he said, indicating the hole at the front of the structure.

Roberts handed his flashlight to Maureen. "Go ahead," he said. "Take a look."

Maureen shone the flashlight into the opening at the front of the manhole and then stuck her head down into it. "I'll be damned," she said, her voice echoing in the hollow space. Withdrawing her head, she passed the flashlight back to the young policeman. "Good job, Roberts."

"Is it the knife?" Charlotte asked Maureen.

"It's *a* knife. I don't know if it's *the* knife. But I'd say it's a pretty good bet that it is."

"Why would he have thrown it away?" Charlotte wondered.

"Maybe he thought he didn't need it anymore, and he didn't want the incriminating evidence lying around. He probably figured that no one would ever find it here." Maureen looked over at the young cop. "He wasn't counting on Roberts."

Roberts smiled proudly.

Reaching into the pocket of her blue denim jacket, Maureen produced a pair of rubber gloves and a plastic evidence bag, which she handed to Roberts. "Be my guest," she said.

"Gladly," he said with the eagerness of the yet-to-become-jaded, and proceeded to don the rubber gloves. Then he got down on his stomach, and gradually shimmied his upper body down into the manhole while Maureen crouched at the side of the opening with the flashlight.

"How're you doing?" she asked after a few minutes.

"Okay," he replied. "But somebody's going to have to hold my ankles, or I might end up standing on my head in here."

Maureen nodded to Charlotte, who took up a position at the young man's feet. Kneeling with her hands on his ankles, she leaned forward with all her weight. She could feel his body twist as he lunged for the knife, which must have been at the limit of his reach.

After several lunges, he finally announced that he had it. Turning off the flashlight and setting it aside,

Maureen joined Charlotte at Roberts' feet, and they proceeded to hoist him back up.

His upper body emerged a few seconds later. As he sat up, he raised the plastic bag triumphantly, a big grin plastered across his face. Then he handed it over to Maureen.

Inside was a silver-hilted dagger with a six-inch blade. The wide end of the hilt was inscribed with a swastika in a circle, and the narrow end, next to the blade, with a lightning bolt, the symbol of Hitler's shock troops. In between were three words in German.

Peering over Maureen's shoulder, Roberts read the inscription: "*Blut und Ehre*. What does that mean?" he asked.

"Blood and honor," Charlotte replied.

12

FROM VILLA NORMANDIE, CHARLOTTE DROVE straight uptown, heading for the Breakers to tell Eddie the news. The Breakers, where Eddie was staying, was Palm Beach's grandest hotel. Built in the 1920's and modeled after the Villa Medici in Florence, it had over 500 rooms, the oldest golf course in Florida, and was situated on half a mile of private beach. It comprised its own little city within the town of Palm Beach: Palm Beach to the nth degree. Ten minutes later, she pulled into the palm-lined driveway, which terminated at an imposing fountain supported on the hefty shoulders of three naked caryatids. Leaving her car with one of the valets, she entered a lobby lined with gargantuan marble columns and hung with Flemish tapestries. Oversized bronze and crystal chandeliers hung from a barrel-vaulted ceiling decorated with Renaissance-style paintings of *putti* darting in and out among the clouds. When she asked for Eddie, she was told that she would find him in the Venetian Ballroom. From the lobby, she headed down what seemed like miles of wide, thickly carpeted corridors lined with potted palms and amply proportioned sofas and armchairs, and arrived at last at the carved wooden doors of the Venetian Ballroom.

The far end of the room was occupied by a stage, on which the music stands for Eddie's sixteen-man "All-American" orchestra had been set up. Eddie was on the stage, consulting with a hotel employee about the lights, which blinked on and off.

"Charlotte!" he exclaimed when he saw her. Stepping down off the stage, he crossed the ballroom to greet her. "What a surprise!" he said, kissing her. Pulling out a chair from one of the tables, he invited her to take a seat and told her he would be finished in a moment.

Though it was less than twenty-four hours since Charlotte had last been with Eddie, she felt a rush of pleasure at seeing him again. Once again, she found herself wondering what it would be like to feel this way all the time.

He joined her a few minutes later. "Is this where the ball's going to be?" she asked, looking around at the huge empty room, with its enormous crystal chandeliers, its peach and beige marble architectural detail, and its classical frescoes of flower-filled urns.

"Yes," he said. "They have a theme each year based on a big band locale. Last year it was the Make-

232

Believe Ballroom. The year before, it was Roseland. This year it's going to be the Rainbow Room. 'Sixty-five stories nearer the stars,' as I used to say on my radio broadcasts from there."

"I remember," said Charlotte with a smile. "I used to listen to those broadcasts, wondering what it would have been like if. . ."

"You did?"

She nodded. "Little did I know that I'd find out years later."

"Little did we both know," he said, taking a seat beside her. "What's going on?" he asked. "It must be very important to have brought you all the way up to the United Nations."

Charlotte smiled. She had told him of her analogies between Palm Beach and Manhattan. In Manhattan, the Breakers would have been located in the East Forties, corresponding to the location of the U.N. "It is," she said, and proceeded to fill him in on the morning's events.

Eddie was as shocked to hear of McLean's murder as Charlotte had been. But after some discussion they both concluded that: one, Lydia couldn't have done it, and two, the murders must be connected with the *Normandie;* there was no other link between the two men. They also decided that the only person with a motive to kill both Feder and McLean would have to be someone else who was involved in Operation Golden Bird. In other words, a fourth man who feared exposure. That is, *if* McLean had been involved in the *Normandie* plot at all. They knew that Roehrer and Federov had been recruited through the count's fascist summer camp, and they knew that McLean had been associated with Walter Welland, and that he

233

would have been acquainted with the camp, but that's all they really knew. They had no proof that he was the Fox. Maybe there was someone else associated with the *Normandie's* command who had fascist leanings and who knew Count Koprosky. The only way to find out for sure if McLean was suspected of being a spy was to make inquires through official channels, as Maureen was now doing. Unless. . .

Charlotte was watching Eddie drum his fingers on the edge of the table when the thought occurred to her. If McLean had been an enemy agent, who would he have confided in? Not his wife, who, in any case, was dead. Certainly not his children. Probably no one, at least at the time he was actively spying. But if he had confided in anybody, it would have been a buddy.

"Eddie," she asked, "was there anyone on board the *Normandie* with whom McLean was especially close? A good friend?"

Eddie immediately grasped what she was getting at. He thought for a moment. "Yeah," he said. "There was! They spent a lot of time together." He stared at the stage at the other end of the opulent room. "What was that guy's name?" he asked himself in frustration.

"What was his position?" asked Charlotte in an attempt to jog his memory.

"He was one of the prospective Navy crew members who came aboard toward the end of January, a couple of weeks before the fire. An engineering officer. They came on first, to learn how to run the ship."

"Maybe we could track him down through the Navy."

"We could track him down through a computer information network if I could remember his name.

My daughter, Sharon, sells them to law firms. They're very expensive to use, but I can use hers for free."

"How do they work?"

"You type in the name and ten seconds later the computer gives you the address of everyone in the country with that name."

"You're kidding!" said Charlotte. More and more, she was feeling like an old fossil these days. She still hadn't reconciled herself to the automated teller machine, much less to a computer information network that could spit out address of everyone with a particular name in a matter of seconds.

"I'm not kidding," he assured her, and then qualified his statement. "Well, not *everyone* in the country, but pretty damn close. I think their database is a hundred and eighty million; it's based on the census records."

"If you exclude minors, the very old, and the socially marginal, that's probably just about everyone," Charlotte said.

He nodded. "Of course, it's not going to be much help if you're looking for someone named William Smith. Sharon checked once, out of curiosity. There were thousands of them. But it seems to me that this guy had an unusual name."

"What did he look like?"

"He was tall, though not as tall as McLean. Round face, genial-looking. I think they knew one another from college. I remember!" he said, his face lighting up. "It was a Chinese name."

"Chinese?"

"It wasn't really Chinese, but it sounded as if it could be. Wang, Wing, Cheng—something like that." He thought for a moment, then looked over at

235

Charlotte. "I'm going to go through the alphabet."

Charlotte sat quietly, watching his lips move as he mentally recited the alphabet, trying each consonant out with a set of vowels. "It's a W word," he said finally. Then he smiled in triumph. "Weg," he announced. "First name Spencer. Spencer Weg. They called him Spence."

"How long would it take you to track him down?"

Eddie called the lighting technician over, and asked him if it would be possible to make a phone call. The man replied that he would look into it and disappeared down the corridor. He returned a moment later with a portable phone.

Eddie dialed his daughter's number from memory. "She has a cellular phone, so I can reach her on the road," he said as he waited for Sharon to pick up.

"Will the wonders of modern technology never cease," Charlotte said.

A moment later, Eddie was explaining what he needed to his daughter. "She's checking now," he told Charlotte. "She was in the middle of demonstrating the system, and she's going to use my request as an example of how it works."

Charlotte withdrew a small, spiral-bound note pad and pen from her pocketbook and passed them over to Eddie.

As Charlotte looked on, he wrote down an address. After hanging up, he passed the note pad to Charlotte. "As luck would have it, we've got us another Floridian, at least during the winter months."

The Florida address was 24 Fairway Island Road, PGA Resort Community, Palm Beach Gardens. The other address was in Weston, Massachusetts, a suburb of Boston.

"Was he the only one in the United States?"

"The only Spencer. Though there were others Wegs."

"That's amazing," Charlotte said. "That took all of a minute and a half. If Sharon succeeds in selling the system, you should act a cut of her commission." She looked at the address again. "Do you know where this place is?"

He nodded. "It's about forty-five minutes from here. It's one of those gated, country club communities. It's also the headquarters of the Professional Golfers' Association."

"A snowbird, I guess."

"And if he's got any smarts, he'll be down here, and not up there," Eddie said, referring to the weather reports, which were predicting more snow for the eastern seaboard states. "Do you want to take a ride out there tomorrow?"

"Yes," Charlotte said.

They dined that night at Château Albert, choosing to do so because they didn't want to be driven out prematurely by admiring fans as they had been on Friday night at Ta-Boó. The dining room was full, but they were in a world of their own. They started with the cocktail that had been served in the Café-Grill on the *Normandie*. Named after the ship, it was half dry vermouth and half cassis. Then they ordered dinner. The food was just as good as it had been on their previous visit, and because it wasn't a special Normandy night, the menu was wasn't limited to entrées cooked in Calvados and cream. They were eating dessert—a napoléon for Eddie and *crème brulée* for Charlotte—when René approached their table

237

carrying two thick black-covered books under his arm. Pulling over a chair from a neighboring table, he sat down and set the books on the end of their table. The cover of the one on top was mounted with a reproduction of the French Line's famous bow-on poster of the *Normandie,* which had served as the model for many ocean liner posters since. The view of the graceful, upswept bow showed as no other angle could the magnificent lines that had made the *Normandie* not only the world's fastest ocean liner, but also the most beautiful. It was the marine equivalent of the Betty Grable pinup. Charlotte remembered René once commenting on the graceful way in which the flanks of the *Normandie's* hull narrowed down to its keel. He had compared it to the way in which a woman's hips narrowed down to her legs. "Ah! *Normandie,"* he had said. "She is just like a woman."

Charlotte looked up from the books to their host. "Scrapbooks?" she asked.

He picked up the top book and showed her the spine. The year 1939 was written on it in white ink. "I thought you would like to look at this," he explained, adding, "I like to think of everything that might please my guests."

"I'm impressed," Charlotte said. "Not only a fabulous dinner in an elegant setting, but memories included as well. Your reputation for thinking of everything is very well-deserved, René."

He beamed.

As Charlotte and Eddie slid their chairs over, René opened the scrapbook to the section marked August 23rd. The first half was devoted to what antique dealers call ephemera: the daily schedules, the menus, the programs for special events. The second half was given over to snapshots of the first-class passengers, all of them clearly identified.

As they flipped through the pages, Charlotte recognized familiar faces from that strange and wonderful voyage. The family of Polish refugees, the director of the movie they'd shot in Paris, the famous children's book author, the woman who had been convinced that her table mate was a spy, the pretty young widow who'd had her eye on René.

And there, whirling around the dance floor in the Grand Salon were Charlotte and Eddie. Looking so young! But then, they *had* been young. Charlotte only twenty, and Eddie twenty-four—barely out of the egg. His hair had still been black, though, as he had told her, it had started turning prematurely white soon after. How dashing he had looked! No wonder she had fallen for him.

"I thought you'd be interested in this photograph because it shows the ruby necklace," René said. "The one you were wearing a copy of at Villa Normandie." He pointed out the necklace around Charlotte's neck.

The ruby necklace that had brought her luck—again, she thought.

The scrapbook contained a number of photos of Charlotte and Eddie: ensconced in deck chairs under steamer rugs, sipping bouillon and probably watching the *Bremen* tailing them off their port side; seated in wicker chairs in the elegant Winter Garden, with its tropical plants and exotic birds in glass cages; holding hands on a settee at the base of one of the Lalique light fountains.

She remembered again that first night, when they had watched the sunrise from the Café-Grill. They had stayed up all night because they didn't want to be

239

separated, and to share the same cabin was still unthinkable. It was to be another twenty-tour hours before the walls of Jericho fell.

"Do you have scrapbooks for every crossing?" Charlotte asked.

René nodded. "Every round-trip crossing: sixty-eight and a half of them. I kept them to help me remember the names of the passengers. So many of those who sailed on the *Normandie* were repeats," he explained.

"So all along you had a crib sheet," teased Charlotte. "And here we thought you were relying solely on your fabulous memory."

He smiled. "My memory's pretty good too," he boasted. He looked down at the scrapbook and said sadly: "Little did I know that this would be the last voyage." Then he closed the cover and reached for the second scrapbook. "The date on its spine was February 9, 1942."

"The day the *Normandie* burned," said Charlotte.

"I thought you might want to see this too," he said, opening the cover. Inside were photographs of the fire, from late in the afternoon, when the public first learned of the disaster, to early the next morning, when the ship finally keeled over on its side.

It also included newspaper clippings. A story from the *Herald Tribune* carried a headline that now appeared sadly ironic: "Investigation rules out sabotage in *Normandie* fire."

But it was the last photo in the scrapbook that tugged at Charlotte's heartstrings. The great ship looked like a living thing that was breathing its last, a great whale that had been beached in the icy waters of the Hudson, a thing of power and beauty that now only looked oversized and ungainly.

"The saddest day of my life," said René.

And as Charlotte looked over, she was surprised to see tears welling in his brown eyes.

Charlotte dreamed that night of the *Normandie* again. But this time, her dream wasn't of a lifeboat drill or of the sinister *Bremen* flying its swastika flag. This time she dreamed of a corridor. It was a combination of the corridor in which Eddie had described finding himself after the fire broke out and her own memory of the *Normandie's* passageways. There was also probably a dash of the long corridors at the Breakers. The one in her dream was tilted at an angle as a result of the list caused by the water that had been pumped into the hold. It was only dimly lighted, as the corridors aboard the *Normandie* had been after the blackout was enforced. Cold air streamed down the passageway. From where? she wondered in the dream. She had an overpowering sense of the importance of finding the exit. The corridor in her dream was also very long, so long that the parallel lines of the ceiling and the floor seemed to converge in the distance. And it was empty except for a solitary figure at the far end, wearing the blue-black uniform of the cleaning watch. In the dream, the figure would appear and then disappear, always with his back to her, always moving away from her, stealthily, silently.

Even in her dream, she recognized that the dark-shined figure played a role in the riddle she was trying to solve, the riddle of who had murdered Feder and McLean. But she wasn't sure if he was hero or villain. Was he helping her find her way out of the labyrinth or was he deliberately misleading her? If only she

241

knew what was behind the doors through which he seemed to disappear.

They drove up to Palm Beach Gardens the next morning. Eddie had called ahead and found that Spencer Weg was not only in residence at his Florida home, but would be delighted to see an old shipmate, especially one who had gone on to become a famous bandleader.

The PGA Resort Community was a huge retirement community that had risen up from several square miles of Florida scrubland. It was comprised of a number of individual developments, each with its own golf course, tennis courts, fitness center, and so on, and each containing all levels of housing, from inexpensive condos to large and luxurious homes. It was the kind of place that Charlotte couldn't imagine anyone actually living in, and in fact it looked as if no one did: it was characteristic of such places that no one was ever seen walking around (except on the golf courses), probably because these homes were only occupied for a few weeks or months of the year by most of the residents. But she supposed that golf lovers were willing to put up with almost any inconvenience—including a housing development that looked as if it had been hit by a neutron bomb—for the luxury of having a golf course right on their doorstep. No doubt there were practical advantages as well: security issues and the like. She herself preferred living in a community where there was evidence of human habitation: dog walkers, window shoppers, children playing, a newstand on the corner.

That was one of the things she liked most about Château en Espagne: its location. For a New Yorker, the midtown location held great appeal. Its envelope of greenery gave it a remote, isolated feeling, but it was only a block from the hustle and bustle of Worth Avenue. At the same time, it looked out over the palm-fringed fairways of the golf course and was only two blocks from the beach. In short, it had the best of all possible worlds. In the back of her mind, she was still toying with the idea of buying the house, imagining what it would be like to sit in the tower room, to tend the plants in the courtyard, to walk over to Worth Avenue for. . . what? Certainly not a quart of milk. What the hell—a diamond necklace.

But she still wasn't sure she was ready to buy her castle in the air.

Spencer Weg greeted them at the door of his home, which was a Spanish-style ranch in a high-priced neighborhood overlooking a lake bordering a velvety green fairway with a gazebo-crowned island at its center. Which was exactly what one would expect of a house with a Fairway Island Road address. After introductions were made (Eddie introducing Charlotte as Mrs. Lundstrom), Weg led them out to a covered loggia by the pool. As Eddie had said, he was a tall man, deeply tanned, with gray-white hair, and a round, genial face. He looked as if he spent a lot of time on the golf course. His wife was also tall and thin, with a long, narrow face and a pleasant smile. Once they were settled in the comfortable patio chairs, Mrs. Weg served coffee and blueberry muffins. While the two men reminisced about their Navy days, Charlotte struggled to make conversation with Mrs. Weg, who was quite pretty and very charming, on the subject of how to make the best blueberry muffins (use only the small, wild berries, and never the fat, cultivated ones).

Finally Eddie got around to the purpose of their visit "I suppose you're wondering why I decided to get in touch with you after all these years," he said.

"I am," said Weg. "Though I was so shocked that you'd tracked me down through a computer information network that I never got around to asking."

"It's about Jack McLean. Did you know he lived in Palm Beach?"

"Yes," Weg replied. "In fact, we get together on a pretty regular basis. He often takes us out for a day of fishing on his boat, the *Sea Witch*."

"I'm sorry to tell you that he died yesterday," Eddie said. He paused to let the bad news sink in.

Weg set down his coffee cup and sat for a moment with his forehead cradled in his hand. With his other hand, he reached out for the hand of his wife, who was sitting next to him. "He was my oldest friend," he said in a broken voice. "We went to Groton and Yale together."

"I know," Eddie said.

"How did it happen?" Mrs. Weg asked.

"He was murdered," Eddie replied.

Weg looked up. "Murdered!" he repeated, his sharp, dark blue eyes questioning how his friend could have been the victim of so horrible a crime.

"Stabbed in the heart while he was out for an early morning walk on the Lake Trail. That's why we're here," Eddie explained. "We were wondering if you could help us find the killer by answering some questions. We think McLean's murder might have something to do with what happened to the *Normandie*."

244

"The fire, you mean?" Weg asked.

"Yes," Eddie said and proceeded to tell the couple about Paul's death, and about their theory that Federov and Roehrer were involved in a plot to sabotage the *Normandie*. "This is difficult for me to say about your friend and my commanding officer, but we think that McLean might have been their contact."

"Contact?" echoed Mrs. Weg.

"We think he may have been the Fox, which was the code name for the *Abwehr* agent who was giving Federov and Roehrer their orders."

"Impossible," said Mrs. Weg, obviously offended that Eddie would dare to level such an accusation. "Jack was one of the most patriotic men I ever met. He won the Navy Cross for extraordinary heroism in Korea."

But her husband's reaction was different: he simply nodded.

Eddie was watching him carefully. "Did you know about this?" he asked.

Weg nodded again.

Mrs. Weg was staring at her husband, open-mouthed.

"I suppose there's no harm in talking about it now that he's dead," he said quietly. "He was an *Abwehr* agent." Weg paused for a moment to collect his thoughts. Then he began: "He had a childhood friend who was involved in the America First movement at Yale."

"Freddie Welland," said Eddie.

"That's him. Through Freddie, Jack was drawn into the movement as well, although only peripherally. He wasn't unlike a lot of patriotic

245

Americans who renounced their association with the isolationists after Pearl Harbor and went on to loyally defend their country."

"Except that he never renounced his association," Eddie commented.

"Not publicly," Weg pointed out.

What did he mean by that? Charlotte wondered.

"Freddie had an uncle who was a rabid fascist. His name was Walter Welland. I always thought he sounded like a nut case, but that's beside the point. Knowing that Jack intended to join the Navy, Welland tried to recruit him. He told Jack that it would be useful to have a fascist sympathizer within the armed forces. Jack mentioned this to a family friend, a high-ranking Naval officer. He didn't want to be taken for a fascist, you see."

"What year are we talking about?" Eddie asked.

"Just after Pearl Harbor," Weg replied, and then continued. "To Jack's surprise, he was contacted by someone from the OSS, the Office of Strategic Services, which was the wartime predecessor of the CIA. Jack had all the right social credentials for the OSS, which was a snob organization. We used to say that it stood for 'Oh so social.' Anyway, they asked him to play along, and he was recruited by the *Abwehr* through Walter Welland."

"Except that he was a double agent," Eddie said. He leaned back in his chair. "What a story!" he exclaimed.

Weg nodded. "The trouble was that the Nazis questioned his allegiances. They thought he was too good to be true. Which he was. When he was assigned to the *Normandie,* they saw it as the perfect opportunity to test his loyalties by asking him to

commit an act of sabotage."

"My God. Spence!" cried Mrs. Weg.

He looked over at his wife. "I could never tell you, honey," he said. "For obvious reasons."

For a moment, they all sat quietly.

In retrospect, the idea of McLean as a Nazi spy was ridiculous, Charlotte thought. People like McLean might have looked on Koprosky as a romantic aberration, a kind of *condottiere* in jackboots instead of egret feathers; they might have tolerated Walter Welland as a deluded eccentric—and they might even have respected Mussolini's ability to make the trains run on time—but they never would have stooped to stiff-armed salutes and *sieg heils*.

"Did you know about this at the time?" Eddie asked.

Weg shook his head. "He didn't tell me until after the war. Anyway, as you know, he recruited the two young men from the count's fascist summer camp and set the sabotage plot into action. His plan was to demonstrate his loyalty to the Nazis by starting the fire, and then to see to it that it was put out. As you know, the *Normandie* was supposed to be unburnable: it had the most advanced fire-fighting capacity of any ship that ever sailed."

"Like the *Titanic* was unsinkable," said Eddie.

Weg nodded. "Actually, the *Normandie's* demise was blamed on the fire, but it wasn't the fire that did it, despite everything that went wrong. The fire was under control by six-thirty. Not as quickly as Jack had hoped, but under control nonetheless. With very little damage, I might add. Had the episode stopped there, she could have been refitted as planned and been carrying troops to Europe within a couple of months.

247

But what he hadn't counted on was New York politics. Mayor LaGuardia, the city fire department, the private fire tugs. Everybody wanted to be the hero of the hour. They kept pumping and pumping and pumping—they were pumping long after more water was needed—until the ship was so full of water that it just keeled over."

Charlotte was reminded of René's scrapbook with the photo of the dead ship lying on its side in its muddy slip.

"After that, Jack became a hero to the Nazis," Weg continued. He had demonstrated his loyalty, in spades. They thought he'd orchestrated events just as they had unfolded. He was posted to Europe as a naval attaché, where he became an intimate in the higher echelons of the Nazi command. I remember him talking about lunching with von Ribbentrop. His mission was to feed the Nazis what the OSS called disinformation, particularly about Allied troop deployments, and in turn to collect whatever useful information he could."

"How did he end up confiding in you?" his wife asked.

"Ah, here we get to the gist of the story," Weg said. "Even thought the fire was extinguished, it wasn't put out as quickly as it should have been. The general alarm wasn't sent in to the central fire station as quickly as it should have been, the ship-to-shore fire alarm box had been temporarily disconnected by the workmen, half the fire extinguishers were out of order, the hydrant couplers didn't couple with American hoses. It was Murphy's Law in full force: whatever could go wrong, did." He looked up at Eddie. "I don't have to tell you this, Ed."

Eddie nodded.

Weg continued. "A hundred and twenty-something men were injured . . ."

Charlotte found her glance shifting to Eddie's hands.

". . . and there were two fatalities: a man who fell off a ladder and another man who died as a result of his injuries a couple of days later. We were very lucky that that there weren't more fatalities. Anyway, Jack held himself accountable, and in fact he became the Navy's scapegoat."

"The conclusion of the Attorney General's investigation was 'There is no evidence of sabotage. Carelessness has served the enemy with equal effectiveness,' " said Eddie.

"That's right," Weg agreed. "The trouble was, that was Jack's conclusion too, as well as the conclusion of a Navy Court of Inquiry, which entered a black mark against his name, and which had no idea of his real role in the fire. After the war, he fell into a depression. It was quite severe. His wife asked me to help. That's when he confided in me. The deaths and the injuries were on his conscience, to say nothing of the loss of the *Normandie*."

"Was that when you took that fishing trip to Ontario with him?" Weg's wife asked. "The one just after Joey was born?"

He nodded.

"Were you able to help him?" Eddie asked.

"I said all the usual things one would say in such a situation: that the deaths and injuries were a consequence of war, that the benefits that accrued to the Allies as a result of his proving himself to the Nazis probably ended up saving many more lives than

249

were lost in the fire, that he shouldn't take the blame personally, and so on."

"But it didn't do any good?"

He shook his head. "Oddly enough, the idea that finally started easing him out of his depression was one that came up in a casual conversation we had one day about the feminine qualities of the *Normandie*."

Eddie looked at him quizzically.

"The ship was so exquisitely designed that one couldn't help thinking of her as a beautiful woman, one who was perfect in every detail: her nails, her hair, her clothes, her figure."

It was the same thing that René had said, Charlotte thought.

"But one of the fascinations of such beauty is its impermanence. One knows that it requires perfect conditions, and what's more, that even under perfect conditions it can't withstand the test of time."

"In other words, that she was doomed," said Eddie.

He nodded. "By the time we got her, of course, she'd been stripped. All the furniture had been removed, the art, the carpets. But the beauty was still there. The French crew that had cared for her were like an army of perfectly trained technicians, priests to the goddess—manicurists, hair stylists, masseurs—all dedicated to maintaining her exquisite attributes. We numbered only a handful, and we were untrained to boot. Did you ever see the plans, Ed?"

Eddie shook his head.

"There were acres of them, all in French. The French just left them all for us. No explanations; there wasn't time. My point to Jack was that she was so complex, so high-strung, so finely tuned, that she was doomed."

"A hothouse plant in the real world," Eddie said.

"Exactly" Weg said. "I once heard her called a blood ship. It's a term used among ocean-liner buffs for a ship that's met a tragic end: the *Lusitania,* the *Titanic,* the *Andrea Doria.* With the *Normandie,* you could see it coming, you knew she would be a blood ship even before the tragedy struck."

"And he understood that?"

"Yes. If it hadn't been then, it would have been some other time. It was like trying to turn an aristocrat into a peasant; it just wouldn't have worked." Weg paused for a moment to sip his coffee and then continued. "Eventually, he snapped out of his depression. He went on to a brilliant career, first in Naval Intelligence and later in the Bureau of Ships. But I don't think he ever recovered fully from the *Normandie* fire. He was never the same after that. He was always withdrawn. I was his oldest friend, but even I never really felt close to him."

Charlotte remembered what Connie had said about his unwillingness to reveal himself.

"The only time I ever saw him really let his guard down was on the *Sea Witch,*" Mrs. Weg said.

"That's true," her husband agreed. "I think being on his boat consoled him. He always said he was happiest when he was trailing a wake behind him."

A career in Naval Intelligence, Charlotte reflected. If she and Eddie had known that, they never would have made the mistake of thinking he was the Fox. They would have suspected right away that he was a double agent. She should have questioned Connie more thoroughly. "Know your victim" was one of the rules of detection always cited by her detective friend, Jerry D'Angelo. "The victim offers as many clues to

251

the crime as the perpetrator," he'd said. It was a rule that they had paid no attention to. Nor had they paid any attention to the common sense dictate that a decorated rear admiral made an unlikely enemy agent. Instead they had madly jumped to conclusions.

Mrs. Weg, whose name was Meg (poor woman—little had her parents known when they named her Meg that she was destined to marry a Weg), had excused herself to get another pot of coffee, and she now refilled their cups.

"Do you have any idea who might have wanted to kill the admiral?" Eddie asked. "Him and Paul Federov. We thought the killer might be someone else involved in Operation Golden Bird—a fourth man. We thought that because of the weapon, a dagger with a swastika inscribed on the hilt."

Weg shook his head. "If there was a fourth man, why would Jack have told me about the others, and not about him? Besides, it was all so long ago. What difference would it make now?"

Which was exactly what Charlotte and Eddie had thought.

13

IT WAS OUT OF THEIR HANDS NOW, CHARLOTTE thought as she drove down Worth Avenue, Palm Beach's main shopping area. After leaving the PGA Resort Community, she and Eddie had picked up some sandwiches at a highway deli and eaten them on the ride back to Palm Beach. Then Eddie had dropped Charlotte off on Worth Avenue and headed back to the Breakers for a rehearsal. But first he would stop by the police station to tell Maureen that McLean had been a double agent. Maureen could then use her CIA connections to pursue the answer to the question of why the participants in an act of sabotage that had occurred fifty years ago were now being murdered. The only theory Charlotte and Eddie had come up with—apart from the fourth man scenario—was that Feder and McLean had been murdered in retribution for a death or an injury that had occurred as a result of the *Normandie* fire, and that it had taken the killer all these years to track them down. It was farfetched, but at least it was *something*. And it should be pretty easy for Maureen to check out, since there had been only two fatalities and a small number of serious injuries. Or maybe the murders had nothing to do with the *Normandie* fire at all. Maybe both victims had been killed by someone who preyed on men who were walking alone on the beach or on the Lake Trail. But then, why hadn't there been other victims? And what about the dagger with the swastika inscribed on the hilt?

Putting the murders out of her mind for the moment, Charlotte turned her attention to a more immediate problem: what to wear to the Big Band Hall of Fame Ball, where she would be the date of the guest of honor. She had decided on a dress—a black sheath she had worn to a recent awards dinner and that she'd asked her housekeeper to ship down to her—but she needed a necklace to go with it. She was thinking about buying a necklace from the *Normandie* collection: not the one she had modeled at the Villa Normandie—half a million was a bit more than her frugal Yankee nature would allow her to spend on a piece of jewelry—but something simpler. But she wasn't sure if she should. On the one hand, she wanted to buy something from the collection as a symbol of her reunion with Eddie, and it had been a long time since she had splurged on something impractical for herself; on the other hand, she didn't want an expensive reminder gathering dust in her jewelry box if things didn't work out.

She arrived at Feder Jewelers a few minutes later. As she approached the store, she took notice of the façade, which had escaped her attention on her earlier visit. It was pure art deco—polished black marble with a door of brushed stainless steel in a geometric design. The art deco lettering read simply: "Feder & Co. Diamonds, Jewels." Though Charlotte doubted that Marianne had chosen her collaborator on the basis of the appearance of his store, it was fitting that her art deco jewelry should be displayed in a shop whose design appeared to date from that era.

A doorman ushered her in, and she was greeted by a salesman, a handsome fellow in his thirties with a heavy French accent. She was about to explain that she was interested in the *Normandie* collection, when a door at the back of the salesroom opened, and Marianne emerged, looking smashing, as usual. She was wearing a chic red thirties-style suit that must have been from her *Normandie* fashion collection, with a red cloche to match.

"Aunt Charlotte!" she exclaimed.

"Hello, Marianne," Charlotte said, kissing her goddaughter on both cheeks.

Then Marianne leaned provocatively close to the salesman and ran her red-lacquered fingernails down the sleeve of his cashmere jacket. "I'd like you to meet someone. This is Nikolai Federov, Paul's great-nephew. He arrived from Paris the day before yesterday to take over the management of the store."

"Very pleased to meet you," said Charlotte, taking note of Marianne's expression as she gazed at the jeweler: jaw protruding, nostrils quivering, sharp brown eyes staring. It was a look reserved for something she had to possess, usually a man. "Like a bird dog with a fix on its quarry," was how Spalding had once described it. She had obviously wasted no time finding another point of light on her path to artistic enlightenment, Charlotte thought, one that was, once again, unsuitably young.

The question was, what type of collection would Nikolai inspire? Actually, Charlotte couldn't remember if Marianne had ever done a French collection. Her designs were usually more exotic, like the Uhuru collection inspired by the African nationalist or the Ballet Russe line inspired by the Russian ballet dancer who had defected to the United States. Maybe it was time for something basic, like a Champs Élysées collection.

Charlotte stepped forward to shake Nikolai's hand. He was a good-looking man, shorter than Paul but with the same strong jaw and striking gray eyes. "I'm very sorry about your great-uncle," she said.

Nikolai shook his head. "He was a great artist," he said. "He taught me everything I know. I will miss him very much. Are you the lady who is interested in buying my uncle's house?"

Charlotte wasn't aware that she had expressed any such intention. "What makes you think that?" she asked, surprised.

"Marianne's daughter, Dede, gave us that

255

impression. She said you admired the house very much. But perhaps she was jumping to conclusions when she said that you might be interested in buying it," he added apologetically.

But as he spoke, Charlotte realized that Dede hadn't been jumping to conclusions at all. She had simply been reading Charlotte's mind. "Is it for sale?" she asked, her intended purchase of a necklace now forgotten.

"Yes," Nikolai replied. "It's going on the market tomorrow. Would you like the real estate agent to show it to you? I could call her right now. There's no time like the present, as the saying goes."

Charlotte thought for a moment. "Yes," she said finally. "I would."

Charlotte had been thinking about Château en Espagne ever since the idea had first occurred to her that she might buy it. It had insinuated itself into her subconscious the way something does that is meant to be. In the back of her mind, she knew that she and the house were fated to spend the rest of her life together. Besides its visual appeal, it met all the basic criteria: convenient to airport, town, and beach, in a community in which she already had good friends. And it wasn't overly expensive, at least by Palm Beach standards. (Where else was she going to spend all her hard-earned money? She had no one to leave it to.) It even had a built-in caretaker. She was sure that Dede would gladly look after the house when she was away. Perhaps because Charlotte had spent so much of her life on the road, the place where she lived had always been very important to her. In her mobile world, the houses she owned were the only places that didn't change. Which was why she moved so infrequently and chose her houses with such care. Besides meeting all the basic criteria, Château en Espagne filled a less obvious but more important requirement. A house was not just a sterile body of molecules, it was an entity with a soul of its own, and the soul of this house resonated with her own.

Waiting now in the real estate office for the agent, who was on the telephone, Charlotte studied the brochure for the house, which was headed *Old World Elegance.* The text read: "Unique 1920's Spanish Revival villa, designed by renowned architect Addison Mizner, with signature exterior tower and spiral staircase. Superbly restored, with all the comforts of modern living. European in feeling, with soaring arches, rich stone floors, and glorious ceilings. With the purchase of Château en Espagne, you will be acquiring a piece of Palm Beach history." From there, the description continued in smaller print: "This three-story Mizner home offers privacy with an in-town location. A pool accents the beautiful, junglelike grounds. The home has high ceilings and two fireplaces, four bedrooms, three and one-half baths, plus a two-car garage and a studio cottage with a bathroom." This was followed by the price—one point seven million dollars—which was enough to support an African village for a couple of decades.

The real estate agent was a pretty woman in her forties named Eileen Finneran with the face of Ireland and the long, curly red hair to go with it. She had a vivacious personality and a leaning toward feminist New Age philosophies, evidenced by the plethora of crystals and amulets—many of them in the form of primitive goddesses—that hung from around her neck, dangled from her earlobes, and adorned the bangle bracelets on her freckled forearms. On the brief ride over to Château en Espagne, Eileen managed to deconstruct Charlotte's fifty-year career in terms of the ascent of the ancient goddess over the modern patriarchal god. Charlotte wasn't quite sure she liked seeing her career evaluated in such simplistic terms (her own talent and hard work had had something to do with it, after all), but she liked Eileen, and they hit it off immediately.

Ten minutes later, they were walking through the empty house. Since Charlotte had last been there, Paul's personal belongings had been removed, presumably by his nephew, though the massive, Spanish-style, Mizner-designed furniture, which was original to Château en Espagne, remained. "Does the furniture go with the house?" Charlotte asked as they entered the dining room, with its rich paneling imported from a Spanish monastery and its views of banana, orange, and palm trees through the undraped French doors.

"Yes," Eileen replied. "Mr. Feder's nephew has already arranged for the sale of his other things, as you can see, but he thought the furniture should remain, since it was designed especially for the house."

"It's lovely," said Charlotte, running her fingers over the antiqued surface of the massive sideboard, and admiring once again the long dining room table, with its sling-back chairs of Spanish leather.

"It's really a wonderful house," Eileen said. "There aren't many like this around anymore. Unfortunately, a lot of them have been torn down. People want to build something bigger, more pretentious."

"Yes, it is a wonderful place," Charlotte agreed. She loved its hidden-away quality, and the way the shafts of sunlight filtering through the vegetation rippled over the walls, like sun shining down through the water.

Without Paul's personal belongings, it was easier for her to see how she might make the house her own.

As they climbed the spiral staircase to the tower a few minutes later, Charlotte could feel herself falling under the house's spell once again. And by the time they reached the tower room, she had talked herself into buying it.

The tower room was empty now—its contents packed up and hauled away, including the album that was missing a couple of photographs, she thought, making a mental note to return them to Nikolai. Looking out at the waving crowns of the palms on the golf course, she could easily imagine herself spending the rest of her life here—or at least the rest of her winters.

But she had at least two reservations about buying her castle in the air. The first was the fact that its previous owner had been murdered. She wondered if that event left a taint on the house. She wasn't superstitious, but she imagined that even unsuperstitious people might hesitate before buying a house under such circumstances.

"That's easy," said Eileen, when Charlotte broached the subject on their way back down the stairs. "There are all sorts of things you can do to purge a house of bad vibrations. You can burn sage, you can conduct a cleansing ritual, you can even call in a priest to do an exorcism," she said. She stopped and turned to Charlotte. "But you know what I'd do?"

"What?" asked Charlotte, who found it hard to imagine herself participating in a New Age cleansing ritual.

"I'd sweep," Eileen said.

"What?"

"I'd sweep. Isn't that what women have always done down through the millennia? Swept in caves, in tents, in tipis; swept in log cabins, tract houses, castles. It's always been the woman's job to get rid of the old stuff. Superimpose their energy markings."

"Swept in one-point-seven-million-dollar Palm Beach houses," Charlotte added, then asked, "Do you mean sweep, literally?"

"Literally, and figuratively too," Eileen replied. "Literally, what you need to do is clean the place up, especially the surfaces. Paint the walls, sand the floors, wash the windows." She waved a bangled forearm around the entrance foyer, where they were standing. "It wouldn't cost that much."

"Not in comparison with what the house is going to cost."

"Besides, the house needs some freshening up," Eileen continued. "And figuratively. In the sense of starting over. Think of living in this house as the beginning of a new phase of your life."

"Sweep!" Charlotte repeated. The idea of sweeping as a metaphor had captured her imagination. She pictured herself in the coral block-paved courtyard with an old corn broom, sweeping the past away: not only the past inhabitant of the house, but her own past as well.

But her other reservation couldn't be dealt with as easily. It had to do with Eddie. She wondered if she should consult with him about buying the house. She

260

didn't want to push things with him, and consulting him certainly presumed a future relationship. But neither did she want to exclude him if he was going to be part of her future. On the other hand, would she want to have a relationship with a man who disapproved of a house that she loved?

Finally, she dismissed the issue altogether. Who said Eddie would even consider leaving Pasadena? There was no point in making a decision based on information that wasn't pertinent. It was Occam's Razor again: she was eliminating all unnecessary elements in the subject being analyzed.

From the entrance foyer, they headed out to the kitchen, which was small and dark—a remnant of the days when the kitchen was the realm of the staff. But that didn't matter—Charlotte didn't cook anyway.

Then Eileen opened the back door. "I have something else to show you," she said, leading Charlotte out to the rear patio.

"The garage?"

"That—and something else," she said mysteriously. After pausing to greet Lady Astor, who was lying down in her lean-to, Eileen led Charlotte into a narrow passageway between the back of the house and the back of the garage.

They emerged a moment later in a small courtyard with a latticework roof from which hung a collection of orchids. Pots of the exotic plants also stood on tiered shelves against the wall, their blooms perfuming the air. The center of the small space was occupied by a wrought-iron table and chairs.

"It's a slat house. For orchids," Eileen added. "Mr. Feder cultivated them as a hobby." She took a seat at the table, on which the sun filtering through the

261

slatted wooden roof had cast a basket-weave shadow. "Just the place to have your morning coffee," she said, quick to point out the house's best features.

"How wonderful!" said Charlotte, thinking that the orchids that hung from the trees in the garden must have been raised here. Stepping up to the shelf of plants, she leaned over to smell an unusual yellow specimen whose petals were mottled with orange. "Are they hard to grow?"

"Some kinds are," Eileen replied. "But a lot are very easy. Most of these are moth orchids, which are very easy. They're called that because the blossoms look like a group of moths in flight."

Taking a seat at the table, Charlotte could indeed imagine herself sipping her morning coffee in the cool, shaded, intimate space, or lying in the hammock that was suspended across the opposite end of the courtyard, reading a script.

"Well," said the real estate agent, "what do you think?"

"I think I'd like to buy it," Charlotte said.

"Excellent," said Eileen with a broad smile.

Reaching into her handbag, Charlotte pulled out her checkbook and set it on the table. Sometimes, she thought, being a goddess had its rewards.

After signing the purchase agreement, Charlotte walked down the street and past the clubhouse of the Everglades Club, following the route that she expected to become a daily part of her future routine. She had wanted to treat herself, and she had. She had bought a house. It was an act so extravagant that she could hardly wrap her mind around it. Like Mizner and Singer, she had come to Florida to recuperate (or

at least to get away from the cold), and she had ended up with a castle in the air. Emerging on Worth Avenue, she turned right at the Spanish-tiled water trough with the "Dog Bar" sign above it (leave it to Palm Beach to have a water trough for dogs) toward the street that she was planning to take back to her hotel. She was so elated about the fact that this walk was to become a daily custom that she felt as if she was walking on air. Charlotte was a walker—a day in her life was not complete without a couple of miles around her East Side neighborhood, and what delighted her about Palm Beach was that it was a walker's town. "It is a great art to saunter," said Henry David Thoreau, one of her favorite philosophers. One could choose a vigorous walk on the beach or on the Lake Trail, or a more leisurely stroll down Worth Avenue, which Mizner had laid out specifically with the needs of the walker in mind. He had incorporated meandering alleyways, which he called *vias,* into his design for the town, which gave it the mysterious charm of an Eastern bazaar, albeit with somewhat overpriced merchandise. Charlotte loved the sense of surprise that came from wandering among the shops tucked away in the vias. One never knew what one would encounter next: a spiral staircase ascending out of sight, a niche containing an urn overflowing with colorful flowers, an aviary filled with brilliant tropical birds, a courtyard occupied by stylish shoppers drinking coffee at umbrella-shaded tables. To say nothing of the exotic and unusual wares—so removed from the oh-so-ordinary merchandise of the standard (for Palm Beach, anyway) Cartier, Gucci, and Tiffany.

And so it was that she found herself entering one of the cloistered walkways, drawn by the intriguing vista of a sunlit courtyard with an elegant marble fountain at its center. Once she reached the courtyard, however, it was the window display in the shop opposite that caught her eye. Standing in the window was a manikin wearing a Russian military greatcoat. It was identical to the manikin that had stood in the tower room at Château en Espagne. Her curiosity aroused, she headed across the courtyard to the store, which was called L'Antiquaire Militaire.

Up close to the storefront, she was able to see that the greatcoat wasn't the only item that had come from Château en Espagne. At the bottom of the window was a display of Paul's toy soldiers. They were all there: the knight of Muscovy in the base of which Dede had found the key, the palace grenadier, the subaltern in the lancer regiment, the private in the Cossack regiment. There was even the photo of the doomed imperial family.

Nikolai must have sold Paul's collection to this shop.

The door stood open to the pleasant air and the sound of the gurgling fountain. Entering, Charlotte found that it was a shop that dealt in military antiques, military artworks, and antique toy soldiers. This was probably where Paul had originally purchased most of his soldiers, she thought as she wandered around, noting the mock-ups of battle scenes that were displayed in glass cases.

She was halfway around the rectangular counter at the center of the shop when a display under the counter caught her eye. It was a collection of Nazi military antiques. There were armbands and helmets and medals, all with the swastika insignia. A sign in the case read: "Every item on display is certifiably authentic."

"May I help you?" asked the salesman when he saw her eyeing a sword with a swastika inscribed on the hilt.

"Do you buy Nazi military antiques?"

"Yes we do."

"I'm interested in selling a piece that I inherited. It's a dagger with a six-inch blade. The hilt is silver, and it's inscribed with a swastika and a lightning bolt. It's very similar to this sword," she said, pointing to the one under the counter, "but smaller, of course. Would you like to see it?"

"Very much," he said. He nodded down at the case. "As you can see, we have a large collection of Nazi memorabilia."

"Can you tell me anything about it?"

"Of course. Daggers of the kind you describe were usually awarded to members of Hitler Youth at the age of eighteen, when they were accepted as full members into the National Socialist Party. They were a symbol of the fact that the youths had become sword bearers for the *führer*."

"It has an inscription," Charlotte said. "*Blut und Ehre*."

"The translation is 'Blood and Honor.' It sounds like it's the kind of dagger that I'm talking about. I couldn't tell you how much I would be willing to pay for it until I see it, though."

"Of course," Charlotte said.

"But I'd estimate that it's worth at least three or four hundred dollars. The value depends on the condition."

"Where would my relative have come by such a knife?" Charlotte asked. "I never really knew him, so

I have no idea."

"Probably from a dead Nazi. The Nazis who had been members of Hitler Youth usually carried them. The Allied soldiers in Europe took them from Nazi corpses as souvenirs, in much the same way as soldiers in the Pacific took samurai swords from dead Japanese soldiers."

The image popped into Charlotte's mind of the spiked German helmet that an uncle had brought back from the Great War; it had been a favorite item in her childhood dress-up trunk.

"They were particularly prized as souvenirs among members of the French Résistance," the clerk added.

"Really!" said Charlotte.

"Yes. They were a status symbol. Having one demonstrated that you had proved yourself by killing a Nazi. Was your relative French?"

"As a matter of fact, he was," she replied.

After thanking the clerk, Charlotte staggered out into the afternoon sunshine. For a moment, she just stood there, blinking. Then she sat down on the rim of the marble fountain. It had come as such a shock: a chance remark from a clerk in a shop that she had just happened to saunter into.

A chance remark that was a key to the puzzle of two unsolved murders.

Her mind was spinning as she walked the four blocks back to her hotel. Ordinarily she would have enjoyed this walk. Ever since her arrival in Palm Beach, the weather had been perfect—sunny, and in the seventies—and this was another perfect day. But her mind was too agitated to enjoy anything. That she had just purchased a house for an almost unthinkable

266

amount of money was by itself enough to throw her off balance, but that had been superseded by the shock of what she had just discovered: the identity of the furtive figure in the dimly lighted corridor of her dream. She now knew why she had seen him in *that* corridor—the corridor on the *Normandie*. She also knew why his uniform was blue-black, though it should have been trimmed in gold braid. She knew what was behind the door into which he had disappeared. She had all the pieces: she had found the exit. Now it was a matter of fitting them together. As she walked, she tried the pieces this way and that and searched among the leftover pieces for the ones that would fill the gaps. It wasn't that she doubted her conclusion, rather that she wasn't sure of the path that led to it.

By the time she sighted the unassuming yellow stucco walls of her hotel fifteen minutes later, she had worked out a scenario for the sequence of events, and all it would take to confirm her conclusions was a couple of telephone calls.

The first was to Wilhelm Roehrer, alias Bill Roe, in Clearwater. She had no difficulty in getting the number from Information.

It was Mrs. Roehrer who answered.

"He died on Sunday," she said.

Charlotte expressed her sympathies, thinking that if the person who murdered Paul and McLean had any intention of murdering Roehrer too, it wouldn't be necessary now. Then she identified herself as the woman who had come to their door the week before with the white-haired man.

"I remember," said Mrs. Roehrer.

"You said that another man had been there before us," Charlotte went on. "You thought at first that we were connected with him. I believe you said you didn't know his name. Is that correct?"

"*Ja*," she replied.

"Can you describe him?"

Mrs. Roehrer thought for a moment, and then spoke in her heavily accented English: "He was of medium height, about sixty years old, very good-looking; dark eyes, gray hair." She paused, and then said, "*Ein Franzose.*"

"*Franzose?*"

"*Ja.* Sorry," she apologized. "I sometimes forget to speak in English. I mean that he was a Frenchman."

Charlotte leaned back on the sofa in the sitting room of her neat little green and white suite and stared at the leaves of the banana tree outside the bay window. She was holding a Manhattan that she had picked up from the bar on her way in and thinking of a quote from Thoreau. "Simplify, simplify," he had said when describing his life at Walden Pond. She and Eddie had concocted a complex plot filled with spies and counterspies and acts of sabotage when all along the murders had been committed for one of the oldest motives there was: revenge. More specifically, revenge for a murdered love. As Eddie had postulated to Maureen earlier that day, Feder and McLean had been killed in retribution for a death that had occurred as a result of Operation Golden Bird. Roehrer probably would have been killed too, had he not been dying already. But it wasn't the death of a human being for which their murderer had taken revenge, but the death of a ship, a ship that he had loved like a woman—more than a woman perhaps—a ship that had been his whole life until that icy February afternoon fifty years ago. "I loved the *Normandie* with a passion one usually reserves for a beloved mistress," he had said.

René Dubord had been one of the priests Weg had referred to, one of the attendants who had worshiped at the feet of the goddess. Even after his workday was through, he had paid her homage, documenting her every whim and passing moment in a series of scrapbooks that he collected over the years. Then she had died, leaving a vacuum in his life that he filled by fighting for his country. Later, he had somehow discovered that the death of his beloved *Normandie* wasn't a tragic accident, but a coldly calculated murder, and he had vowed to track down his mistress's killers and take their lives in revenge. He wasn't a stranger to killing: he had killed in the Résistance—quickly, quietly, professionally. And he would kill again. He would take the lives of the hated Boches who had murdered his mistress, using a weapon he'd taken from one of them during the war. Over the years, he had doggedly hunted down his mistress's killers. Until, one day, he found them—ironically enough—right under his nose. As it turned out, only one had been a Boche, but that didn't matter. The second had been a Russian fascist and the third had been on the same side as he, but that didn't matter either: in his mind, they were all murderers, no matter what side they had been on.

But, Charlotte asked herself, was love of a ship sufficient motivation to drive a man to spend fifty years hunting down her murderers? There must have been something more, she thought as she sipped her drink. Combing her memory for clues, she latched on to the photograph of the original Château Albert, which hung on the wall in the barroom at René's exclusive dining club. The elegant family château, centuries old—lost as a result of debts incurred by René's father in the high-stakes gambling salons at Deauville. He and his mother reduced to living in the bakehouse on their former estate, the mother no doubt obsessed with the lost glories of her past life. Later, the massacre at Oradour-sur-Glane in which the SS had taken the lives of six hundred and forty-odd inhabitants of his village, including his mother and all his relatives. She realized now that for René, the *Normandie* had been more than just a beautiful ship, a ship that he loved as he would a mistress. It had been the symbol of—and the replacement for—the elegant Norman château and the acres of fields and woods that his father had so callously gambled away at Deauville's felt gaming tables. It had been the symbol of a life of wealth and privilege which was his birthright, but which had been snatched away before he was old enough to claim it. It had been the symbol of the grandeur of France, which had been gambled away by a weak, collaborationist government as callously as his father had staked the family patrimony on the deal of a hand. The elegant *Normandie* had been a memorial to his past: his castle in the air. In striking down her murderers, René had been taking revenge for more than just the death of a ship: he had been avenging the loss of his family's honor, the defeat of France, the shame of it all. He had been taking revenge for the Nazi savagery that had destroyed everything he knew and loved.

Setting aside her empty glass, Charlotte picked up

the tulip shell on the lamp table, the shell she had found on the beach. With her finger, she traced the path of the narrow brown band as it coiled its way around the body of the shell in an ascending spiral. René had been coming back to the same spot for fifty years, but instead of circling upward, he had been stuck on the same plane. For fifty years, he had been going around and around in the same path, until a deep groove had been worn into his soul.

Sitting back, she found herself pondering the remaining gaps in the puzzle. How had he found his way to Roehrer's tract house in Clearwater? she wondered. For that matter, how had he found out that the *Normandie* fire wasn't an accident? Then her mind made one of those connections that is the serendipitous result of aimless daydreaming, or maybe the effect of a stiff drink. Reaching over to the table, she picked up the phone again.

The second call was to the Jewish Documentation Center in Los Angeles. She explained to the person who answered that she was following up on an investigation that was being conducted by Mr. Edward Norwood into the career of Nazi *Oberscharführer* Wilhelm Roehrer, and was immediately transferred to someone else. After several more transfers, she was finally connected with a woman who was able to help her.

She told the woman that she was interested in the positions held by *Oberscharführer* Roehrer in the months immediately preceding V.E. Day. "I'm Mr. Norwood's secretary," she said. She didn't want to get into an elaborate explanation as to why she needed the information, not knowing on what pretext Eddie had originally queried the center, or even if a pretext were

271

needed.

But as it turned out, the woman asked no questions. "That should be easy," she replied. "We have all that information on our computer."

"Wilhelm Roehrer was his real name," Charlotte said. "The alias that he used in this country was William Roe—Bill."

"It doesn't matter," the woman said. "We have the information cross-referenced under all the aliases. Sometimes there are a dozen of them."

Charlotte could hear the computer keys clicking. "I have him," she said after a minute. "Born in Köln, emigrated to the U.S. with his parents in 1933 when he was fifteen; active in the German-American Bund; returned to Germany in 1942. What else did you want to know?"

"The position he held at the close of the war. Just before V.E. Day. It would have been in the spring of 1945."

"He was a warder at a prison in France," she said. "It was in Fresnes, just outside Paris. It says here that it was a prison for political prisoners, mostly members of the French Résistance."

"Thank you," Charlotte said, and hung up.

14

THEY ARRIVED AT CHÂTEAU ALBERT AN HOUR later. There were three of them: Charlotte, Maureen, and Roberts, who, since his discovery of the dagger, had been promoted to the position of Maureen's sidekick. After passing through the tall, clipped ficus hedges that concealed the club from the plaza they made their way up the front path. Crossing the cobble-stoned courtyard, they rang the bell at the door of the quaint half-timbered building with the steeply pitched roof. Standing by the French flag that hung from a flagpole, it struck Charlotte that this private dining club—so carefully constructed by craftsmen whom René had imported from his native province—was also a memorial to his aristocratic heritage and to the glory of France, just as the *Normandie* had been. He had spent an entire lifetime trying to resurrect his lost past.

The door was answered by a member of the kitchen staff who informed them that the club didn't open until eight. Upon asking for René, they were escorted into the kitchen, where they found him hunched over a counter, going over the menu with the chef. He looked only moderately surprised to see them, but then, he was a master at maintaining his composure. As usual, he was elegantly dressed in a navy blue double-breasted blazer and gray flannel slacks, and as usual he wore the red and black rosette of the Médaille de la Résistance on his lapel. Excusing himself to the chef, he escorted his visitors to a private dining room with red and white toile wallcovering, where they all sat down on rush-seated ladder-back chairs around an antique table under a large painting of Normandy peasants in wooden shoes harvesting apples.

Then he beckoned to a waiter and asked him to bring them a bottle of pastis and some tumblers. "The drink of Marseille," he announced. As an afterthought, he also asked the waiter to bring them some olives.

If he was going to be arrested, Charlotte thought, he clearly wanted it to be under civilized circumstances.

When the bottle arrived, René set tumblers before everyone and poured out the amber-colored liquid. Ever the attentive host, he then added water from a small ceramic beaker, which turned the aperitif a distinctive cloudy yellow color. Finally he passed around the saucer of olives. "Imported from southern France," he said, as he popped one into his mouth.

"Miss Graham has a story she would like to tell you," said Maureen, introducing the subject as they had previously agreed. She sat tensely at the table, her glass of pastis untouched.

"If you have a few minutes, that is," Charlotte said, maintaining the pretense that this was a casual visit.

René gestured with his hand as if to say, I have all evening.

"It's a love story," Charlotte said. "About a man who was desperately in love with a woman. A woman of enormous beauty, grace, and charm. A woman sometimes of wit. A woman to whom the man had devoted his entire life." She took a sip of the sharp-flavored anise apéritif. "Then one day, this woman's life is prematurely cut down by a terrible tragedy."

René also took a sip of his drink.

"It's a common enough story," Charlotte went on. "It's the story of Juliet and Aïda and Madame Butterfly."

"And Camille," added René, picking up another olive.

Charlotte nodded. "Except for two aspects that make this story different. The first is that the woman doesn't die as a result of suicide or from disease. She is

274

murdered. The second is that the woman isn't a human being, but a ship. A ship with sleek lines and beautiful decor, a ship that symbolized the greatest artistic achievements of France. As the man who loved her put it, 'the world's most perfect ship.' " She paused to gauge René's reaction, but there was none. He removed the olive pit from his mouth, and set it on his napkin.

"The name of the ship was the *Normandie*," she continued. "And her murderers were Nazi fifth columnists, fascist saboteurs whose goal it was to see to it that she would never carry troops to Europe to aid the Allies. At the time it occurred, the *Normandie's* lover thought the magnificent ship's death, which was caused by a fire, was just a tragic accident, but later on—as a fighter in the French Résistance—he found out differently." She looked up at René, who stared directly back at her.

"It's a very interesting story," he said. He sat stone-faced, sipping his pastis. Then he turned to Maureen. "Don't you agree, Miss White?"

Maureen returned his stare. "Yes," she said. "I do."

Charlotte continued. "As fate would have it, the man who loved the *Normandie* was destined to come face to face with one of her murderers. Toward the end of the war, he was captured by the Nazis and incarcerated in the same prison where one of the *Normandie's* saboteurs was working as a guard. The prison was in Fresnes, just outside of Paris."

René nodded as if to confirm her story and then ran his thumb along the waxed surface of his dapper mustache.

"At this point, I'm not entirely clear how the story

275

goes," Charlotte said. "It may be that the man who loved the *Normandie* overheard a conversation among the guards, or it may he that the saboteur bragged about having started the fire that led to the ship's death. In any case, our lover discovered that the tragic end of the ship he had held so dear was not an accident, but a murder for which the prison guard was one of those responsible."

She glanced at Roberts, who was sitting next to her, hands in his lap. Though he looked relaxed, Charlotte could see from her vantage point that his right hand rested lightly on the grip of his gun.

"It was at that point that he vowed his revenge," she continued. "He resolved to track down the men who had murdered the *Normandie* and murder them, in turn." She leaned back in her chair. "A bit extreme, you might say," she noted, looking around at her audience "After all, the *Normandie* wasn't a woman, she was a ship." Charlotte had picked up a creamer from the table. It was from the *Normandie*. On its side was the CGT logo of the French Line. Setting the creamer down, she went on with her story:

"But as it turned out, the man had other reasons to hate the Nazis. Not only had they killed his ship, they had executed many of his colleagues in the Résistance. And they had murdered his mother and his relatives in the Oradour-sur-Glane massacre, one of the Nazis most heinous war crimes. The SS shot all the men and locked all the women and children in a church, and then burned it down. He didn't know who had killed the members of his family, but he did know, or could find out, who had murdered the *Normandie*."

She looked up again at René. Tears were welling in his soft brown eyes, and he blinked them away.

"In this man's mind, the saboteurs of the *Normandie* became the scapegoats for the loss not only of the *Normandie*, but of all he held most dear."

René had refilled his glass, and he took a long swallow from it.

"After the prison at Fresnes was liberated, our lover was free—free to indulge himself in his determination to track down the *Normandie's* murderers. It became a hobby for him, in the way that tracking down one's ancestors might be for a genealogy buff. He started with the Nazi technical sergeant who had been the prison guard. He became a detective: making inquiries, looking into old records, following up on leads. What he didn't know was that he had made his job much more difficult than it really was."

"How is that, might I ask?" René interjected.

Charlotte explained. "He was like a genealogy enthusiast who does all the legwork himself— traveling to distant countries to study the records in libraries, churches, and city halls—when he might have consulted a genealogy database. He was an avenger who had yet to enter the computer age. Unbeknownst to our vengeance seeker, the Nazi hunters at the Jewish Documentation Center in Los Angeles had already done all his work for him; the information he needed was in their computer records, available for the asking."

René shrugged.

"Eventually, he tracked the prison guard down; it took him nearly fifty years. The guard's name was Wilhelm Roehrer, and he was living in Clearwater, Florida, using the alias William Roe. But there was no point in killing Roehrer, because he was terminally ill.

Roehrer was useful in another respect, though. With the aid of a bribe, he was induced to reveal the name of his accomplice in the sabotage plan, Operation Golden Bird. The accomplice was a Russian fascist by the name of Paul Federov."

There was a subtle shift in positions around the table as Charlotte drew near the dénouement of her story.

"With a little detective work, the man who loved the *Normandie* discovered that Paul Federov was the prominent Palm Beach jeweler, Paul Feder. He had tracked Feder right to his own backyard. Feder was to be a guest at a preservation association benefit with a *Normandie* theme, for which our lover would be the caterer. How fitting that the *Normandie* benefit should be the venue of the saboteur's death! Especially when the party was taking place on the fiftieth anniversary of that very act of sabotage."

"And so our lover planned the murder of the man who had killed the ship he had so dearly loved. He would wait until Feder was alone, and then stab him with a knife he had taken from the corpse of a Nazi during his days as a *résistant*—a knife he had saved all those years specifically for that purpose. On that fateful evening, he was able to carry out his scheme exactly as he had foreseen it. Our lover, you see, was a man who had devoted a lifetime to making certain that events unfolded according to plan."

Charlotte continued, looking directly at René. "How satisfying it must have been for him to finally have taken his revenge! But the score wasn't fully settled yet. There was a third man: the *Abwehr* agent who had masterminded the sabotage plot. His *Abwehr* code name was the Fox, after a character from the fairy tale from which the plot took its name. What our lover didn't know was that the Fox was an impostor: he wasn't really an *Abwehr* agent, but a counterspy working for American intelligence."

René looked up in surprise.

Charlotte had risen from her chair, and now stood behind it, her hands resting on the top rung. "That's right," she said. "He was Lieutenant Commander Jack McLean, and he was the officer in charge of the *Normandie* conversion. The *Abwehr* had solicited his participation in Operation Golden Bird as a way of verifying his allegiances. McLean's plan was to start the fire in order to demonstrate his loyalty to the *Abwehr,* and then to put it out and save the ship. But his plan went awry: the fire boats pumped and pumped until the ship foundered." She turned and paced toward the fireplace on the opposite wall. "I don't know if it would have mattered to the man who loved the *Normandie* that McLean wasn't an *Abwehr* agent, but I suspect not. In his eyes, McLean would still have been accountable for the *Normandie's* death."

Reaching the fireplace, she reversed direction and returned to the table. "I have no idea how the man who loved the *Normandie* tracked McLean down, since neither Roehrer nor Federov knew his identity," she said, standing once again behind her chair. "But track him down, he did. Like Feder, to his own backyard. And so Admiral John W. McLean the third became his second victim—stabbed in the heart with a Nazi dagger while walking on the Lake Trail." As Charlotte spoke, it struck her that McLean had done penance with his life for the crime for which he had carried the guilt for most of a lifetime.

René had regained his composure and sat quietly sipping his drink. "But, madam," he protested with his debonair little smile, "you have left out the most important part of the story."

"And what is that?"

"The identity of this . . . man who loved *Normandie*." His eyes had hardened, revealing the soul of the French Résistance fighter beneath the charming, pleasure-loving façade.

"I will leave that part of the story to my friend, Detective White," said Charlotte, looking over at Maureen.

She resumed her seat, and the audience's attention shifted to Maureen. In fact, Charlotte had turned matters over to Maureen because she had no idea where to go from there. She had expected René to admit to being the character in her story, but it was clear that his legendary savoir faire wasn't going to crack.

"Before Detective White takes over, I would like to offer my guests a cigarette," said René. Leaning back, he removed a cigarette case from the pocket of his navy blue blazer.

It was the $200,000 gold-enameled case from the *Normandie* collection, the case that Paul had said rivaled the artworks of Fabergé for its craftsmanship, the case that Paul's murderer had removed from his body.

Opening the lid, René slowly and deliberately offered the case to each of those assembled around the table. Then he removed a cigarette for himself and lit it. Finally he picked up the bottle of pastis and refilled his glass.

The others sat in silence, mesmerized by his

performance. As they looked on, René raised the glass of milky yellow liquid.

"*À la revanche*," he said looking at them through the smoke of his cigarette. "*Douce revanche*," he added, and proceeded to down the contents of the tumbler.

Then he threw back his head and laughed.

It was three days later, and Charlotte had spent the morning sweeping. Not sweeping exactly, but cleaning out. Not even cleaning out, which was her excuse for being there, as much as daydreaming. Once she had signed the purchase agreement, she had been eager to get into Château en Espagne, to get a feel for her new house. The real estate agent had indulged her whim, though the actual closing wouldn't take place for several weeks. She had spent the morning sweeping up dead palm fronds from the courtyard with a corn broom that she had bought in West Palm Beach, and admiring the paving blocks of cut coral, which made the house seem like an organic part of the coral bedrock of the island. Because the courtyard was the part of the house that had first captured her heart, she had chosen to attend to it first. When she was finished sweeping, she cleaned the dead leaves and other debris out of the fountain, and then pruned and watered the lemon trees in the terra-cotta pots lining the entrance walk, and the potted gardenia plants in the courtyard. Then she tended to the neglected orchids in the slat house, immersing the pots in water to simulate a tropical rainfall, as directed in a book on orchids she'd picked up at a bookstore on Worth Avenue. After a ham sandwich eaten at the patio table in the slat house, she had spent the early afternoon in the empty house, sitting, thinking, wandering around. Ever since she'd decided to buy the place, she had been mentally running up and down the stairs, peering into empty rooms, and arranging the furniture. In short, building castles in the air.

Now she was sitting with Dede in a sling-back chair on the flat roof of the guest cottage, taking a break. They were eating pistachio nuts and drinking iced tea and enjoying the view, which was similar to the one from her tower (she liked that—*her* tower!), but even better because they were out in the open. The design of the flat roof continued the Moorish theme that had been established by the interior design of the cottage. Looking out over the barrel-tiled roofs of Palm Beach, with their various pitches and angles and shades of red, Charlotte felt as if she could have been in old Morocco.

"Does the fact that I'm soon to become your landlady mean that I'll have the excuse to come up here and drink iced tea with you when I come calling for the rent?" Charlotte asked as she looked around at the roof garden, whose floor was covered with raffia matting, and which was casually decorated with beach furniture and gay pots of flowering plants.

Dede laughed, revealing the charming gap between her front teeth. "It is wonderful, isn't it?" she said, gazing out at the Atlantic Ocean with her sea-green eyes. "I come up here sometimes to sleep under the stars," she added, nodding at a chaise lounge in the corner.

"Shouldn't you be drying raisins or dates or something up here too?" asked Charlotte. "I thought that was the way it was done. Sleep on the roof with your dried food, and keep the animals downstairs."

"I do keep the animals downstairs, usually," said Dede. "Or rather, animal." She leaned down to scratch the neck of Lady Astor, who lay at her feet, and who had managed quite gracefully to climb the spiral staircase.

Leaning back, Charlotte turned her face to the sun. The temperatures over the past few days had been cooler—in the sixties during the day and the forties at night—and the warmth of the sun felt marvelous in the cool air.

After a moment, Dede said, "I'm glad you came over. You can help me celebrate. I have some good news."

"What?" asked Charlotte, turning to face her.

"The board has named me director of the preservation association," she announced with a wide smile. "I just found out."

Rising from her chair, Charlotte went over and gave Dede a hug. "Congratulations!" she said. "That's wonderful! It's impressive that they're putting their confidence in someone so young."

Dede nodded. "I was hoping I'd get the job, but I thought they'd choose someone from outside. Though they have separated the administrative function from the financial end. They're going to hire a financial officer too."

"I can understand that," said Charlotte.

"I'm really looking forward to it," Dede continued. "I never would have said this before, but I think I can safely say it now. Lydia wasn't a very effective administrator."

Charlotte wasn't surprised.

"And it's too important a job for an incompetent. One of the first things I want to do is try to save more of these old Spanish-style houses. Palm Beach was really the result of the vision of one man, Addison Mizner, and it's a vision that I want to do as much as I can to preserve."

Dede was really quite a remarkable young woman, Charlotte thought. She had it all: her grandmother's beauty, her mother's drive and creativity, and her step-grandfather's sense of social responsibility.

"It's going to be a tough job," Dede went on. "What Lydia did really hurt us. It's not the money so much. Between the Dupas mural and the fidelity bond, we'll more than cover what she took. But that can't make up for the loss of public trust. People are going to think twice before giving us money."

"Yes," Charlotte agreed. "But the public also has a short memory. And you have the flair it takes to be a successful fundraiser." Charlotte wished her the best. "And what's happening with Lydia now?" she asked. "I saw her right after Jack McLean died. Her house was on the market."

"Another house that needs preserving," Dede commented. "She's been very depressed, but she'll be all right. She's going back to Flint, where, as Spalding says, being the widow of the bumper king will always count for something, even if she does end up doing time for embezzlement."Charlotte smiled. Spalding was right.

"What about you?" Dede asked. "Will you be going back to New York soon?"

"Yes," Charlotte said. "Right after the Big Band Hall of Fame Ball on Sunday. I'm going to be filming a movie for public television in London." She wondered briefly if Eddie's upcoming tour included any London gigs. "But I expect to be back for the closing; and then I'll stay awhile. I want to fix the place up."

"Are you leaving on Monday morning?"

Charlotte nodded.

"That's when mother's leaving too. You might even be on the same flight. She's going first to New York and then to Paris."

"With Nikolai?" Charlotte asked.

Dede smiled. "They're an item, despite the fact that he's twenty years younger than she. She's already talking about doing a collection with a French theme. I wonder what she could call it."

Charlotte looked over at Dede, and smiled mischievously. "How about *Mésalliance*," she suggested, and they both howled in the sparkling sun at the continuing escapades of the irrepressible Marianne.

After her work-break with Dede, Charlotte returned to Château en Espagne. First she called Jeannie Stavola, as promised, and spent a good forty-five minutes filling her in on the case, including the fact that René was now in jail, awaiting arraignment on murder charges. Though the evidence against him was circumstantial, there was a lot of it, including the fact that he had been seen on the Lake Trail on the morning of Jack McLean's murder. After her conversation with Jeannie, Charlotte opened all the doors and windows, allowing the ocean breeze to fill the house with the crisp, salty smell of the sea air. It was another form of sweeping, she reasoned, allowing the fresh air to scour the rooms. Then she resumed her mental decorating. She had just repainted the living room for the fourth time—she'd gone from ochre to sand to rose and back to ochre again—when she heard a knock on the door. Opening it, she was surprised to see Eddie standing there with a bottle of champagne in one hand and a hanging flower basket overflowing with geraniums in the other.

"Connie said I would find you here," he said. He held up the bottle of champagne. "This is to celebrate your first day in your new house. And this"—he held up the flower basket—"is just for the hell of it."

He was dressed in typical Palm Beach style: a white guayabera shirt and tan chinos with sandals.

Charlotte kissed him, and was surprised again at how compact he felt by comparison with the other men she had known, most of whom had been bigger. Then she set the flower basket down in the courtyard and led him through the pecky cypress gate to the swimming pool, which was the only place on the grounds, apart from the slat house, where there were still any chairs.

Next she went back into the house to look for glasses, returning a moment later with two of the antique silver mint julep cups in which Paul had served the rum cocktails on the night of his dinner party. She had found them among the jelly jars at the back of a kitchen cupboard, where they had apparently been overlooked by the movers.

"Well," Eddie said, once they were settled in with their cups of champagne. "Here we are." He looked around at the lush tropical vegetation surrounding the pool, which made it seem like a natural pool in the rain forest of a tropical paradise.

"Yes," she agreed, "here we are."

"I liked the inn at Hadfield. Very picturesque and all that. But I *really* like this," he said, gazing out at

286

the pool with its colorful Spanish tiles. "You know, I could get used to a life like this."

"Could you?" Charlotte asked, with her signature arched eyebrow. He looked over at her and smiled. Then he changed the subject.

"What's happening with the case?" he asked. Charlotte had already told him about René being linked with the murders through the dagger, and that he'd had the cigarette case taken from Paul's body.

He also knew that René had been seen on the Lake Trail. but he hadn't yet been filled in on the latest news.

"I talked with Maureen this morning, as a matter of fact," Charlotte said.

"There weren't any fingerprints on the dagger that were complete enough to tell anything from, but there *was* blood, and it matched McLean's. Plus, René's cleaning woman is willing to testify that she saw the dagger in his apartment."

"Has he admitted to owning it?"

"To owning it, but not to using it. He says it was stolen from his apartment last year. Naturally he didn't report the theft. He says he took the dagger from from the body of a Nazi that he killed in the course of blowing up a railroad, just as the clerk at L'Antiquaire Militaire had suggested."

"What does he say about the cigarette case?"

"That he found it on the beach."

"He just happened to find a gold-enameled cigarette case that's worth two hundred grand on the beach?"

"That's his story. What puzzles me is why he chose to take it out during our interview at Château Albert. I decided that it must have been an act of defiance,

287

that he was saying, Nah, nah. I did it, but you can't prove it."

"Of course," Eddie agreed. "He was flaunting it."

"I also decided that he's stuck in a time warp. In some section of his mind, he still thinks that this is wartime, and that he's a *résistant* who can murder the enemy with impunity I think he's in for a rude awakening, because the police *can* prove it. Oh! I forgot to mention the footprints."

"What about them?"

"The castings the police took of the impressions on the beach and at the tree match those from a pair of his shoes. The soles had a distinctive pattern—the shoes had been purchased in France. And there's another thing: a possible answer to the question of why it took him so long to track down his victims."

"What is it?"

'We don't know for sure, of course, since he's not admitting to anything. But Maureen's connection at the CIA speculated that he might have tracked the *Normandie* saboteurs down through *Abwehr* archives that were only made available to the public after the Berlin Wall came down two years ago last November."

"Is that how he found out that Roehrer had settled in this country under the William Roe alias—through the *Abwehr* archives?"

"Maybe. He did travel to East Berlin, or what used to be East Berlin, last summer. It might also be how he found out that McLean was the Fox."

Eddie nodded.

"But I suspect that how he tracked his victims down will remain one of the mysteries of this case. The other mystery is the event that set us on the path toward the solution in the first place, namely a dormant memory that suddenly pushed its way to the surface after being buried for fifty years."

"That's not a mystery. That was simply a matter of the circumstances being re-created exactly as they were on the *Normandie*. Speaking of circumstances," Eddie said, "I have something for you." Reaching into his pocket, he pulled out a small blue leather box with "Feder & Co." embossed in gold on the lid.

"I have the feeling that I've seen a box like this before," Charlotte said as he handed it to her.

She slowly opened the lid. Inside was a pair of earrings in the shape of seashells. They were made of gold, enameled to look like mother-of-pearl, and they were inset with tiny diamonds, rubies, and sapphires.

"Oh, Eddie!" she said, gazing at the lovely earrings. She had wanted to buy a piece of jewelry to commemorate her reunion with Eddie, and he had bought one for her. Their minds ran on the same track. It was an encouraging sign.

With her forefinger, she slowly traced the path of the delicate gold braid that wound itself around the body of the shell, like the coil of brown on the tulip shell she had found on the beach. "A spiral," she said.

"Yes," said Eddie. "Always moving onward and upward, but always coming back to the same place."

"Kind of like us," she said.

15

CHARLOTTE WAS SITTING AT A TABLE AT THE BIG Band Hall of Fame Ball, wearing her black sheath and her seashell earrings from Eddie. On the table in front of her was the *minaudiére* that Marianne had given her, with its elegant lacquered compartments for comb, lipstick, and mirror—the souvenir of what was supposed to have been a restful vacation in Palm Beach. She was seated with Connie and Spalding and the honorary chairmen of the ball, who included several actors with whom she had been trading notes. The Venetian Ballroom looked quite different than it had when she had last been here. The crystal chandeliers blazed, the round wooden tables had been dressed up with pink tablecloths and centerpieces of pink roses, and the room was filled with Palm Beach's most influential residents, twelve hundred in number, each of whom had paid $300 for the privilege of being present at the induction of Eddie Norwood into the Big Band Hall of Fame. On stage the music stands for Eddie's sixteen-man orchestra each proclaimed "Eddie Norwood and His All-American Band," in glittering gold script. Seated behind the stands, the members of Eddie's band, wearing white dinner jackets and red plaid ties with matching cummerbunds, awaited the nod from their leader, who was being lauded as the "King of Dancebandom" by the Palm Beach society matron who served as general chairman of the ball. Above the stage, a banner announced the theme of the evening, which was New York's Rainbow Room, the legendary club at the top of the NBC Building, which had been the site of Eddie's radio broadcasts for so many years. If for only an evening, the Breakers' Venetian Ballroom would be "sixty-five stories nearer the stars," as the slogan of Eddie's radio show had proclaimed.

After an address from the mayor, the chairman of the ball delivered a speech in which she likened the country's big band musicians to Picasso and Rembrandt, and then went on to describe the plans for the Big Band Hall of Fame Museum in West Palm Beach, which would include—in addition to thousands of photos and pages of sheet music—such memorabilia as Jimmy Dorsey's trombone, Benny Goodman's clarinet, the mirrored ball that once hung in New York's Roseland Ballroom, Xavier Cugat's music stand, and an autographed baton from Eddie Norwood. Finally, she briefly described Eddie's career, as a prelude to presenting him with an award for lifetime achievement.

The scenario was very familiar to Charlotte. Having worked so hard to get where she was, she was reluctant to be ungracious about such awards, but in fact it seemed as if a week hardly passed these days without her being honored by someone or other. As she was sure was also the case for Eddie. And so it was that her attention drifted off to the question of what to do about the kitchen at Château en Espagne before she realized that Eddie had already been presented with his award, and was now mounting the stage.

He was wearing a white tail coat and a red bow tie. The white of his coat accentuated the white of his hair and his deep tan. He looked wonderful. It was no mystery why he had been such a success for so many years; he had that glow that the Hollywood moguls called "presence."

Looking up at the stage, Charlotte caught his eye. He smiled at her, and her heart skipped a beat. Then he proceeded to announce that the first song of the evening would be dedicated to Miss Charlotte Graham.

Connie beamed at her from the other side of the table, where she was seated next to Spalding. Blue eyes sparkling, she leaned forward and asked, "How does that make you feel, Charlotte?"

The audience had burst into applause at the mention of Charlotte's name, and she could feel their eyes upon her as she spoke in Connie's ear: "Sixty-five stories nearer the stars."

As Eddie turned to the band, Charlotte's thoughts turned back to that first night in the Café-Grill, when he had played their song on the white baby grand as the sun rose in the tall windows at the stern of the ship.

It had been " just one of those things"—then. With both of them married to other people, it could hardly have been anything else. But she wondered if that would still be the case, or if it was destined now to be something more.

Then Eddie raised his baton and the band began to play.

But the song that Eddie had dedicated to her wasn't "Just One of Those Things," as she had expected. The band was a few bars into the melody before the lyrics started coming back to her: they had to do with being under the stars while an orchestra played by the shore, and palm trees swayed in the breeze.

She leaned back in her chair and broke out into a

wide smile. She was reminded of the saying that Palm Beach was a place in which many things ended but few things began. Whoever had said that was wrong.

Because she and Eddie were about to begin the beguine.

Dear Reader:

I hope you enjoyed reading this Large Print book. If you are interested in reading other Beeler Large Print titles, ask your librarian or write to me at

Thomas T. Beeler, *Publisher*
Post Office Box 659
Hampton Falls, New Hampshire 03844

You can also call me at 1-800-251-8726 and I will send you my latest catalogue.

Audrey Lesko and I choose the titles I publish in Large Print. Our aim is to provide good books by outstanding authors—books we both enjoyed reading and liked well enough to want to share. We warmly welcome your ideas and suggestions for new titles and authors.

Sincerely,

SOUTH HUNTINGTON PUBLIC LIBRARY

3 0652 00046 8464

DISCARD

LT
M

Matteson, Stefanie.

Murder under the
palms.

$24.95

DATE			

99

05

RECEIVED APR 1 1 1999

SOUTH HUNTINGTON
PUBLIC LIBRARY
2 MELVILLE ROAD
HUNTINGTON STATION, N.Y. 11746

BAKER & TAYLOR